ON THE SUBJECT OF UNMENTIONABLE THINGS

ON THE SUBJECT OF UNMENTIONABLE THINGS

Julia Walton

RANDOM HOUSE NEW YORK

All rights reserved. Published in the United States by Random House Children's Books,
a division of Penguin Random House LLC, New York.

Random House and the colophon are registered trademarks
of Penguin Random House LLC.

Visit us on the Web! GetUnderlined.com

Educators and librarians, for a variety of teaching tools,
visit us at RHTeachersLibrarians.com

Library of Congress Cataloging-in-Publication Data is available upon request.
ISBN 978-0-593-31057-1 (trade)—ISBN 978-0-593-31058-8 (lib. bdg.)—
ISBN 978-0-593-31059-5 (ebook)

Printed in the United States of America
10 9 8 7 6 5 4 3 2 1
First Edition

For my kids, who will have questions someday:
please ask them

I thought about making my second tweet a little-known fact about the human penis. But I changed my mind.

There were hundreds of alerts on my phone, my follower count was climbing by the second, and I didn't want to lean into my new "viral" success with a fact about male genitalia.

Starting with something about the male body, no matter how obscure, seemed like a betrayal. I mean, focusing the study of sex on men is what everyone expects you to do. Because it's what everyone else does. Right?

I looked at the sentence I was about to post and deleted it. I'd only ever wanted to have my blog, *The Circle in the Square*, as a depository for my research, not a Twitter account. But everything changed when someone alerted Lydia Brookhurst, our wealthy town embarrassment, to the existence of my work.

"Phoebe, maybe you'd fall less if you weren't texting while rollerblading?" Cora sped past me and swerved to an elegant stop that made her look part figure skater, part hockey player, and more coordinated than I would ever be.

Meanwhile, my follower count jumped by a thousand in a five-minute time span.

What. Life. Is. This.

I lost my balance and fell spectacularly on my ass, still clenching my phone in my fist.

Cora looked down at my face.

"Actually," she said, "you're fine. Keep texting." Then she leaned forward to pull me up.

"I miss our old Thursday routine," I complained, still clutching my phone. I could almost feel it pulsing in my hands, even though I'd turned vibrate off hours ago.

Cora had no idea what secrets I was hiding, but she'd definitely know something was up if I missed our regular Thursday plans. Even though I was still bitter that we'd been forced to change them.

Thursdays used to be for romantic comedies. We'd spend hours eating junk food and watching people fall predictably in love with their worst enemies. But when Cora's parents threatened to sign her up for yet another beach cleanup group because they were afraid she was spending too much time inside and not enough time communing with nature, we decided to try something else.

"Rollerblading?" I'd whined.

"It is making a comeback," she'd said. "And it's fun!"

It is not, I'd thought.

"And can you believe I found these two brand-new pairs of Rollerblades by a dumpster?"

Yep. I definitely can.

My butt cheeks might be permanently bruised from our first week on wheels, and even though I can mostly move without falling now, she's probably right about the texting.

But if she knew what was happening right now on my phone, she'd—

"Oh my God, Phoebe! You're never going to believe this," Cora shouted.

She let go of my hand, and once again I fell hard on my ass. Exact same spot.

I stared up at the sky with my ponytail pressed against the pavement, wondering if I'd ever be able to sit comfortably again and why I'd chosen to sacrifice a butt cheek for the sake of our friendship.

"Pom! The one who writes *The Circle in the Square* is from Linda Vista!" she screamed.

"No way," I said—convincingly, I hoped.

That had been an accident. I'd posted my bio, but I hadn't meant to post my location. By then it was too late to fix it.

Pom
@CircleintheSquare

Author of The Circle in the Square: Sex Ed for
Teens by a Teen
Linda Vista, California

I wanted to tell Cora it was me. I really did. At least that's what I told myself.

If I'd actually wanted her to know, I would have told her when this whole thing started. Back when I created the blog.

But I'd kept it a secret.

I was grateful that Cora couldn't see me sweating underneath

3

my helmet, and secretly jealous that she was doing elegant figure eights in the empty church parking lot.

"Oooh..." She whistled, stopping to look down at her phone.

Lydia Brookhurst had posted a link to *The Circle in the
Square* with the comment:

> **@TheRealLydiaBrookhurst:** Look at this blog! This
> is disgusting. I miss the old days where people
> understood that constantly talking about sex leads
> to more sex. Obviously!

So this morning I'd responded with:

> **@CircleintheSquare:** Ah yes, the old days of crabs
> and gonorrhea and other rampant STDs. I too am
> nostalgic. Obviously!

A few people retweeted this, and then Brookhurst responded with a flood of hypothetical questions:

> **@TheRealLydiaBrookhurst:** Do we really need to
> talk about condoms in school?

> **@TheRealLydiaBrookhurst:** Isn't talking about safe
> sex just another way of telling our kids we think it's
> okay for them to have as much sex as they want?

4

@TheRealLydiaBrookhurst: YES! SEX IS FOR PROCREATION. WHY IS THIS SO HARD TO UNDERSTAND?

@TheRealLydiaBrookhurst: SEXUAL RISK AVOIDANCE IS THE ONLY ADVICE THEY NEED!

Ah yes. All caps. The language of agitated people. It's almost as if someone screaming on the internet will, in fact, have an effect on whether anyone has sex. And fun fact: abstinence-only sex education is also called sexual risk avoidance education. That's the more modern term that means no sex is the only sex teens should be having or thinking about.

Can we just accept that the sex is going to happen anyway? Because it is.

Can we also assume that teenagers look for answers to very basic questions that are both embarrassing and reasonable?

Because they do.

The "wait until you're married" and the "you're too young to know about this stuff" groups are making the issue less about sex and more about control. They think that the minute you know about it, you'll want it, so they want to control how much information you get and when you get it.

The response to curiosity should be: "Here's the information. Safety first."

Not: "Nothing to see here! Move along!"

> **@TheRealLydiaBrookhurst:** If we allow this blog, where do we draw the line?

> **@TheRealLydiaBrookhurst:** Don't let Linda Vista become Los Angeles!

Judging from the responses to Brookhurst's posts, there were a lot of people who agreed with me.

> **@OrangeSwedishFish75:** Reading the blog now—so good!

> **@Salgoudthetalldude03:** @CircleintheSquare is 🔥 Don't @ me Brookhurst.

> **@EclairQueen_21:** Pom is a genius

"Phoebe. Look at this! Pom has only existed a few hours. *Hours!* Everyone we know is following this account! Brookhurst must be so pissed!"

So as I stood there trying to keep my balance on Rollerblades that Cora had found by a dumpster, I watched my follower count climb.

Cora eventually drove me home, promising to update me on all the Brookhurst-related drama later.

She had no idea she'd be updating me on my own blog,

which, as I later found out, had more visits in one day than it had in its entire lifetime.

I pulled off my Rollerblades and peeled off my sweaty socks before walking into my room to process what had happened.

Sex education is *my thing*, and now that I have a Twitter and a following, I can correct people who are willfully spreading lies. And the best part is no one knows it's me.

I responded to Brookhurst with a series of tweets:

> **@CircleintheSquare:** Yes we need to talk about condoms.

> **@CircleintheSquare:** No, safe sex education doesn't encourage sex. It encourages SAFE sex.

> **@CircleintheSquare:** No, sex is not ONLY for procreation.

> **@CircleintheSquare:** No, sexual risk avoidance is not the only advice they need.

The problem is that when you try to argue with someone who thinks discussing sex is off-limits, you come off sounding more aggressive about it than you mean to be.

I might say that we need to discuss sex openly and honestly so people make smart choices as they mature sexually, but the person I'm talking to, who has rejected everything I'm about to say, is already picturing me dropping condoms and sex toys from a hot-air balloon over the high school parking lot.

I'm really nice and polite in person. But Brookhurst is, in fact, a moron.

Because instead of responding to my tweet, she retweeted it to her followers with the following message:

> **@TheRealLydiaBrookhurst:** POM? WHO ARE YOU? I'll pray for you, honey.

Then Cora texted:

> OMG. She just continues to get owned on Twitter. This is absolutely delicious.

No one in our town would have cared about the blog at all if I had been from anywhere else, but the possibility that the infamous Pom might somehow be "living among us" was just too much for my tiny, conservative town to handle.

Now I had a responsibility not just to respond to idiots but to tweet about sex ed. And alas, I kept coming back to penis facts, because that's how this whole quest for truth started.

I was fourteen years old the first time I saw one. The crew

team at Camp Golden Lake had stolen some guy's clothes, and he was forced to run naked across the open field in front of our cabins. I don't remember the kid's name or what his face looked like as he parted the crowd of laughing campers, but I definitely remember his penis, flapping in the breeze as he raced toward an open locker room door.

To be clear, I was *not* leering at him; I was just curious. Everything I thought I knew about penises was wrong. It wasn't what I'd imagined, and its movement suggested a complete lack of control. I'd always pictured a tiny arm with the bizarre ability to pick up small objects or sense danger. But that's probably when my research started, exactly at the moment that I realized everything I knew about the male anatomy was wrong. More specifically, everything I knew about sex was wrong.

My mom *did* give me the basics, though. The whole his-thing-goes-there conversation. But she was so embarrassed about it that I felt guilty prolonging her agony. She doesn't handle awkward well. When I started my period, she gave me all the information in a whisper, on a need-to-know basis, and I had to figure out how to use a tampon by myself. I'm not sure she's ever even said the word "vagina" out loud.

I couldn't do any of my early research online because my laptop at the time was ancient, and anything beyond using Word documents for school would have killed it. So I started with everything I could get from a book, but finding the material was difficult.

I got my big break when a gynecologist three streets over died and her husband had an estate sale of all her medical stuff. The room to her office was open, and all the medical journals, books, magazines, and dissertations were just lying in boxes. No one asked any questions when I paid for three boxes of what they thought was miscellaneous junk. I kept looking over my shoulder as I wheeled all of it up the street on a squeaky old dolly while my parents were at the farmers' market buying blood oranges and bok choy. The hard part has been keeping everything hidden.

Even though I don't use this stuff for research anymore, I still keep it all hidden in my room. I have one of those beds with drawers on all sides for storage, but that's where I keep my clothes. The research material is accessible only when I remove the largest drawer on the bed frame and reach inside the hollow opening. The floorboards beneath hold the most "sensitive" information. Basically, anything that has a visual goes there. I don't need my mom to accidentally find my giant plastic vagina (the kind you find in doctors' offices) or my illustrated copy of *The Kama Sutra*. These are not necessary for research, and I hardly ever look at them anymore, since most of my research is online. But they were in my original haul of stuff, and it would be weird to get rid of them. They feel important in a way I can't explain. Maybe because this is where it all started. And yes, I know it's strange to be sentimental about a giant plastic vagina.

I should probably repeat the facts that:

1. it's a research obsession;
2. I'm not a pervert.

I still needed somewhere to put all this information.

Somewhere to write everything down. Then a few months after the estate sale, my old laptop finally died and my parents got me a Mac. I finally had access to the internet, and the blog was born.

But even now, two years later, I'm not sure why I put it online.

Part of me wants this blog to make all this research available, because I'm putting it out there for people my age in a clinical, totally not-gross way. So sex won't be such a secret. Not that that's a problem. I seem to be getting good at secrets, though. Which is great because I'm not ready for people to know my secret identity.

I know now that you're supposed to create your online identity with a clear vision for your platform, but when I needed to pick a name, I just looked at stuff in my room.

There were two paintings hidden safely under my bed from the gynecologist's estate sale. The first was a picture of a vagina.

I mean, I'm not *really* sure. That's just what I thought it was when I first pulled it out of the box. There are swirling bits of color. Light reds and blues and purples innocently surround what is probably the clitoris, and strange wavy yellow lines dance around what I believe is the vaginal opening.

The second painting was obviously a nod to Eve eating the fruit from the tree of knowledge and thus dooming all of humanity, because whatever you do, you don't eat the fruit. You do not reach for knowledge.

The fruit on this tree was a pomegranate.

Therefore, my pen name became Pom.

Mainly because Colorful Vagina seemed a little too attention-seeking.

But my desire to research all comes back to the faceless boy with the floppy penis, running for his life. There is so much I didn't know and so much I still have to learn. Now that people know the blog exists, and now that some adults have warned their kids against reading it, I'm guaranteed an audience.

And for the record, I didn't intend to jump on Twitter to fact-check anybody, but it's hard to sit back and listen to people say stupid things.

I mean, lie.

Only thirty-nine states currently require sex education.

Only seventeen require that it be medically accurate.

Bite me, Brookhurst.

2

A few weeks ago my follower count was 0. Today I have 62,447 followers, minus one guy who followed me and then sent me a message saying he would unfollow me if I didn't follow back. Interesting. So 62,446 followers, I guess.

That's what I was thinking about when Cora walked into the newsroom and waved her hand in front of my face.

"Phoebe! I know Neil is a senior and he's got that hot-nerd look going for him, but you can't stare like that without looking like a fangirl," said Cora, appearing out of nowhere in her black jeans and sitting down next to me. She had just downloaded that app that tells you what celebrity you look like, and it had proclaimed Jameela Jamil and Meghan Markle her doppelgängers. I could tell by her face that she was still gloating about this inside. Third period wouldn't start for another few minutes, and Cora is not the type to arrive anywhere before she absolutely has to, but of course she'd walk in and notice me at the exact moment I was staring.

It's true he goes by Neil, but in my head he will always be Cornelius, for reasons even I don't fully understand. Though

I'd like to note here that the fact that I'm also a little bit in love with Cornelius Norton had no impact on my decision to join the school paper.

Seriously.

I've always enjoyed writing and I've always had a thing for research, even the kind that doesn't deal with penises and vaginas and make other people uncomfortable.

I'm not even sure "love" is the right word to use when describing my feelings, but "like" is the way people feel about ice cream or really good Mexican food and not how someone should feel about a person who can recite Atticus Finch's closing argument in *To Kill a Mockingbird*, like he did on the first day of school for the whole newsroom. That is attractive in a totally intellectual way. Maybe it's my body telling me that I want to have sex with his brain.

So there's that.

"Crap. Was I staring? Make it your mission in life to tell me when I'm doing it."

"That sounds boring, so pass. But this is me telling you to practice looking normal."

"Noted," I said. "What are you doing here, anyway? You're not on the newspaper."

"I know, but I'm ditching fourth period, and I want you to turn this in for me. We have a sub, but he's collecting our essays. And David's mom is at the chiropractor, so . . ."

"So you'll be . . . ," I prodded, raising an eyebrow.

"Catching up on math homework," she said. "Obviously."

"Okay, well, practice safe calculus, then," I said, putting her essay in my bag.

"Speaking of that," she said, pulling out her phone and flashing the screen in my face. Excerpts of my own writing stared back at me. I'd already read the article, but seeing it in Cora's hand somehow made it seem real, like my secret identity was on display for everyone. I was inexplicably filled with the desire for a cape and a pack of magic condoms.

"Seriously," she said excitedly. "Have you read this blog?"

"I may have glanced at it," I said, trying to keep my face free from emotion.

Cora rolled her eyes.

"I know it's not really your thing, and I don't really read blogs either. They're old-timey websites trapped in the early two thousands. But I've read every entry. I mean, every question I've ever had is answered here. Even questions I didn't know I had. It's like talking to a doctor. A doctor who gets it. You should read this."

"Why would you say that?" I asked, smirking a little.

"Just because you won't make use of this information now doesn't mean you won't *ever* need it. Maybe you'll get that swoon-worthy kiss even sooner than you think," she teased.

"You know that's condescending, right? And you know I have been kissed before, *right?*" I said.

"Yes to both," said Cora. "But the kiss doesn't count. It was at camp during truth or dare. And if I recall, the guy you kissed was also trying to win a bet in his cabin for longest time without a shower. So let's just ignore that, shall we?"

Fair point, I thought, watching Cora examine her sparkly black nail polish.

"Oh, and," she said, pretending to look around and over

her shoulder for eavesdroppers, "some people think the writer goes here."

"And that's a good enough reason to read something?"

She shrugged. "No, but at the very least it should give us hope that not everyone who lives here is incapable of talking about more *interesting* topics. Maybe before you head off to Stanford, you could read this and have a little fun." I frowned as she looked at Neil, then winked at me before hopping out of her chair and slipping out the door.

She knew any mention of Stanford annoyed me. It was the one thing in the world that I was superstitious about, so much so that when my parents got me a Stanford sweatshirt for Christmas last year, I made them take it back, saying I didn't want it unless I got in. Owning the sweatshirt felt like I might jinx my chances. I had stupidly made the possible acceptance into my dream school the alpha and omega of my life. But the obsession was deeply rooted now, so I just had to go with it, and as my best friend, Cora knew that.

I had met her when she was an argumentative five-year-old who showed up to school in a rainbow tutu. My mother had eyed her nervously as I carefully folded my pink cardigan into my cubby and stood back so my mom could use the lint roller on my navy-blue overalls. During art class our teacher, Mrs. Tippindort, told Cora not to paint her trees purple because trees were supposed to be green.

"Not jacaranda trees," I said. "Jacaranda trees have purple flowers."

Mrs. Tippindort smiled in a pained sort of way that suggested she wanted nothing to do with small children and eventually walked off to crush some other young artist's dreams.

"You're smart," Cora said.

"I like your jacaranda trees," I told her. No one had ever called me smart before, but when she said it, I believed her. Also, it doesn't take much to make friends when you're five.

Though under normal circumstances Cora would never have become my best friend. Her parents, Astrid and River, are hippies who own their own T-shirt company and make custom designs.

They come from a long and established line of what my incredibly conservative grandfather would have called "hairy-legged women" and "bearded men with Hacky Sacks and ukuleles."

River was a real estate agent once, and before he quit, he managed to sell a yurt to a couple who wanted to go off the grid. Actually, what they said was that they wanted to raise their peacocks in peace.

"Seriously," Cora had told me. "That's what they said. They want to raise their peacocks in peace. Their nasty, aggressive, bejeweled birds who shit everywhere need peace."

Anyway, a yurt is a fancy tent. This one was pretty luxurious with high ceilings, two bathrooms, and a meditation area.

That is my favorite River story.

Cora's parents always encouraged her to pursue all creative endeavors and question authority whenever possible. In contrast, I spent the first few years of my life thinking my name was No Phoebe!

"Okay, everyone," said Neil, standing and trying to bring

the focus back to him. "We're handing out assignments for this week." He ran his fingers through his hair, and I wondered why I was suddenly spending so much time staring at him. It was possible he'd gotten hotter over the summer, but it was more likely that I was so desperately lacking in romantic experience that I was now completely fabricating this ridiculous attraction to my editor.

My editor with perfect brown hair and just the right amount of geek chic. I could write a sonnet about his nerdy glasses and the way they rest on his beautifully freckled nose.

"Did you find out who writes *The Circle in the Square?*" someone shouted, and a few people laughed.

"No," said Neil. "But I've just finished reading the whole thing, and that, my friends, is excellent writing. Organized, succinct, brilliantly researched, and—"

"Dirty," said a girl at the front of the room in a deep, sultry voice. More people laughed, and I felt my face get hot. Monica Hansen is the kind of girl who can get away with interrupting someone without everyone thinking she's a jerk.

She doesn't do anything overtly terrible. It's the small things. The tiny backhanded compliments she offers with a smile. Inside jokes that she likes to have on hand just so she can exclude people from them. It's the casual meanness that gives her power.

But she's only cruel to select individuals. She can't go around being awful to everyone. It would blow her cover. She has to be nice enough to some people to cast reasonable doubt on the comments of those she torments, so they can use this phrase:

"Oh, really? But she's always been so nice to *me*."

Guess what? People who are selectively nice are not actually nice.

"There's nothing dirty about it," said Neil, who grinned, bringing me back to the newsroom. "It's a well-researched trove of information. And whoever it is is—"

"Horny!" yelled someone toward the back. Neil held up his hands to quiet the laughter again.

"Look," said Monica wickedly. "You're all making Phoebe blush."

I tried to ignore her, but I could already feel my face getting hot again. *Damn it,* I thought. Even though I was good at keeping my expression neutral, Monica was good at getting a reaction. It had been this way since middle school.

"Anyway," said Neil. "The blog is closed to comments. It's like someone just wrote a research paper and posted it. And everything is cited."

"And they're from here," shouted a girl directly in front of me. My stomach tightened. "It mentions Dilly's Drugstore on Main Street as a place to get free condoms and birth control."

A few people laughed at the mention of condoms.

I tried hard not to smile even though Neil was obviously impressed with my work. He ran his hand through his hair again, and I looked down, remembering what Cora had said about looking normal. Though I'm not sure avoiding eye contact *completely* was what she meant, especially when he was talking directly to me.

"Phoebe?" he said once everyone had dispersed to work on their assignments.

"Sorry—yes?" I said, trying to look like I had been thinking about something important and journalistic, and not about what the soft curl across his forehead might feel like in my fingers.

"I didn't give you an assignment."

"You didn't? I mean, I know."

Cora is right. I am a colossal idiot.

"Don't you want to know why?" he asked.

"Well, I'm sure you'll tell me," I said.

Nice, I thought. *Very smooth. That's way more normal. Well done, Phoebe.*

"I didn't give you an assignment because I was hoping you'd conduct a couple interviews for me."

"What kind of interviews?" I asked.

"Well, I was hoping you'd handle our staff spotlights for a while. Pick a few teachers. Ask them a few questions about their background. Maybe come up with an interesting angle to make each story seem . . ." He spent a little too much time searching for the right word.

"Unique?" I offered.

"Yes. Unique. That's a great way to put it." He beamed at me a little too brightly, and for some reason it made me suspicious.

"Why do you want me to do this?" I asked.

"You're a solid writer," he said. I raised my eyebrows a little.

"Okay, you're also on track to be valedictorian, and you get along with all the teachers. We've had a few people on staff go rogue with these interviews before, and it turned out, well, badly."

I remembered the previous year when one interview in

particular had been embarrassing for the school's vice principal. The interviewer went into detail about the items in Mrs. Rodriguez's office, which included (among other, more mundane things) a bong that had been confiscated from a locker during a drug inspection.

The bong in question had been planted in an empty locker as a test for one of the new canine trainees, but the interviewer failed to mention that it was (1) a tool used by police to train their dogs and (2) not the property of Mrs. Rodriguez. A retraction was printed immediately, but the damage had been done. And it probably could have been avoided if certain adults actually did their jobs, like Mr. Edmundson, the track coach who was *supposed* to review articles before they were printed but who spent most of his time napping at the back of the newsroom with his mouth open.

"So you think they'll be more eager to let me interview them because I'm boring?" I asked innocently.

"No, of course not! I think you'll be able to get the story. And you won't ruffle any feathers," he said amicably. I secretly loved that he used the phrase "ruffle any feathers" instead of "piss anyone off." It was just the right amount of charming nerdiness.

"So . . . will you do it?" he asked.

Of course I would, but I played it cool.

"Sure," I said. "Do you have someone in mind, or do I just choose any staff member I want to interview?"

Just then Neil's phone started buzzing in his pocket.

"Anybody you want," he said, looking down at his screen. "Just make it, you know, splashy. Unpredictable."

"Not boring?" I offered.

"Exactly. Thanks, Phoebe!"

I forced myself to keep my eyes on the desk as he walked away. There was no need for me to stare at his butt right now, and I could practically hear Cora's voice.

Stop trying to eye-fuck his brains out, Phoebe.

Cora is pretty crass.

But something Neil had said made me think.

The blog is closed to comments. What if I opened it up for questions? . . . And posted responses on Twitter?

Judging by the number of hits *The Circle in the Square* was still getting on a daily basis, people were curious about my research. Well, actually, what it proved was that people were curious about the *subject* of my research. Some of them even went so far as to express their outrage. They thought it was bold to discuss unmentionable things like female masturbation or wet dreams or the existence of the clitoris. As if the clitoris were some mythical beast that granted wishes.

But none of these things should be secrets.

My identity, though—yes, that should still be a secret. My parents would die of embarrassment, and I don't want to deal with the assumptions people would make. It's amazing what people will assume just because you know a lot about a subject. Like that you're easy. Or really open about your body. Or an experienced sex-haver. And even though there's definitely nothing wrong with being open about your body or sexually active, I'm neither of these things.

I'd just rather nobody know I'm Pom.

There's freedom in this secret identity. I can slip on my

mask, say whatever I want, and I don't actually have to be quiet, reserved, completely predictable Phoebe.

That night after my parents had both fallen asleep watching reruns of *West Wing*, I closed my door and opened the blog. My only regret was that I hadn't gone with one of my cleverer titles. In the beginning I'd toyed with calling it *Musings of an Extra-Virgin Sexpert* or *The Orgasmic Truth*, but in my effort to keep it as clinical and noncutesy as possible, I'd decided to call it *The Circle in the Square*.

A condom. You get it.

I thought about Neil's praise, and it made me smile.

He thinks my research is good.

He called it a trove of information.

He wants to find out who Pom is.

All of these thoughts buzzed happily in my head, and I realized I could let him ask his questions without revealing myself. I played with a few of the settings and leaned back in my desk chair before making the changes final.

If anyone was paying attention, the blog was now open for comments, and I'd added a Q&A section as well. There was no guarantee that anyone would notice these changes. It was entirely possible that the attraction to the blog had actually faded and the hits it had received recently were just lingering moments of curiosity.

But there was also the chance that the attraction hadn't faded and that Neil might be able to get an interview with Pom after all.

3

Turns out people are still interested. And it turns out that every time Brookhurst tweets something and mentions Pom, I get new followers. Because the woman doesn't understand that talking about someone is essentially free advertising. She kept retweeting and commenting on my posts.

And tweeting *POM REVEAL YOURSELF!* is a little dramatic.

There were new messages waiting for me when I woke up, but I couldn't log in to respond until later. *Never work on the blog in public.* That was one of the rules I'd adhered to since I began this unconventional hobby. It would be too easy to get caught by someone reading my phone over my shoulder. Plus, my parents were still home, so I couldn't look on my laptop even if I'd wanted to. My mom moves like a panther; I'd never hear her coming.

Dad had turned on our local-access channel to watch the town council meeting from the night before, and just as I was about to step into the shower, I heard a shrill voice talking about something that needed to be eradicated immediately. I distinctly heard the words "profane" and "disgusting."

"It's filthy and it is polluting our children's minds," the woman said.

I opened the door a crack and heard my dad sigh.

"Lydia Brookhurst. Does she have nothing better to do?"

Dad has followed local politics obsessively since he moved here from Hawaii, but he's never participated in elections beyond putting the occasional sign on our lawn.

"Well, I bet Lydia thinks this blog is bad for business. I mean, she *does* sell purity rings," said my mom, who was pouring my dad another cup of coffee.

Lydia Brookhurst is the president of the Citizens' Coalition for Responsible Censorship, a group that regularly holds protests in front of movie theaters when the subject matter is deemed wildly inappropriate. By "wildly inappropriate" I mean her group once famously stood outside the multiplex theater in town for two straight hours in the rain to protest a children's film that featured a purple koala bear of indeterminate gender.

Nope, not kidding.

Her family still owns a large apple orchard that has been the cornerstone of the town's economy for over fifty years, and Lydia definitely used some of their funds to open a Christian bookstore and coffee shop. She's also a huge donor to all the schools in town.

But she's most well known for her beauty pageant days.

Publicly she's known for sinking into a perfect split, center stage, during someone else's talent performance. But in some private circles, and unbeknownst to the judges, she's rumored to have lodged a nail in the first runner-up's stiletto before the swimsuit competition, slicing her heel wide open. Lately her business has been doing exceptionally well because she managed to secure a huge contract with a chain of jewelry stores that agreed to carry her abstinence rings. They were marketed as Promise Rings in the large chain, but in our town they were sold with a note that said:

Choosing abstinence is just another way of choosing Jesus.
God bless.
Stay pure.

"Ms. Brookhurst," said a town council member who sounded like she was using up her finite stores of patience. "With all due respect, there are actual pornographic websites that are just as easily accessible as this bl—"

"But this is labeled as an educational blog!" she shrieked. "Children are being bombarded with sexualized material everywhere they turn, and now this blog, no doubt pushing some political agenda, is threatening their innocence."

"Again, Ms. Brookhurst. Like all material that a parent deems inappropriate, it can be blocked and—"

"I am aware that it can be blocked, as it most *certainly* is in our home, but I'm concerned about the other children whose parents don't know what harm they are subjecting their children to by being negligent about their unsupervised internet time. This writer, whoever he is, is a pervert! And according to some very specific details, we know that he is a teenager and lives in our town! You can say whatever you want in this country, but that doesn't mean you should. So, Pom, I am speaking directly to you now. Delete your blog. Delete your Twitter account. And Linda Vista, if he doesn't, it's up to us to take out our own trash."

"Well, that's enough of that," I heard my dad say as he turned the TV off.

"She hasn't changed since we were in school," my mom said. "Always outraged about something . . ."

"Yeah, well, privileged people with a buttload of money and a business they inherited can afford to waste time getting offended for no reason," said Dad while my mom pursed her lips.

"Do you have to say 'buttload'?" my mom asked. "It sounds like money she actually pulled from her . . ." She cast around for another word, then gave up and let the sentence die.

" 'Buttload' is actually a unit of measurement for wine or whiskey," Dad said. He looked really pleased with himself.

"Whatever," said Mom, pouring herself more coffee. "It's gross." Dad laughed. Sometimes he just likes to bug her.

"Phoebe, leaving in twenty, okay?"

"Okay, Mom," I called through the door, before jumping in the shower.

Brookhurst's comments distracted me for a bit. So much so that I shampooed my hair twice. *Take out our own trash.* Was that a threat?

I comforted myself yet again with the fact that she had no idea who I was. Even if she was trying to pick a fight, that's pretty hard to do when you have no idea who you're fighting.

And with that thought, I got dressed and slid into the backseat of Mom's car while my parents discussed their agenda for the day.

They're both risk analysts, with about twelve insurance designations between them, which means they work primarily with large companies addressing hazards and the general possibility of bad stuff happening.

They can provide the statistical probability of a future event occurring and advise companies how to reduce that risk.

They also know, among other things, when you are most likely to die and how much you are worth when you do.

They are quietly brilliant people who have managed to succeed in life with hard work and very little confrontation. On Thursdays they teach a class together for one of their corporate clients.

If you go into my parents' home office at any given time, you are sure to find diagrams of people lifting heavy objects correctly, ergonomic keyboards, and lists of things to remove from a work space to avoid expensive claims.

To be honest, I can't imagine either of them addressing a crowd of people. I love them, but every conversation we have in our house feels like a whisper. Thursday must be rough for whoever sits in the back of the room.

When they dropped me off at school, my mom's eyes narrowed at my shirt. I tried to ignore it, but I knew what was coming.

"That one is getting a little snug, isn't it, sweetheart?"

Boobs, Mom. I have boobs. You can say the word out loud.

"I got it from Cora," I said, knowing this wasn't an acceptable answer.

"It's a little formfitting. Probably not something I'd want you wearing again to school."

I sighed deeply.

"Don't you think so, Matt?" She turned to my dad, who has zero opinions on how I dress.

"Just don't wear it for our Heavenly Bodies Clients, okay?" He winked.

Mom pursed her lips, and Dad patted her on the knee as I got out of the car.

It is a nickname. Their Heavenly Bodies Clients are the ones they meet with on Thursdays. They are a huge collection of churches, mosques, and synagogues that take risk management classes together.

They are ultraconservative, and my mom is always concerned about me showing too much skin or curvage in front of them. They *are* responsible for quite a bit of the extra income we've enjoyed over the last two years, and one of the reasons they signed with my parents was because they thought they were "morally upstanding people."

Whatever that means.

I looked down at the breasts my mom never wanted me to show and wondered briefly what could be done about them.

If my breasts are really so insidious . . .

But then I stopped myself because a supervillain called the Insidious Breast would be hilarious.

I hate Thursdays. I have two classes and a zero period, which means I start school at 9:00 a.m. But one of my classes is gym and the other is health. I must have spoken to every counselor at school to try to get out of my health requirement, but I was unsuccessful. One vice principal even went so far as to say, "Phoebe, I know the subject of sex might make you squeamish, but you have to take this class. This is important information you need to know."

I was annoyed, but I get it.

And I love the fact that there's so much still to learn. I post information to *The Circle in the Square* all the time. Whenever I learn something, it goes up.

And of course I wouldn't necessarily call myself an expert on sex yet.

But.

I'm also not going to disregard the amount of research I've done.

I can explain the female menstrual cycle *and* draw an accurate diagram of a human penis (including placement of seminal vesicle, prostate gland, urethra, vas deferens . . . etc.) *and* explain in excruciating detail what happens from arousal to ejaculation using clinical terms, *and* I bet my knowledge of male circumcision is on par with the average pediatrician's.

But instead of saying this to the VP, I nodded, accepted my fate, and died a little inside every time Coach Snowden, who is also the health teacher, opened his mouth to say something. Anything. In fact, everything he said was just a tiny bit wrong, making the class just a tiny bit pathetic, and not just because we were getting valuable, life-changing health-related information from the head football coach.

While I was thinking about this, Cora was standing in front of me wearing a T-shirt that featured a scowling rainbow unicorn leaning against a brick wall. I'm not sure how long she stood there waving her hand in front of my face.

"You are completely oblivious to life," she said, sitting down on the wall outside my health class and handing me a latte.

"I'm not oblivious," I said, taking the drink. "I'm just choosy about what I pay attention to."

I actually am a little oblivious.

"Right . . . but hey, so fourteen days!" she whispered dramatically, the straw from her disgusting pseudo-coffee concoction secured between her teeth.

"You are so weird."

"How can you not be excited about getting your braces off! You were, like, the last person in the world to get them. Don't you miss biting into sandwiches? Smiling without worrying about half-masticated food hanging from those tiny metal cages?"

"I guess I just haven't thought about it much," I said.

This was sort of true because I had accepted braces the moment I got them as a robotic extension of me, but of course I missed sandwiches and biting into pizza. And opening my mouth after a meal without wondering what gross combination of food was still lingering there. And I never wanted to see those tiny brush-behind-the-wire toothbrushes again.

"Well, that's just bizarre, but I don't have time to talk about it right now. Pedicures after school, right?"

I grimaced a little.

"Oh, c'mon! Your toes are not that bad. You hardly ever get ingrown nails anymore, and I want this to be a thing we do together until we're super old and living with a bunch of cats."

"So we can quit rollerblading?" I asked hopefully.

31

"No, we keep blading for sure. You're getting better! And I got us light-up wheels."

"Perfect. That's totally going to help me not suck."

"You'll be fine. See you after gym."

She ran off, leaving a kind of neon image in her wake. Just as I was about to launch myself into health class with the same enthusiasm my grandmother would reserve for a colonoscopy, someone stopped me.

"Phoebe!"

It was Neil.

"Yes, Cornelius, what can I do for you?" He looked at me for a minute and I froze, remembering that I'd only ever called him Cornelius in my head or with Cora. But never out loud like an idiot.

"Wow. Formal today," he said with a bemused expression.

"Yeah, apparently, I'm all business," I said. "Sorry."

Stupid, I hissed at myself.

"No worries. It's my name, after all." He put his hand on the back of his neck like he wanted to ask me something, and I was momentarily distracted. I'm not sure what it is about a man's neck that is so attractive. There is no evidence to suggest that attraction to someone's neck is even a rational thing, but there I was, staring at it.

"Listen," Neil said, "I was wondering if you could do the sports write-up for a couple weeks."

"Uh . . . ," I said. I couldn't imagine anyone on the planet knowing less about sports than I did.

"I know it's not your thing and you're already working on the staff spotlights, but I'm really desperate."

"Well, that's flattering, I guess."

"Please, Phoebe. Sports recap. Player spotlight. It's easy, and I wouldn't ask unless I really needed your help. Just a couple weeks." He did look desperate, and it's not like I wasn't thrilled to be doing him another favor.

"What sport?"

"You're serious?" he asked. I looked at him and nodded.

"Football," he said slowly.

"Right. Football," I said.

He looked worried. "That means you have to actually, you know, go to the games."

"Obviously," I said. "Who is the spotlight athlete?"

I've never been to a football game in my life.

"Jorge Cervantes."

"And he's the . . . ?"

"Quarterback."

"Right. Okay."

"Awesome. Here's his email," he said, handing me a scrap of paper. "I told him you'd be in touch."

"Gotcha," I said, and I could tell Neil was anxious about this assignment.

"It's just, we've had a few people quit the paper to run the school's social media accounts instead, and . . ."

I nodded. It's more fun running around campus taking pictures for Instagram than it is writing articles about losing teams.

"Thanks, Phoebe," said Neil. "When this is all over, I owe you a coffee. I really appreciate your help."

"No problem," I said.

No, that's not a date, I told myself.

33

It was totally professional.

I'd seen him getting coffee with other writers in there before.

I'm not an unlovable swamp beast or painfully irritating, but there *was* an incident about a year ago. Monica was on the winter mistletoe delivery team, and she handed me a bundle, saying it was from Neil. When I smiled and reached out to take it, she grinned and said, "Oops, my mistake. This one isn't for you. But imagine if it *had* been from Neil."

The bell rang, and I walked into health, grabbing a seat at the back near the door. It was the only class in which I'd actually made an effort to distance myself from the teacher.

Coach Snowden's faults were many. His own ignorance of the subject he taught was unfortunate for a teacher, but the most inexcusable thing about him was his smell. It was a combination of Axe body spray, Doublemint gum, and coffee that overwhelmed me the moment I was within six feet of him. Apparently, he ran to school in warm-up pants and a rain slicker, which allowed his natural musk to bake at a steady ninety-five degrees. This aroma still wafted over the back row occasionally, but my preferred seating did at least spare me from the feeling of going to class inside his armpit.

"Okay, ladies!" Coach Snowden barked over the crowd of thirty kids, half of whom were not "ladies." The football players in the front row barked back, and I wondered briefly how most of them managed to squeeze into the tiny 1960s desk-chair configuration that our school hadn't yet abandoned.

But before he could get started, a young woman walked in carrying a stack of pamphlets. She wore a pantsuit, and her hair hung in a long ponytail. I couldn't make out her name tag from the back row, but I could see she looked irritated, like she'd rather be anywhere but here.

"Oh, right. Nurse Reyes," said Coach Snowden. "Class, we have a guest spea—"

But before he could finish talking, Nurse Reyes shook her head and handed him the stack of pamphlets.

"Not speaking, just dropping these off for the class. If anyone has any questions, you know where to find me," she said tersely before nodding to us and stepping out abruptly.

Everyone started muttering at exactly the same time, and I heard a girl in the row in front of me whisper to her friend: "She got in trouble for using *The Circle in the Square* as a sex ed reference during a school board meeting for a bunch of teachers and parents. That's probably why she's not doing a presentation. She's the reason Lydia Brookhurst found out about it."

My ears perked up at that. Nurse Reyes was the one who'd alerted Brookhurst to the existence of the blog. The one who'd essentially made it go viral. Like the blog's fairy godmother or something.

This was the first time I'd actually seen her in person.

Coach Snowden dropped the pamphlets onto his desk.

"Well, okay then. No guest speaker!" He clapped his hands together. "Which is fine because today I have prepared a presentation on puberty," he said, turning off the lights. He pulled out an ancient projector and turned it on. Laughter erupted as Coach Snowden sighed at the picture someone had drawn on the lens: a penis with a smiley face. He wiped the projector clean, looked out over his football players as if they were naughty children, and proceeded to write the list of topics to be discussed.

"So, puberty," he said. "Pay attention. I know many of you will have questions about all those funny feelings you've been having." There were some noises followed by laughter from the front of the room, and I clenched my teeth. If anyone *did* have questions, they certainly weren't going to ask them now.

Most people took out their phones, but I watched the Power-Point the way someone might watch a car accident in slow motion. It was painful, but I couldn't look away.

A description of masturbation that only addressed boys.

A detailed account of male arousal (including helpful tips on how to hide an erection), but nothing to suggest that girls have similar feelings.

A lengthy explanation of wet dreams that included a lament about the potentially embarrassing situations young men might endure during orgasm.

I'm not sure why I was annoyed. It's not like I expected it to be better.

I sent Cora a message to tell her what she was missing in health, and she responded a few minutes later with a short one-act play to illustrate the difficulty that young men face when forced to interact with women.

Hey Michelle

Oh hey Ben

takes off jacket

becomes visibly uncomfortable as alarms go off around his penis

Looks down Oh Ben I'm sorry! *Throws jacket back on and zips it all the way to her neck*

Phew! Thanks Michelle! *Alarms stop sounding* For a minute there I thought I was going to be distracted from my education by your magnificent breasts!

Cora added: *Toyed with the idea of throwing in a "merciful heavens" or "heaven forbid" but didn't want to detract from the power of the piece.*

I turned my attention back to Coach Snowden just in time to get his take on the developing female body. When the subject of a girl's period was mentioned, Coach had this gem to share:

"Period cramps are not actually *that* bad."

That's when I started drafting my interview questions for the player spotlight. Ten questions seemed appropriate. It was a stupid interview, after all, so I emailed them to Jorge and asked him if he was okay with skipping the in-person interview and just going with email responses. It was not a top priority, and I wanted it checked off my to-do list.

When the bell rang, I bolted from the room to get to PE. Oddly enough, the gym smelled better than Coach Snowden's den of manliness.

Cora talked through our entire pedicure while the women doing our nails shook their heads every so often and looked at me sympathetically, as if offering their condolences for my hideous feet. I have no nail on the baby toe of my left foot, and the rest of my toenails are short and cut at odd angles.

"Sorry," I told them. "Just do the best you can."

My phone buzzed three short beats, signaling a new email. I opened it while Cora described the kind of flower she wanted painted on her big toe.

Phoebe,

These questions are a waste of time for both of us. This isn't something you genuinely care about, so why put in the effort, right?

But some of us use articles like these for college admissions, resumes, etc. . . .

Judging from your past work on the paper, I thought you might be up to the challenge, even if sports aren't your thing. Research, you know? Like a journalist? That's why I asked Neil if you'd do it.

Anyway, I'd rather do the in-person interview,

maybe before the game on Friday? You have to be
there anyway to cover it.

Jorge

The embarrassment must have shown on my face, because
Cora immediately asked me what was wrong. I showed her the
email.

"Wow," she said. "What a dick. He knows how to hit you
where it hurts. How bad were the questions you sent?"

I opened my original email and felt my face flush again.
Cora looked through them and tilted her head to the side.
It was a move that acknowledged that they were, in fact, not
great interview questions, but how dare he say so.

"Poor, whiny athlete. He's worried he's not getting enough
attention because you're not asking thought-provoking questions about what it's like to pat another guy's ass before the big
game? What balls he has to email this to you."

"He's right, though, isn't he? These are boring questions,
and this piece is already crap, right?"

"So don't make it crap. Give them something they're not
expecting. Tell the whole story. Sweaty jockstraps and all."

"That is so beautiful, Cora."

The number of messages in my inbox had grown significantly
by the time I logged in to the blog that night. I scrolled through
a few congratulatory comments and zeroed in on the Q&As.

39

There were a few questions on condom use and size and a few worried queries about other contraceptives. For these I was able to refer readers to other sections of the blog. But one question in particular stood out:

> How do I give my girlfriend an orgasm without having sex?

There were some questions I understood from a research perspective but not from a personal perspective.

This was one of those questions.

I liked it for its straightforwardness. I also liked that this reader recognized the fact that there are ways to experiment sexually without penetration. There is no shortage of information on how to handle an erect penis, but vaginas are mysterious, unmentionable things.

We do not speak of them.

We do not acknowledge their existence.

I made sure my response was simple.

> For most women, clitoral stimulation is the most effective means of achieving orgasm. I will direct you to the diagram in the visual section of this blog.
>
> It is important to note that the "clitoral hood" (see diagram) has a similar role to the male foreskin (for uncircumcised penises). Light touching

> over this "hood" followed by rapid movement at
> your partner's request is usually a good method.
> However, each woman is different, and it is
> important to talk to your partner about her pleasure
> preferences. Communicate with your girlfriend
> about what feels good for her.
>
> And even if you are not having intercourse that
> involves penetration, please follow the safe-sex
> practices listed on this blog.

I felt good about this response when I sent it, and then I looked at the open email response to Jorge on my other monitor and sighed. I knew I had to respond but wished that I had it in me to lie and sound indignant about the accusation that I hadn't put much thought into my questions.

Something along the lines of:

> How dare you besmirch my honor, sir!
> I am a serious journalist and I will not tolerate
> such flagrant disrespect for my craft!

Instead, I wrote:

> Dear Jorge,
> You're right.
> I'll see you on Friday before the game.
> > Thanks,
> > Phoebe

I sent the email, but I still wasn't tired, so I went back into the blog and there were two more comments on my Q&A page. One of them was most definitely from Neil.

> Hi Pom! Noticed you allow questions and comments now so I'd like to formally request an interview for the Linda Vista High School Chronicle. Can I pick your brain about why you created this blog and what you hope to accomplish?

I smiled and told myself I'd get back to him in a couple of days, to give myself some time to come up with a good response. Then I turned my head and saw the new, folded non-formfitting shirt my mom had gotten me. It was just another way of keeping me safe and an extension of her job training. Wardrobe risk avoidance.

Basically, lock up your boobs. She would die of shame if she knew what I was doing here.

I was going to close my computer when I remembered the other assignment Neil had asked me to work on.

He'd said to pick any staff member I wanted. He'd said to make it "splashy." He'd asked for unpredictable.

> Dear Nurse Reyes,
> Would you be willing to give an interview for the

school paper about your thoughts on the popular blog *The Circle in the Square*?

Thank you,
Phoebe Townsend

Email sent.

Then another comment popped up on the screen.

> If you're writing this because you're trolling for dick, I can help you with that.

It was creepy, so I deleted it and went to bed. But it took me a while to fall asleep.

Someone must have explained to Brookhurst that taking a screenshot of a Twitter post reduces the amount of traffic or attention that the original post gets. She used this new skill to screenshot my mini orgasm how-to seminar and commented with her favorite word: *Filth*.

She was annoyed because she had been tagged in a lot of my thank-you messages on the day I went viral. You know, all in a day's work, I guess. My favorite so far was:

> @CircleintheSquare, the blog that launched a thousand orgasms

Then I noticed that Brookhurst had tweeted something completely unrelated.

> **@TheRealLydiaBrookhurst:** Here are a few LOCAL businesses I'd like to spotlight! Thanks for making us proud! @LindaVistaStationery @TonysBurgers

Coincidentally, they were also the businesses directly across the street from where I was sitting with Cora at that exact moment.

"Jesus, he asked you to go to the locker room?" Cora asked, handing me a California burrito while she emptied the contents of a tiny tub of guacamole onto her quesadilla. We'd stopped at the food trucks before leaving for the game because Cora knows this is my happy place.

"No one is going to be naked or anything. He wants me to get a good sense of the game. He wants a 'real' story."

I tried not to let *that* get under my skin.

"Yeah, well, you have the most sensitive nose on the planet. You're going to get a lot of 'scents' of the game," she said, pointing to her nose, clearly thinking she was a genius.

"Hilarious," I said, clutching my notebook. "I have no idea what I'm doing."

"That isn't even a real burrito," Cora said, eyeing my massive, absolutely real burrito and effectively changing the subject.

For someone who was pretty open-minded about every other aspect of human life, she was a remarkably picky eater and a would-be vegetarian if she didn't secretly still love chicken fingers more than life itself.

"It's better. A California burrito contains carne asada, guacamole, tomatoes, cheese, sour cream, *and french fries.* Let that sink in," I said for what felt like the millionth time. Cora shook

45

her head as I slammed my hand down on the edge of the table to keep a stack of napkins from flying onto the ground.

What started as one taco truck has evolved into Food Truck Village, the most amazing culinary experience our tiny cookie-cutter town has to offer. The row of food trucks is about a ten-minute walk from school. It runs parallel to Main Street, next to an old flower shop and an empty lot that no one has developed yet. The food truck owners got together and turned the lot into a covered picnic-bench area surrounded by star jasmine bushes, creeping grapevines, and palm trees.

Food Truck Village's very existence is comforting. There is something magical about a place where you can get earth-shattering Mexican food, Korean barbecue, Soul Food, sushi burritos, vegan sandwiches, and smoothies all in one spot. I love everything from the anthropomorphized sushi burrito statue greeting customers to the ridiculous cartoon squirrel painting on the side of the vegan truck with a speech bubble that reads: I'M NUTS ABOUT KALE!

That is delightful. Pure and simple.

I heard some of the owners are trying to get the town to let them put a little playground at the far end of the lot. At night they hang twinkle lights, and it really is beautiful.

Linda Vista *is* a striking place. Loosely translated, it means "pretty view," because even though the natural streams and three-hundred-year-old sycamores are, in fact, pretty, the people who eventually named our town were very beige with their adjectives and not Spanish speakers. Southern California was once mostly Mexico, so I guess the white guys who took it over thought Spanish words might be a good idea.

"Pretty view" is okay, I guess. It doesn't win any points for imagination, but there are definitely some pretty spots.

So they weren't wrong. Just boring.

I breathed in the smell of the food and the jasmine, while Cora searched her purse for gum.

"Okay," she said. "Now that you've been nourished by the talented chefs of Food Truck Village, can we go be with people?"

"Do we have to?" I asked.

But Cora was already clearing our trash.

Awesome.

As we left the picnic tables, I noticed that Tony's Burgers, directly across the street, had started offering 50 percent off lunch purchases to students.

"They're getting desperate," said Cora, pointing to the sign.

It was Friday, the air was crisp, and for normal people, going to a football game was a perfectly lovely event, but I was absolutely dreading it. Football to me has always been the equivalent of a battle to the death in the Colosseum, where giant gladiators fought against their will for Caesar's favor. I know the players choose to be on the team, and no one is supposed to get killed, but it feels less like a sport and more like a public flogging when someone needs to be carried off the field to the medic after every play.

Not to mention the fact that it *is* painfully boring.

"You'll be fine," Cora said, leaning into my shoulder as we walked toward the football stadium entrance. "Try to focus on the stuff that doesn't have to do with the sport. Adds color to the story." She waved to someone over my shoulder, and I saw

David, her bearded, lanky hipster boyfriend, leaning against a tree with a mustard-yellow beanie on his head and a giant grin on his face. She told me where they'd be sitting and then immediately ran over and started making out with him. Immediately. No words were exchanged before she latched her face on to his.

There's really no appropriate response when your best friend shoves her tongue down some guy's throat, so I turned to follow the crowd edging its way toward the stands and veered off in the direction of the locker rooms. I made a mental note to sit somewhere else when the interview was done, and then text Cora later and say I couldn't find her. David's kissing technique is erratic, and I preferred not to listen to slurping while I tried to pay attention to the game.

I had heard Jorge's name a lot in recent months because of football and was pretty sure I had health class with him, but he sat at the front with the rest of the football team, and all I ever saw of them was the backs of their heads.

All the players seemed to be expecting my arrival, because no one looked surprised when the gravel under my boots crunched against the linoleum floor.

One face looked up at me as I moved toward the crowd of oversized shoulder pads, and I knew it was him. He was thin, but not in a gawky way. He had the weird, overly enthusiastic look of someone who enjoyed the gym. His eyes were dark, and there was something about them that made him look like he was seconds away from laughing. Then, once I got close to him, I noticed the cleft in his chin.

He nodded in my direction and pointed at a chair a few

feet away. I was close enough to see and hear everything that was going on in the huddle, but far enough that I didn't have to touch anyone, which I appreciated because they all looked pretty, well, moist.

"Gentlemen," said Coach Snowden as I wrinkled my nose. Even among the group of abnormally large athletes who had presumably been warming up outside, the scent of Coach Snowden was distinct. He cleared his throat importantly and I lifted my pen, ready to take notes.

I mean, I tried. I really did.

A few phrases buzzed through my ear canal. Things like "stay focused" and "be aggressive" and "stick to the game plan." That's when I remembered what Cora had said: *Focus on the stuff that doesn't have to do with the sport.*

The players' faces and body language made it seem like they were going into battle. Most of them fidgeted with their pads, and a few of them stared blankly ahead. One guy picked his nose and casually flicked a booger away. After a while Coach Snowden stopped talking, and the team got together to pump each other up, which was a little frightening for a casual observer.

"Come watch the game from the bench," said a voice. Jorge was standing next to me as the rest of his team was filtering out into the stadium. He was remarkably light on his feet, and I was momentarily stunned at how quickly he'd moved to my side.

"I don't need to do that," I said. "Really, I can see fine from the stands."

"C'mon," he insisted. "An actual postgame interview from the bench."

"Postgame?" He'd asked to do the interview before, not after.

"Yeah, why not? You're going to try and escape before the game is over?"

I raised my eyebrows at him.

"Please?" he asked.

I nodded and followed the players out into the stadium.

As the team warmed up, I looked up at the crowd of people sitting on the bleachers and tried to feel something. If someone were to caption this chilly September Friday, with kids under blankets watching athletes injure themselves for our amusement, I think they would go with: "America."

"Phoebe, will this work?"

Jorge had cleared a spot for me on the bench and lined it with a plaid blanket.

"So your butt doesn't freeze," he said, bowing, and I could feel a small smile flash across my face, despite the fact that this was the last place I wanted to be.

He ran off and the game started.

It was loud and obnoxious and exactly what I expected the experience to be despite never having sat through a game. I took about ten pages of notes, determined to be a journalist.

Which is why the fate of those notes is particularly sad.

It is impossible to explain the appeal of dousing a coach in Gatorade when your team is victorious. It becomes exceedingly more difficult to explain the appeal when the giant plastic container gets lifted over the coach's head, only to come crashing down on the oblivious reporter trying to take a picture of the scoreboard for her article.

The edge of the heavy container hit me in the face, and I felt the tiny metal wires spring from my braces directly into my gums before I passed out with a mouthful of blood.

I vaguely remember being carried by a giant, sweaty football player who would not stop apologizing. I think I told him to shut up because I wanted to vomit, but I can't be certain. I remember someone calling my parents, who had to bring me in for emergency orthodontic work. I remember the sweet relief of painkillers. I remember Monica Hansen's face swimming overhead as she tried to get a picture with her phone. The weirdest thing I remember, though, is what I did to distract myself from the rising panic in my chest when I felt the thin pieces of metal crumble in my mouth.

Sometimes when you're nervous, it's comforting to imagine that you're someplace else. Safe. Warm. Happy. But the only thing that has ever helped me relax is recitation of facts.

It's almost like retained information reminds you of all the things you can hold on to, no matter what happens, because it's tucked away in your memory somewhere. So in usual Phoebe fashion, my brain did a recall of information from the blog that was both soothing and a little unconventional.

Sexual positions. Erogenous zones. Sexually transmitted diseases. Safe-sex practices. *The Kama Sutra.* The production of semen. The lining of uterine walls. Lubrication. Condoms. Contraception. Female erections. Ejaculation.

My thoughts rolled through my brain like a teleprompter and kept going until everything went dark.

When I woke up, my mouth was completely numb and my braces were gone. The orthodontist had opted to pull them early. I ran my tongue over my teeth in shock, surprised at the slimy feeling in my mouth and all the extra space now that the hardware was gone. I was actually worried that my lips were going to slide off my face.

"How are you feeling?" Cora asked. I groaned. "Hey, silver lining! You got them off already!" She was sitting cross-legged in a chair about a foot from me, reading a magazine. "Your parents are filling out some paperwork, and then they're taking you home."

"Where's David?" I asked, looking around. It didn't really bother me that he wasn't at my bedside, but he'd been with Cora at the game, so I wondered where he'd gone.

"He went home to paint. Got inspired at the game."

I used an extreme amount of force not to roll my eyes at this. I also decided it was probably not a good idea to ask whether it was the game or the crushing blow of the Gatorade container that had inspired him.

"I see," I said, looking at her while I touched my cheeks.

"Just don't, okay?"

"Don't what?"

"Make that face. It reeks of judgment."

"I see," I repeated. She glared at me. "What?" I said.

"Can you just try to like him?" she asked.

I was a little annoyed that she was lecturing me about not liking her boyfriend enough right after I'd had my braces smashed into my face. "I don't dislike him," I said.

"But you don't like him."

I chose to say nothing.

"Phoebe, you are my person. My laser-focused superdork. I think you can try to like this guy, since you're making zero effort now."

"Maybe we should have this discussion when I'm not feeling so groggy." She frowned at me.

The truth is that I don't actually dislike David. He's fine. He's cute in a quirky way, and he's artsy, like Cora. What I don't like is that she's become David's Girlfriend, like it's a title she acquired with land and responsibilities. At least, that's how it feels to me.

She quit her water polo team when it clashed with the interpretive dance class they started taking together, which no matter how many times she explained it to me still sounded like mime practice. She even stepped down as the organizer for Poetry Slam Night because she never seemed to have enough time to read and comment on all the submissions before Wednesday evening.

I didn't want to tell her that she was letting a guy steal the twinkly things that made her special, because I didn't want to crush her feminist spirit and make her feel like she couldn't have it all. She deserves to have a boyfriend if she wants one. She also deserves to have a supportive best friend who reserves judgment for things that are actually bad for her. Like smoking. And drugs. And her weird obsession with British royalty.

And I can't pretend that I'm actually sad about her quitting water polo, though I'd never tell her so. I didn't really enjoy wincing every time someone came close to drowning her when she had the ball.

"The guys are worse," she'd said when I complained. "You don't know the kinds of things they hide in their suits."

"Their Speedos?! What could you possibly hide in there?" She never gave me specifics, and I've spent way too much time thinking about it since.

"Did anyone grab my notes?" I said, changing the subject in a very obvious way.

"I saw what was left of them on the field, but the Gatorade . . ." She trailed off. I wanted to scream, but even as the irritation built, I realized something else was off.

"Why does my hair feel shorter?" I said, noticing that there appeared to be several inches missing when I ran my fingers through it.

"Oh, that," said Cora. "It got fused to your sweater with blood that I'm pretty sure was yours, and instead of trying to ease it off, or get it wet, or do something sensible, the dumbass guy in the ambulance cut a massive chunk of it on one side. . . ."

"Mirror," I said quietly. She pulled one out of her bag and stepped back, frowning. There were streaks of dried blood on my cheeks and a very noticeable void where several inches of hair should have been. I looked like I'd been run over with a lawn mower.

It reminded me of one Christmas when I was small and my parents had taken me to Hawaii to see my grandparents. Tutu had been horrified that my mom had cut my hair, because she'd had her heart set on me starting hula lessons with long, flowing locks.

In this moment, I understood Tutu's rage.

"You should know Jorge Cervantes is waiting outside too."
I looked at her and felt my face get hot. "He looks awful," she
added.

"Good," I said. "He wanted a thorough interview. He wanted
me to experience the game. Done and done."

"C'mon, Phoebe. He's not that bad. I thought he was a huge
asshole too, but then when you got hurt, he—"

"Felt guilty because it's his fault I was there in the first
place?"

"I'll tell him to go home, then," said Cora, standing up. I
nodded. "Can I get you anything?"

"A pen," I said angrily, still tasting blood in my mouth. She
pulled a bright teal one from her bag and handed me a notebook before stepping into the hall to tell Jorge to leave the
premises if he valued his life.

Football Injuries, I wrote. *A Firsthand Account.*

5

Brookhurst wasn't too busy on Twitter, but she did manage to get me a few more followers.

Her first tweet was about the high school football game. The second one was about the blog. Both included me because the universe clearly has a sense of humor.

> **@TheRealLydiaBrookhurst:** Great game Linda Vista Wildcats! Good effort! Hope that poor Linda Vista High School Chronicle reporter is OK!

> **@TheRealLydiaBrookhurst:** Hey @CircleintheSquare—Just a reminder. Your blog is disgusting. Your graphic depictions of sex and mast*rbation are offensive.

Several other Twitter accounts expressed their support of Brookhurst's message.

> **@LindaVistaStationery:** That blog MUST GO

@Gails_Nails_On_Main: Disgusting. Absolutely Agree.

@MelsPookieBear27: BROOKHURST FOR PRESIDENT!

@THERIGHTSTUFFLindaVistaBrch475: VOTE THIS WOMAN IN!

My response:

@CircleintheSquare: Thanks for reading! Glad you found the information useful.

I have never been considered funny in my life. Or cool. But that's beside the point. When I got back to school on Tuesday morning, after taking Monday off, I was met in the newsroom with a round of applause. I'd emailed Neil my football article, and apparently, he'd shared it with everyone.

"Holy shit, Phoebe. I didn't know you were funny," Neil said.

I'd spent the better part of Saturday and Sunday lying on my couch writing the sports recap while my mom tried to force-feed me soup and applesauce. The cuts in my mouth made chewing regular food quite painful, though I'm not sure sloshing liquid and squishy food over the open wounds was any better.

I hadn't been able to get over my irritation with Jorge to

write the player spotlight, but I had managed to write a decent summary of the game. There may have been a few extra details about butt sweat and the aroma of the locker room, but what people really seemed to respond to was my complete lack of understanding regarding the sport itself and the detailed account of being knocked unconscious and escorted off the field.

"Nice article," Monica said from the front of the room. She swiveled her chair all the way around to face me, and though I was used to her casual indifference, her interested expression stopped me for a minute. "And I like the look."

"Thanks," I said, unsure if she was serious or not. My hand went instinctively up to the soft chopped ends of my hair that now hung about an inch below my shoulder.

Monica never complimented anyone, so it was natural for me to feel a little uneasy about her attention. With my new hair and without braces, my face had transformed in a way that I was not used to yet. I was still doing a double take in the mirror to make sure it was me.

My mom, who had never shown the slightest bit of interest in my hair before, had taken me to an expensive salon. The stylist had given me layers that were supposed to frame my face, but they made it impossible to get all my hair in a ponytail, though I'm fairly certain the whole elegantly-falling-out-of-the-ponytail thing is the point.

Just as I was about to leave, Monica pulled out a ziplock bag filled with a few loose sheets of paper.

"Don't think you need these anymore, since you wrote the article already, but here are your notes," she said, handing them over. "Interesting observations," she added.

"Oh, great. Thanks," I said, taking the notes and trying to picture Monica Hansen scooping them off the field. But I was also trying to understand her motivation. It was uncharacteristically thoughtful for someone who once convinced our entire fifth-grade class that I'd asked to be called Fo-bo the Hobo instead of Phoebe.

Diabolical.

Even after we'd finished our strange interaction, her eyes followed me, and I pretended not to notice.

I packed up my stuff when the bell rang, but Neil stopped me.

"Hey," he said. "Glad you're okay. And seriously, that article was great. You were always a solid writer, but I guess I just hadn't seen you do anything like this before. It was a whole different side of you. I like it," he added.

"Thanks," I said, recognizing the patronizing AF comment but blushing like an idiot anyway.

"So are you free for that coffee on Friday?"

"Friday?" I asked.

"Yeah. I owe you, remember?"

"Right. Sure. Friday works," I said.

That was totally cool. You didn't sound desperate or creepy at all, I told myself.

"Great. You have a free period at eleven too, right?" he asked. I nodded, wondering how he knew that.

"Perfect. Let's do it then." He turned to leave, then turned back, remembering something else. "Oh yeah, and the player spotlight. You're sending that over to me, right?"

"Oh," I said. I knew it was still due, and I knew I had to get the information from Jorge, which was problematic because

I'd decided that I'd rather avoid him at all costs, but for some reason I felt no sense of urgency to complete this particular assignment. It was like I'd decided that it would just write itself if I ignored it long enough.

"So can I have it tomorrow?" he asked.

"Is that when it's due?"

"It's due yesterday," he said. "And the staff spotlight deadline is coming up."

Crap. The spotlight. Nurse Reyes had not responded to my first email and follow-up.

"I was just distracted because Pom finally emailed me back. You know," he whispered, "the writer of *The Circle in the Square.*" He looked pretty smug about this, and I tried not to look pleased with myself because (1) hello, it's me, and (2) I'm also working on a great interview that will be both *splashy* and *unpredictable.*

"Nice work," I said, focusing on my surprised face. It had taken me nearly two hours to craft a response to Neil, and it was only a few lines long:

Hi Neil,

Thanks for contacting me.

I'd be happy to answer any questions you have on the blog, but here are the ground rules:

Interview must be conducted online through Q&A portal in the blog.

My identity will not be revealed, so please don't ask.

You may publish the responses in the

newspaper, but you must cite the blog as a
reference.

10 p.m. Thursday—I'll send you a link.

Thanks,

Pom

"Yeah," he said. "I'm hoping they change their mind and
decide to reveal themselves, but I'm okay with just getting the
information for now." He sighed. "So you'll have the player
spotlight for me tomorrow?"

"Tomorrow it is," I said, touching my hair.

He noticed the way my fingertips lingered over the ends
and smiled.

"Your hair really does look good like that," he said.

"Thanks. It was time for a change, I guess."

Casual acknowledgment of a compliment without denying the aes-
thetic appeal of new look. Nailed it.

Neil nodded and I spent half a second too long watching
him walk away.

"You're going to make his butt blush."

I rolled my eyes. I'll never understand how she manages to
be there every single time I do that.

"I know you're still basking in the glory of your article,
but you need to read this, okay?" Cora said, handing me her
phone.

"What is it?" I asked, squinting at the screen.

"The latest Q and A on *The Circle in the Square*. Just finished. I may have casually left it open on David's laptop. A
little educational reading, I think."

I looked at the response I'd written about how to give a woman an orgasm without penetration.

"Good, right?" Cora asked.

"Yeah. But why am I reading this?" I asked her.

"I think it's healthy for us to study the ways that some people choose to express physical love," Cora said.

I snorted.

"'Physical love'? Since when do you talk like this?"

"Since David and I have been thinking about taking that step in our relationship," she said.

"But you two already . . ." I trailed off. Cora was open about her current experiences with David and all past experiences with other guys. I was privy to all information, from her first French kiss in seventh grade to the over-the-sweater boob-honk from an eighth-grade boyfriend that earned him a throbbing red welt across his face during the bus ride home from Disneyland. It was a little strange because I'd been led to believe that sex was already happening, when apparently it was not.

"No," said Cora. "We haven't."

"Okay," I said.

"I want to. But I also want to be on the pill for a full month before," she said.

"And you want to use a condom," I added, unable to stop myself.

"Phoebe, he hasn't been with anyone else," Cora said.

"You still want to use a condom," I said, aware that I was stepping slightly out of character.

"Well, I've heard it doesn't feel as good," said Cora.

"Use it anyway," I said.

Cora gave me an annoyed look that very clearly questioned the authority with which I was speaking.

"I think my boyfriend and I can decide what his penis will be wearing when it makes its grand entrance," she said flatly.

Stubborn Cora made an appearance every now and then when she thought someone was trying to tell her what to do. I should have realized that she would push back strongly if I phrased my response the way I did, so I backtracked a little.

"I'm sure you can. But I'm not saying use protection because I think David is having wild orgies. I'm saying use it because whenever a penis and a vagina get together, pregnancy is *always* a possibility."

Cora was silent for a minute, and when she nodded in agreement, I felt a tiny rush of relief.

"'Whenever a penis and a vagina get together'?" she asked, smirking.

"Yes," I said. "As they do."

"Who talks like that?" she continued. "Seriously, read the blog. Sounds like you should."

"Maybe you're right," I agreed.

My parents called to say they would be home late and that I should order pizza, so I luxuriated in the freedom of an empty house by sitting on the couch in my pj's with my laptop open to my blog. I was about to start reading the Q&As for the day when the doorbell rang.

My immediate response was to drop to the floor.

I'm not sure when this started. As a child, I once saw my mom hide from a pair of Jehovah's Witnesses at the door, and the image left a lasting impression on me. A grown woman hiding behind the curtains in her own house. I'll never forget the way she mouthed *Don't move* to my father, who was trying to walk to the family room with a cup of coffee. Eventually the couple on our doorstep gave up and left, even though I'm sure they could hear my parents whisper-arguing, but we still watched cautiously from our window as they disappeared down the street.

To be fair, my mom hides from anyone who comes to our house unexpectedly, so I thought this was totally normal growing up. I know that you don't *have* to ignore everyone who comes to the front door, but my initial response is still to hide, which I see now is completely bizarre.

I got up and walked over to the front door and stood on my tiptoes to look through the peephole.

No one was there.

Seriously, people still doorbell ditch?

I opened the door a crack and found a basket covered in a blue dish towel on our doormat.

My first irrational thought was, *Thank God it's too small to be a baby.* I'm not sure why my mind went there, but the thought was still with me as I looked around for signs of whoever had left it.

I pulled the cloth back to reveal a pile of fruit.

Turning one of the grapefruit over in my hand, I noticed that someone had written *I'm sorry* on the peel.

Then I took out one of the tangerines.

My sincerest apologies was written all the way around it.

Then a banana had a more specific message: *It was stupid of me to ask you to sit on the field at the game. I am an asshat. And I am sorry.*

Every piece of fruit bore some kind of apology.

I took a picture of the banana with the basket in the background and sent it to Cora, who immediately responded:

> OMG. He. Signed. Fruit.

> FORGIVE HIM.

As if writing an apology message on a banana were the equivalent of a troubadour playing a ballad on their lute outside my bedroom window.

I texted her.

> Really? That's all it takes?

> He's also super-hot and in my honors English and History classes. You could do worse. Listen to the fruit!

> So this fruit is basically asking me to do the interview?

No, Phoebe. It's fruit.
It's not saying anything.

But I should do the interview
right?

Didn't you tell Neil you'd
do it anyway?

Yeah, but I could email the
questions and be done with it.

You could.

but . . . ?

But nothing. He's cute and
he apologized with fruit. If it were
me I'd be driving back to
school already

I knew Jorge would be done with practice around five-thirty,
all thanks to Cora's stint as a runner during our first year at
Linda Vista High. She had to wait until the football team was

done training to use the track, so she had their schedule fully memorized.

She is still pissed about that.

When I got to the stadium, I spotted Jorge immediately with a few other teammates, packing up their bags to go home.

He looked up and saw me, and for a moment he shuffled his feet. The other players headed out of the stadium while a few runners stretched on the track. Then it was just the two of us standing on the grass.

"Got your sorry fruit," I said. "Thanks."

"Would've sent figs too, but they were too ripe to write on."

It was such a weird thing to say, but I refused to laugh or ask him about that even though I wanted to. I was still holding on to some of the resentment from his first email and his demand for a good interview. But there was something nice about the way he shifted uncomfortably, something honest.

"I'm sorry I made you sit on the bench at the game," he said. "And I'm really sorry you got hurt."

He meant it.

The sky was turning a pretty orangey-pink color as I pulled out my notebook.

"So you want the interview or not?" I asked.

We talked for a while on the field in the middle of the stadium until the lights came on. I pressed him for details on how he trained. What it felt like to be on a team. What he said to people who thought football was stupid.

He laughed at that one.

By the time we'd finished and I had enough information to create a fairly comprehensive assessment of his character, I thought of one thing I hadn't asked.

"Is your family supportive of all your athletic endeavors?"

"Yes," he said. "Mom is a professor. And Dad is a contractor. Mom is in the hospital a lot for dialysis, and Dad is there with her when she has to go overnight, but they're both really supportive. They catch as many games as they can, especially since scouts started showing up. Mom stopped teaching full-time, so a scholarship and maybe loans is how I'm getting to college."

I looked up at him and felt something hard fall into my stomach. He seemed to sense this and his mouth set in a hard line.

"Off the record," he said. "I don't need you to feel sorry for me. Football might be stupid to you, but it's not just about the game. Colleges provide more scholarships for football players than any other sport. And whatever happens, I don't want my parents to have to pay for me."

"Right," I said, unable to think of anything else to say.

"Got what you needed?" he asked.

"Yeah," I replied. "I got it."

"Thanks for doing that," he said.

"I hope everything is okay with your mom. I mean, I hope she's well again soon." It sounded weak as I said it, but Jorge smiled reassuringly.

"Thanks," he said. "Me too."

I got up to walk away, but as I leaned over to zip up my

backpack, my stack of Spanish flash cards fell onto the grass. Jorge bent over to pick them up.

"'Ferrocarril?'" he asked, the word flowing out of him like music as he looked down at the first card in the stack.

"Vocabulary quiz," I muttered. "'Ferrocarril' is 'railroad,' right?" I said, flipping the card over to make sure I was right.

"Yes, but you have to roll the *r*'s," he said, raising his eyebrow.

I frowned. I could not for the life of me figure out how to move my tongue to make that sound.

"¿Quieres ayuda?" he asked.

"No, gracias," I said, trying not to laugh at the stupid grin on his face. He was clearly enjoying himself. "I don't need help."

"Okay," he said. "But if you did want some advice, which you don't, I'd say, when rolling your *r*'s, try pressing your tongue behind your front teeth and breathe the word out. Don't force it. Let it roll."

"Thanks," I said, deliberately using English this time to avoid embarrassment.

He walked off toward his car, and when he was far enough away, I practiced it like he'd said.

I was mildly annoyed that he was right.

My mom and I got home at exactly the same time. She slammed her car door with her hip, and she carried two armfuls of groceries to the house.

"Thanks, sweetheart," she said as I took one of the bags. She kissed me on the cheek before bending over to take off her shoes. "This woman really is something else, you know." She handed me a flyer she'd stuffed into one of her reusable bags.

"That was on my windshield at work."

It read:

Citizens' Coalition for Responsible Censorship:
Boycott immorality.
Do you know what your children are doing online?

Below that was my blog's URL and another line that read:

If you stand by your blog, why are you anonymous?
It's only a matter of time before someone discovers who
you are.

I nearly dropped the groceries I was holding as ice slipped into the pit of my stomach. It wasn't a threat to expose me, and she wasn't demanding my identity or asking other people to find out who I was. But it was almost like she was posing the question: Wouldn't it be a shame if someone found out who runs this blog and ruined their life?

Relax. Nobody knows it's me. I breathed.

"Did you know she's running for mayor now?" my dad chimed in, lifting a heavy box of policy binders out of the trunk of the car. "Scary thing is she has a following. Can you

70

believe she's rallying people against this blog?" He tripped a little, trying to kick off his dress shoes without untying them.

"I mean, I'm not a fan of the blog either, but she's got hundreds of flyers. That's over the top," Mom said, taking some green beans out of the fridge to wash.

"Why aren't you a fan of the blog?" I asked, then immediately regretted it. Mom didn't look up from her green beans.

"It's just unnecessary. Feels like the kind of thing someone would write just to push buttons."

"Have you read it?" I asked, but before she could answer, my dad dropped a carton of eggs on the kitchen floor.

I looked down at the flyer again.

A small white dove holding what looked like an olive branch in its beak. Underneath it was BROOKHURST FOR MAYOR in gold lettering.

My family is not religious, but even I recognized the obvious Christian symbolism. For the first time since starting my blog, I felt dirty. It wasn't because of anything I'd written. It was almost as if Brookhurst's ignorance was turning my blog into something it wasn't. For some reason she thought it was an opinion piece.

The Circle in the Square was just a bunch of facts about sex.

There were larger issues at play here, things I couldn't quite wrap my head around yet. So I helped my parents put groceries away and tried to settle my thoughts.

When I sat down at my computer, I noticed the ziplock bag Monica had given me earlier. The pages were a pulpy mess, but there were a few discernible scribbles of notes, which were useless now that I'd written the article already. There were scores and jersey numbers, but there was one line she'd gone to the trouble of circling. And I froze for a moment when I read it.

I'd accidentally made a list of injuries that would complicate a player's life . . . sexually. Thankfully, the other, more embarrassing notations had been washed out by the Gatorade. The one note that survived, however, was *crushed scrotum/possible testicular trauma*. I couldn't imagine what Monica had made of that, but I felt uncomfortable knowing that she'd seen it.

I tried to distract myself with the blog to help brush off the unease that had started to build, but that only worked until I got to the last few comments in the Q&A section. Some of them were definitely in response to the orgasm entry. And some were just angry.

Are you a doctor? If not, you have no business writing this blog. If you are, I'd like to see some credentials.

This blog is a crime against God.

Ur going to hell

Love your new Q&A section. Talk to your girlfriend about what feels good? How about you just tell her what feels good. She'll learn to like it.

The last one scared me. There's something eerie about the way commenters post on a blog about sex. Something unnatural about the way people want to control information because they feel like the facts alone are dangerous. It makes my skin crawl.

I liked my anonymity, but there were moments when I wished I could take off the mask and be honest with someone.

I followed up with Nurse Reyes again but still got no response.

6

Brookhurst tweeted again.

> **@TheRealLydiaBrookhurst:** It appears there's a Q&A section of the sex blog. So our kids can get answers from a pervert? Reckless.

It was a fairly benign tweet, and not unexpected. But the next day, when I got out of bed and walked across the hall to the bathroom, I caught a glimpse of Lydia Brookhurst. The actual, *real* human person had just appeared in *my* home like a blond phantom.

I'd never really understood the phrase "shit your pants" until that moment, when my guts had a reaction to her physical presence. Of course I panicked, launching myself back into my bedroom before anyone could see me.

By leaving the door open a crack, I managed to get a better view of her through the reflection in our hallway mirror. She was perfectly coiffed, with a long string of white pearls around her neck, and completely at ease in my living room, where my mom was perched on the edge of the sofa like an anxious cat.

For a frightening nanosecond I assumed my life was over, that I had been discovered, and that I would have to begin a new life as a wandering sexpert in suburbia. But then I heard some bits of the conversation.

"So it's really important that we address this liability, and I'll need a full consultation on all my locations, and . . ."

SWEET RELIEF. Thank God it is boring insurance risk analysis.

It was bizarre watching her movements because her voice and presence filled the room even though she was barely taking up any physical space on our couch. In fact, her butt might have been floating mere centimeters away from the upholstery as she gesticulated wildly with one hand and grasped my dad's favorite mug with the other. It was the one my mom got him the last time we visited family in Hawaii. It had a picture of a giant wave, and it said EDDIE WOULD GO.

Dad was looking at Brookhurst's perfectly manicured fingers wrapped around his mug with an expression of determined avoidance.

She was asking my parents for help with risk analysis, and even though they were usually so professional with clients, both of them seemed uneasy about this meeting. Mom's eyes darted back and forth between my dad and Brookhurst while Dad asked a series of questions about her property. To anyone else, he would have looked like a normal human being conducting business, but he was also clicking his mechanical pencil and letting bits of lead drop on the floor. To anyone who knows him, that's weird.

Dad doesn't make messes.

I continued watching their meeting in the reflection of the mirror through the crack in my bedroom door and made the mistake of leaning too hard on the wood panel. It creaked just enough to draw attention from the three adults, and I panicked again, grabbing a random dirty backpack with a broken zipper and pretending like I was getting ready to leave. The backpack was empty, so I filled it with a stuffed animal from my bookshelf and two books off my floor before stepping out into the hall.

"Phoebe, you remember Ms. Brookhurst?"

I nodded at my dad.

"Hello, Phoebe. What a charming backpack!"

The stuffed animal's foot was sticking out of the zipper.

What a weird thing to compliment.

But I was wearing sweatpants and a ratty tank top, so really it was the only option she had.

"Thanks," I said.

Shit, I thought. *I've forgotten how to smile naturally. Pull up both sides of the lips and appear to be a reasonably content human being.*

My dad made a face at me, so I guess I wasn't convincing.

Luckily, Brookhurst was oblivious.

"I hear you write for the school paper. I might just give you an interview," she said. Her face lit up like she was offering me a once-in-a-lifetime opportunity, and I resisted the urge to scowl.

"Really?" I asked. Then, luckily, my dad stepped in.

"She's a brilliant writer," he said. "But her assignments come from her editor, I think."

76

Nice save, Dad.

"Well, I must meet this editor," she said, still smiling as she looked down at her watch. "Oh, is that the time? I really must dash. Town council meeting tonight. Fiona, send the contracts over tomorrow and I'll sign them immediately. Here's all the financial information you requested." She pulled a huge file from her bag and handed it to my mom. Brookhurst rose, birdlike, from our sofa and fixed me with a smile that looked forced. Then she winked, twiddled her fingers in an asinine baby wave, and raced out the door.

"So we work for that woman now?" Dad asked, looking at the file in my mom's hand. There was a large, obnoxious cursive *L.B.* on a Post-it note.

"It's more money than we've ever made on one contract, Matt."

"She's a political candidate."

"For a small town in a local election. We don't have to get involved in that. It doesn't even affect us."

Dad frowned. He followed local politics pretty closely and he attended the town council meetings.

"It always affects us," he said. "And even if it didn't, it still matters if it affects other people."

They argued politely for a minute about this while my stomach clenched as I remembered what my mom had said about the blog.

I'm not a fan of the blog either.

Now their biggest client was the one person on the planet more interested in my blog than I was. For very different reasons, of course.

My parents had no idea they were actually aiding my enemy.

My poor, quiet, unsuspecting parents . . .

Sometimes I wonder if the blog is a direct response to the fact that my parents have always treated sex like a taboo subject.

As a kid, I remember my dad fast-forwarding romantic scenes the minute someone leaned in for a kiss.

"Whoa, nothing to see here," he'd say quickly.

Cartoons that displayed any kind of sexual tension made both of my parents squeamish in a way that seemed over the top even for them. They loosened the reins on my TV viewing as I got older, but I'll never forget the look on my mom's face once when something too sexy appeared on the screen and she tripped over the coffee table to lunge for the remote.

"Let's go out for ice cream!" she'd said from the floor, rubbing her shin.

It was weird.

And going to Cora's house as a kid was the exact opposite.

Her parents respected the fact that my mom and dad monitored nearly everything I read and watched, and didn't put on anything too provocative for us whenever I was over, but there were still things that slipped through the cracks. Even the love scene between Nala and Simba in *The Lion King* when they frolicked in the jungle to "Can You Feel the Love Tonight" would have freaked them out.

And what's strange is that even though my parents never really display physical affection in front of me, they're incredibly loving toward each other.

They've always appeared to enjoy each other's company, and even their arguments are respectful, which I guess is more important than having no memory of ever seeing them kiss.

But still a little weird.

I've always wondered how they would react to my research. If they would think I was some kind of freak for having any interest at all in sex. But then I'd let the moment pass and just be glad that I would never have to find out what they thought. That's the beauty of anonymity, which was proving to come in quite handy as Brookhurst continued her campaign.

In addition to her personal vendetta against my blog, Lydia Brookhurst had managed to add Food Truck Village and plastic bags to her growing list of concerns as a political candidate.

Her campaign against the food trucks was threefold:

1. They blocked the side street next to her store.
2. They damaged the aesthetic appeal of her storefront window.
3. She has said on numerous occasions that she does not like the smell of "ethnic food."

Most young people were choosing to spend their money at the food trucks and not at the old establishments. So naturally, Brookhurst had support from the owners of three restaurants within walking distance of the trucks. They also believed that

Food Truck Village was an eyesore, added noise pollution, and greatly damaged the traditional Main Street feel they were trying to preserve. It was also a convenient excuse for people to dust off some subtle and not-so-subtle racism.

"Ethnic food," my ass . . .

As for plastic bags, it might seem like a nonsense issue, but there are actually a lot of people in our town upset about the fact that they were basically outlawed in California to help lessen the environmental impact of our wasteful consumer habits. Supermarkets now require you to pay for bags if you do not bring your own, and it has become quite clear that there are people who would literally strangle the last unicorn on the planet if it meant they didn't have to walk back to their car to get their reusable bag.

Lydia's tweets on this issue were more specific:

> **@TheRealLydiaBrookhurst:** 25 cent charge for plastic bags at the market if you "forget" your "green" reusable bag?!

> **@TheRealLydiaBrookhurst:** Stop charging people for plastic bags! Stop forcing reusable bags on regular people!

> **@TheRealLydiaBrookhurst:** And don't get me started on the hideous Food Truck Village! It is RUINING our beautiful Main Street!

Her loyal minions agreed:

@ShinyPatty76: You're absolutely right Lydia! So annoying to have to walk back to my car!

@RadDadRoadTripin_88: It's a corrupt charge for no reason! Brookhurst for Mayor!

@GrannyKate: Those Food Trucks have got to go! They are taking business away from the REAL Linda Vistans!

@XmarkstheSpot: The Food Trucks are garbage. Linda Vista, Vote Brookhurst in NOW.

So if we examine the facts, it would appear that Brookhurst was running an anti–sex ed, anti–food truck, pro-pollution campaign, and the creepy part was that some people thought this was fine.

A few hours after Brookhurst visited our house, my dad came back from the town council meeting in a political-nerdified stupor. He'd recorded the meeting before he left, and now it was paused on our TV, Brookhurst's face frozen in her trademark megawatt smile.

"It was strange the way it happened," he said, lifting a spicy tuna roll to his mouth with his chopsticks. "People just started showing up to the meeting. And a bunch of them were supporting Brookhurst."

"I'll never understand why you didn't go into local politics," my mom sighed, watching my dad's eyes light up as he talked about the campaign. "How could you tell they were supporting her, anyway?" my mom asked.

"They were all wearing little buttons that had her slogan on it. 'Brookhurst for Morality.' It was fascinating."

Mom scowled.

"That's not a word I'd use," she whispered.

"Why not?" I asked, since my dad's mouth was full.

"Because 'fascinating' is a word you reserve for things of substance. Lydia is a spokeswoman for stupidity."

Dad and I both stared at her.

"What?" she asked.

"Um, I don't think I've ever heard you say anything like that in my life. That wasn't . . . *nice*," I said.

"It wasn't meant to be," said Mom, lifting the remote and hitting Play on the recording of the televised meeting. Dad and I moved closer to the screen. We listened to the crowd muttering around an empty podium until Lydia Brookhurst, wearing her signature bright red business dress, cleared her throat importantly and they all fell silent.

"Good evening," she said. A few people muttered "good evening" back.

"I love our town. I think it is without a doubt the most remarkable place in the world to live."

Applause.

"But," she said quietly, in a low, seductive voice. The audience laughed. "We can do better. And you know what? We *deserve* better."

More applause.

"I know this is a small town. And this is just a mayoral election, but isn't it time we stop letting political correctness invade every aspect of our lives?"

More applause.

"Maybe if someone uses the wrong word to describe someone else, we could, I don't know, use a little common sense and stop jumping down other people's throats. Maybe we could stop spending so much time getting offended about every tiny thing. Maybe we should *cancel* cancel culture!"

More applause, followed by whistling.

"You know, when my great-grandparents lived here, their orchard was something special. They taught me that traditional values are best and people who claim otherwise have just not spent enough time with Jesus."

"Amen!" a woman shouted.

"And we need to protect our *established* businesses. Fight to preserve our traditional values. Get back to our roots! And most of all, we need to stand up to the crude, disgusting, sexualized nature of the information that the media wants to shove down our throats."

Thunderous applause.

"I am running for mayor of our beautiful town against Helen Rubinowitz because I believe she will ignore opportunities for growth and will damage the image of our home with foreign businesses."

At this point the applause was so loud it was difficult to hear her closing remarks.

"We deserve better!" she shouted. "And I'm going to give it to you!"

Then out of nowhere someone started chanting:

"SPLITS. SPLITS. SPLITS. SPLITS. SPLITS."

More people joined in, until finally the whole group was shouting and clapping.

"Oh, I don't do that anymore," she said, giggling.

Almost immediately she lunged into a perfect split, which was followed by thunderous applause.

My mom clicked off the TV and looked at my dad with a serious expression.

"Lydia is not clever. She always surrounds herself with people who are smarter than she is. But she *is* malicious, and she does not stop until she gets what she wants."

"Honey," said my dad, who looked a little alarmed at my mom's sudden anger, "there's no way she'll get enough votes. She can't possibly win."

"She made a motion to ban the food trucks downtown," my mom said. "And she's got a lot of support on that one so far. Restaurants have been losing the lunch crowd."

"All right," said Dad, "but that's just business. She's trying to stifle the competition. It's cutthroat, but it's not illegal."

"I saw a bunch of new signs on Main Street today. They've started putting up displays in the windows of the restaurants facing the food trucks."

When Dad and I shrugged, Mom pulled out her phone to

show us a picture. There was a row of large white signs facing the food trucks, each with a Brookhurst dove at the bottom. They said things like:

Celebrate Our Roots!
Support Local Business!
100% American!
Let's Bring Linda Vista Back!

"It's what she's saying to get people angry," Mom said quietly. "And the way she tries to create friction."

I must have made a disgusted face at this point.

"She can't win with this," my dad said quickly. "'One hundred percent American'? What kind of racist crap is that?" He sighed. "Plus, she's a beauty pageant winner who is just trying to make money. People will see through that."

"You don't know Lydia Brookhurst," said Mom dejectedly. "She was a few years ahead of me in school, and there were weird things going on with her family. There were rumors about things that were hastily covered up. Nasty things. But I know they happened. And everyone in her creepy circle of friends knew too."

"Fiona, you are the one who said you want her business!" Dad said, exasperated. "If you're having second thoughts, now is the time to say something and cut her loose."

"You don't need to agree with someone to work with them," she said softly.

We ate the rest of our dinner in silence.

Minus the uncomfortable dinner conversation, I was able to temporarily ignore the Brookhurst flyer and mayoral campaign by throwing myself into the Q&A section of the blog, knowing that Neil's online interview was only a couple of hours away.

To kill time, I tried to answer something that Cora had asked under her breath the other day while reading the blog. I'm not even sure she knew she'd said it out loud. And since I'd gotten vagina and pubic hair questions from other commenters as well, I didn't worry much that Cora might think it was strange to receive such an immediate answer. But they were good questions, so I drafted responses.

> Please do not put hot wax near your genitals.

Okay, I didn't respond with this, but I was tempted.

Aside from the obvious interest because this was a question someone had asked me, it was also another one of those questions I'd posed to myself in my diary on my computer. I write all the facts in the blog, but the diary is for me. It's the place I put all the questions the new information brings up.

Like how I wonder if pubic hair actually matters to anyone at all. Or if removing all your pubic hair is another strange beauty standard imposed on women to arouse men. Or on a much grosser level, if this is another way of infantilizing women.

I had no answers to these musings, which is why they didn't belong in the blog.

The Circle in the Square is for facts; the diary is for feelings.

I did, however, manage to draft a few responses that addressed the concerns in a more scientific way.

Pubic hair does serve a biological purpose. It provides a buffer against skin irritation and also protection from some bacteria.

Please follow the link below to the section of the blog that addresses safety and health concerns for reproductive . . .

No, Brazilian bikini waxes (complete removal of all hair in the pubic region) are not inherently dangerous, but they may cause skin irritation. They may also leave certain areas of the vagina more vulnerable to the spread of disease. In addition to this, the removal of hair with hot wax in a sensitive region of the body can be uncomfortable and, in some cases, painful. Be sure to use a hygienic, reputable facility. If the skin is broken, be sure to keep the area clean and . . .

Once in a while I'll look at a question and imagine how Cora would answer.

My vagina has a smell. How do I get rid of it?

Cora: You don't. It's your vagina. It's vagina-scented.

I laughed despite the fact that I was getting a little nervous about my interview with Neil. It had seemed like an innocent thing to agree to when I sent the message, but now it seemed reckless, especially with Brookhurst poking around. It wasn't that I thought Neil would figure out who I was or reveal my identity if he knew. I think part of it was that I hadn't come up with answers to the questions I knew he was going to ask.

His first question was probably going to be about why I'd started the blog, for which I didn't have a solid answer. I could talk about curiosity all day long, but I'm not sure that's really the reason I started writing the blog. I love research. I love biology. I like the idea of being an authority on a subject someday. But none of these reasons explain why I secretly collected information that, if found and connected to me, would be embarrassing. And I knew Neil was going to try to get me to reveal myself if he could.

I didn't believe he had any malicious intent. He was just trying to be a journalist. Trying to dig up as much information as possible. I'd probably do the same thing if I were trying to get this story.

The last hour rolled by slowly. I made sure my parents were both in bed and that my blinds and door were closed.

Neil logged on to the blog through the link I'd sent him, and I took a deep breath as he typed.

Neil: Hi, Pom. Are you ready?

Pom: Go for it.

Neil: So the purpose of this interview is to get a little more information about why this blog is necessary. Don't people just know about sex?

Pom: No.

I wasn't going to make this easy for him. He could do better than that.

Neil: Um. Care to elaborate? Why is it, do you think, that people don't know the particulars about sex?

Pom: That's a better question, but I don't think that's exactly true. It's not about not knowing the particulars. People—more specifically, teens—don't always ask questions about sex because it is a taboo subject. Parents want their children to know the basics, but the subject matter is embarrassing and therefore difficult to discuss. The mechanics of sex are pretty easy to explain, but those aren't the questions teens generally ask.

There is also a great deal of misinformation on the subject. Even in schools. No discussion of consent. Incorrect definitions of rape. Mixed messages about birth control. It's difficult for anyone to know what to ask if they're not even being given correct information.

Neil: What is one thing that you want teens to get from your blog?

Pom: I just want them to have a safe place to find information.

Neil: But why did you start a blog about sex?

Pom: I don't know.

I hit Send and immediately regretted it.

Neil: I think you probably do have an answer for that question. It would be hard to believe that you have no idea why you started writing this in the first place.

Pom: I think it's because I once had questions and I just assumed other people do too.

Neil: Fair enough. Can you tell us anything about yourself and your background?

Pom: No.

Neil: Okay . . . Well, this is a well-researched blog and it clearly has taken you a great deal of time to create it. Why is your anonymity so important? Why are you afraid to publicly own your blog?

I had to think about this for a minute before typing.

Pom: If, as you say, this is well researched, then it doesn't matter who I am or what my background is. It matters that the blog exists as a resource.

I was relieved when Neil didn't follow this up with more questions on the same subject.

Neil: Are you familiar with Lydia Brookhurst's mayoral campaign?

Pom: I am.

Neil: How do you feel about the fact that she is so opposed to your work?

Pom: I find it interesting that someone would be so opposed to my blog. It is not an opinion piece. It is a living document that cites every single source. I have quoted medical journals and medical professionals. Her issue does not appear to be based in fact—or reality, for that matter.

Several moments passed before Neil typed his next question.

Neil: Lydia Brookhurst recently made a statement that she took issue with the definitions of abortion, sex, and virginity on your blog. She also criticized your recent addition of a Q&A section as "reckless" and has called you a "pervert" on several occasions. What do you think of this accusation?

Pom: I think that Ms. Brookhurst's views are framed primarily around religion, which is her choice. But it is problematic to view scientific fact through a religious lens. I know people who are

religious but still have the ability to respect
facts as they are presented without damaging
their faith.

To say that I am a pervert is incorrect.

To say that I'm reckless for giving teens the
opportunity to ask questions about a subject that
concerns them is also incorrect.

Her argument is weak.

Neil: Would you say that you believe Lydia
Brookhurst is a weak candidate?

Pom: I don't make political statements.

Neil: As a researcher, then, if presented with a
candidate who wanted to block websites and seek
out the identity of people whose opinions differ from
their own to be publicly shamed . . . does that serve
the best interest of science and research?

Pom: No, it does not.

He spoon-fed me this answer, and it was at moments like
this that Neil really was swoon-worthy.

Neil: Then I'm asking, as someone who reads
and respects your blog: What would you say to
voters? And how would you respond to Lydia
Brookhurst, who has been a loud voice against
anything but "abstinence only" birth control in sex
ed classes and who has characterized your blog as
"pornographic smut"?

I paused. I'd never intended this to become a political thing. I'd literally *just* said I didn't make political statements, but . . .

Pom: If you are asking me to answer politically, I would tell voters to look at the facts and vote for the individual whose platform and experience speak to them.

As for Ms. Brookhurst, I hope she will become irrelevant. I hope that her stance against information is seen for what it really is: pathetic and dangerous. Sexual risk avoidance taught as the only form of birth control is absolutely absurd. It makes a pretty bold statement that sex is inherently wrong and therefore should not be discussed in its entirety because it is the discussion alone that will lead to *more* sex.

When the reality is that healthy discussion leads to more *safe* sex.

As for my blog being "pornographic smut," I would delicately explain that pornography is intended to elicit arousal. My blog is intended to present information.

Her misunderstanding of this fact is perhaps evidence that she should actually read the blog herself and develop a better grasp of the subject matter. She might learn something.

Neil: Thanks for the response! One last question: What would you say to a parent of a teenager who doesn't want their kid reading this stuff?

Pom: It is absolutely a parent's right to oppose this blog and keep their children from reading it.

It is not, however, appropriate or legal to censor scientific fact from the public simply because you don't like the subject matter.

When I signed off a few minutes later, I noticed that Cora had sent me some text messages. One was an outfit suggestion for my coffee with Neil, and the other was a photo of what looked like a box of condoms.

I sent a thumbs-up emoji back to her, but even that felt like too much.

Truthfully, I didn't know how to respond. It seemed strange for me, a wannabe sexpert, to even think about advising anyone against sex, but I thought she was moving too quickly. I thought she was looking at sex as something to be checked off a list of things to do before she went to college. And I thought she was being typical Cora. Doing something because she felt like it was an experience she should have, like a social experiment, not because she actually wanted to do it. But I didn't know this for certain.

And if I've learned anything beyond the facts of sex, it's that it is a personal choice. The right time is different for everyone.

So I gave her a thumbs-up emoji for the condoms because safe sex is worthy of praise. And she's my friend, so I did what I thought needed to be done to be supportive.

7

I wasn't planning to go on Twitter for long, but there are moments when I say that and I get lost in a wormhole of other people's comments. And then sometimes Brookhurst opens her stupid mouth, and that's hours of distracted, completely unfocused energy plus the addition of more followers.

> **@TheRealLydiaBrookhurst:** Young people. Please save yourselves for marriage. Protect your virginity! STOP READING THE BLOG!

It reminded me of some of the questions I'd received on the blog, the ones that always started with "Am I still a virgin if..."

I have anal sex?
I have oral sex?
I let someone finger me?
I let someone perform oral on me?
I use a tampon?

I posted a screenshot of Brookhurst's tweet with a link to my blog.

> **@CircleintheSquare:** For more information on the nature of this belief in protecting a woman's virginity, please follow this link to view the definition of hymen. . . .

Having a hymen and being a virgin are not the same thing, but it felt necessary to address people's medieval perception of the term.

And I posted my response before leaving for my not-date with Neil.

It was a confirmed not-date.

But really, coffee during your free period at eleven in the morning is a date, right?

I mean, Neil paid for the coffee, and both of us were dressed moderately well, which was a little confusing given the signals he'd been sending.

It was the coffee shop right next to the high school, so it was pretty packed with kids from school. The owners were going for a New York City feel, but it was clear that they had (1) never been to New York and (2) ordered all of their decor from various tourist shops online.

Neil wanted to talk about the staff spotlights I was supposed to be submitting.

He wanted to talk about the football piece I did.

"It was one of the funniest articles we've ever run for the paper," Neil said.

I'm sure that I was cool about him saying this, but inside I had completely melted into a puddle of goo on the floor.

When he wanted to talk about my future as a journalist, it started to feel a little bit like a job interview.

Then he touched my hand lightly, and I was unsure how to proceed.

"Glad you liked it," I said casually, grateful that I was holding a coffee, so that I had something to do with my hands.

Monica Hansen was sitting two tables over from us with two girls from my health class. Her eyes traveled to my new boots and then to Neil, where they rested quizzically. Neil was an interesting hybrid of nerd and normal. He could discuss books without appearing too cerebral and laugh with people who didn't exactly share his appreciation of language. It was impressive to see the way his approach shifted depending on whomever he was talking to.

"Your spotlight on Jorge was perfect," he said, taking a sip of his coffee. He'd ordered it black, and he leaned back in his chair, giving me an appreciative smile. "I really liked the way you rounded it out by giving him a real personality."

"Thanks," I said, bristling a little. "But he actually *has* a real personality. I didn't give it to him."

"Of course you didn't," he said quickly. "Look, I need to ask you another favor."

"Not sure how many more pieces I can cover for you, Neil," I told him, still playing it cool.

Well done, Phoebe.

"Oh, don't worry. That's not what I was going to ask." He smiled and even blushed a little bit, which made me feel strangely powerful.

"I was actually wondering if you'd join me at the Kids Take Center Stage Media Gala. I was given two tickets, and since you've written the most articles for us so far this year, I thought . . ." His voice trailed off.

High school newspapers weren't normally invited to the KTCS gala. I wasn't sure they'd ever been. There were some college periodicals, magazines, and online journals that went, but it was mostly big publications and a few local cable channels that came out to mingle and raise money for a bunch of kids' charities by dragging rich people to dinner and a play. It was a big deal, and going to the event practically guaranteed you contacts with some of the most influential people in the field.

"Sure," I said. "I'd love to go."

Nice. Way to pretend it isn't a big deal. You get invited to these things all the time.

"Excellent," he said. Then he looked at his watch. "I have to fact-check an article before tonight, so I have to run." I could practically feel the heat radiating from my face. "Thanks for coming," he said seriously, and though I knew it was biologically impossible, I felt my heart drop to my stomach as Neil got up from our not-date.

I watched his butt leave the coffee shop and then stopped once I realized I was doing it.

When I looked up, Monica was leaning against the wall

of the coffee shop with a pink Frappuccino of some kind. No one should look that smug drinking fake coffee. I could never understand why anyone would want to drink something that smelled like melted gummy bears and Froot Loops.

"So Neil invited you to the KTCS gala," Monica said. It wasn't a question, but I wasn't sure how she knew, since it had just happened, and I didn't think Neil was the kind of person who chatted about his weekend plans. Maybe she could read lips?

"Yeah," I said, my hands instinctively traveling up to my hair in a protective sort of way, remembering her last compliment after my emergency haircut. The self-conscious middle schooler in me cowered.

"Nice," she said. "He's always had a thing for the smart, mousey types. You two make a cute couple."

It's amazing how the addition of one word can make a statement completely diabolical. "Mousey." Without it, I might have been able to look at the rest of her comment as a weird, insincere compliment she was just tossing out to unnerve me.

She grinned, but I didn't smile back. These were the kinds of things she'd gotten used to saying over the years. There was even a time, probably when she coined the phrase "pube head" regarding my short wavy bangs that had sprouted out of control during puberty, when I couldn't speak around her.

"You have a little piece of strawberry in your teeth," I said, pointing to her face. While she tried to get it out, I said, "You know what, you probably need a mirror for that—it's huge and way in there."

She froze, still trying to pick her teeth, then blinked at me while I grabbed my stuff. She looked like she was getting ready to say something else before I added, "But your outfit is *supercute.*"

I didn't tell Cora about my Monica encounter when I met up with her later because I couldn't deal with all the cheering and pretend tears I knew would follow. The addition of Monica Hansen to my life had been the addition of a villain to *both* of our lives. Though Cora was arguably much better at dealing with her. She'd gotten used to her role as my defender, and I'd probably relied on that a little too much.

"C'mon," said Cora, spotting me from across the hall. "They're going to announce homecoming court in the quad."

"And I need to be there?"

"It's a human experience you might need to write about," said Cora.

I couldn't argue with that, so I went. In the hall I bumped into someone else.

"Hi," said a voice. I looked up to see Jorge looking down at me.

"Hi," I said.

"Can we talk?" he asked.

"Sure," I said uncertainly.

"See you at the quad, Phoebe," said Cora, flashing me a mischievous grin that I hoped Jorge missed.

Jorge was wearing a cotton T-shirt and shorts and looked

like he was heading to practice. His hair was tousled, but it didn't look like it had been done intentionally because he still had two or three pieces of dark hair sticking up in the back. Plus, the tag on the collar of his shirt was standing up against his neck, so it looked like he'd just changed and run out of the gym. I resisted the urge to fix it.

"I wanted to say thank you for the spotlight you did. Well, actually, my mom wanted me to thank you. She's shown it to everyone—like, strangers at the supermarket. It was a really great addition to the stuff I sent the scouts this week. So I really appreciate it."

"That's great," I said, meaning it, but I noticed that he still looked like he wanted to say something else.

"Was that it?" I asked.

"No, not really," he said.

"Okay, so what's up?"

He touched the back of his neck and shuffled a little. "So I'm not *just* into football, as evidenced by the fruit I apologized with."

"Yes, I remember the sorry fruit," I said, grinning, because he was clearly getting ready to ask me for a favor, but I had no idea what.

"Well, I'm writing about hybrid plants for my college admissions essay, and I've edited it myself and had my mom take a look at it. But I feel like it's missing something. Can you read it and tell me what you think? No editing. Just want your opinion. And I understand if you're busy or . . ."

He trailed off.

"You want me to read it?" I asked.

"I mean, if you have time," he said without making eye contact. He waited a beat and looked up at me. There was something vulnerable in his expression that was impossible not to like.

"Sure," I said. "I'll read it."

"Great." He grinned broadly. "I'll send it over in a few days."

He walked off, and I smiled to myself, definitely not flattered that he'd asked.

Cora was already sitting in the quad, staring up at the table where the Associated Student Body was set to announce the court. Today she was wearing another one of her mom's T-shirt designs. A Mother Earth with hairy armpits stomping on a litterbug. One of her favorites.

I looked around and remembered why I rarely venture into the quad if I can help it. It has a very eerie mob-mentality feel to it, like a human stampede could start at any given moment for no reason.

Like someone could yell "FREE PIZZA!" and a bunch of us would be instantly crushed to death.

"Just sit and try to pretend you enjoy human interaction," Cora said.

"Do I have to?"

She raised her eyebrows at me. I smirked a little as I sat down next to a couple who were making out more vigorously than any two people I have ever witnessed before in my life.

"Try not to stare, Phoebe."

But even she looked at them with distaste.

The weird thing about the homecoming court announcement this year was that it was outside and at the end of the day. I guess it hadn't really clicked that this was odd until someone mentioned the fact that it was always announced during a pep rally in the gym.

I watched everyone settle awkwardly into a spot on the concrete steps in the quad. It's impossible to *not* do something awkwardly in a group of this many people.

The microphone squealed to life, and everyone cringed as ASB broke their huddle onstage and our ASB president, Tiffani Stevens, stepped forward.

She is a question talker.

Every single sentence she speaks drifts upward at the end like she's not sure what she's saying is true.

"Today we're here to announce this year's homecoming court based on your votes? And here's Principal Wiley to get us started?"

Principal Wiley looks like a cartoon character in a really cute old-man-who-feeds-pigeons kind of way. He'd actually be pretty easy to draw. He wears the same short-sleeved blue collared shirt and khaki pleated pants every day with the same clicky pen in his pocket. It's almost like somewhere in his closet there is a row of light blue shirts with the pen already strategically placed.

"Thank you all for being here today!" he shouted into the microphone.

Smattering of applause.

"Well, let's see what Gramps has to say today," said Cora.

It's common knowledge that Principal Wiley is like everyone's grandfather. He's well liked and tells just the right number of corny jokes to make him almost vintage. So he gets away with a lot.

He smiled in a bemused sort of way to the crowd and said, "Today, before we announce our court, I'd like to introduce our town's Junior Olympic acrobatics team!"

I'll be honest and say I had no idea that such teams existed in our town, but the minute they were announced, they burst out from behind the stage with such force that some of the people in the front row actually shouted in surprise.

"Holy shit balls, Batman," said David, who'd appeared out of nowhere and was busy weaving his fingers through Cora's. It's the kind of move that would be cute in a rom-com but is painfully awkward in real life.

The gymnasts leapt across the stage with magnificent choreography and an absurd amount of energy.

After four minutes of acrobatics that included several painful-looking splits and twelve quick front handsprings, the gymnasts filed offstage to scattered applause. Most of us were too shocked by their sudden appearance to fully appreciate the difficulty of flinging their small, muscled bodies into the air for our entertainment.

Two smoke machines on either side of the stage began to spew purple smoke over the front row, but it evaporated almost immediately, filling the air with a weird hissing noise and the smell of burned waffles.

"Probably not the effect they were going for," said Cora as a few people moved away from the stage, coughing.

"What's she doing here?" I asked, noticing a familiar face just behind the stage.

Principal Wiley waved some of the purple mist out of his eyes and said, coughing a little, "It is my pleasure to welcome this year's homecoming sponsor, Lydia Brookhurst, to announce our court."

The blond phantom promptly walked to the center of the stage with a well-practiced twirl and shook Principal Wiley's hand, before flashing the crowd a smile.

"Thank you, Principal Wiley. It is an honor to announce your homecoming court!"

She opened the envelope and began to read the names, alternating between boys and girls. "Anthony Winchester, Emily Nguyen, Jeff Saunders, Rachel Henderson, Jorge Cervantes, Tatiana Mauna, Hector Rojas, Monica Hansen, Jamal Lee, Dela Schwartz, Aditya Patel, Cora Antonov . . ."

Cora looked absolutely mystified as several people pushed her toward the stage to get her bouquet. While all the other girls smiled for the yearbook photo, her upper lip curled into an unmistakable grimace.

"Congratulations to this year's homecoming court!" ASB shouted in unison.

Brookhurst signaled someone behind the stage, and suddenly hundreds of white doves were released from a cage I hadn't noticed until that moment.

Well-fed white doves, it would seem.

They soared overhead, and just as the court tilted their heads upward to get a better look—

"Oh my God, they're shitting everywhere!" Cora screamed. She was close enough to the mic that her voice was blasted through the speakers, and the word "shitting" echoed over the concrete steps.

Two other girls onstage now had fresh dove excrement dripping down their hair, while one of the homecoming princes shouted, "Dude! That bird shit in my eye!"

Everyone dispersed quickly after that, even as Brookhurst tried to convince the crowd to stay.

David and I moved over to the side of the quad, where we waited for Cora to stomp offstage holding her bouquet like a sword.

"Your Highness," David said, kneeling before her. Luckily for him, he stood up fast enough to block the roses that Cora had sent flying at his face.

"Is this real?" Cora asked.

"Is what real?" I said, picking up the bouquet of roses and inhaling deeply.

"This nomination," she said.

Cora was involved in a lot of extracurricular activities, and almost everyone knew who she was because of her parents' T-shirt business, so even though she wasn't classically popular through cheerleading or sports, she definitely knew a lot of people.

"Yeah," I said. "See what happens when you go outside and talk to people?"

David laughed and put his arm around her while she scowled at me.

"At least the birds missed you," David said, kissing her cheek.

One of the gymnasts ran past crying, her hair streaked with bird poop, and I noticed that at the bottom of her shorts there was a tiny emblem I hadn't seen before.

A dove marked with the letters *LB*.

Lydia Brookhurst.

And under that, in smaller cursive letters: *for morality.*

I realized that although his name had been called, Jorge had not been onstage. He was probably already walking to practice or the weight room or the field . . . wherever it was that football players went when they were not playing football.

My parents had an argument.

This wouldn't be new for most people, but for me it was the first time I could remember ever hearing my mom and dad discuss something in raised voices for longer than a minute. They agreed on almost everything, which is why it was so unnatural listening to a fight about Brookhurst. It was like hearing a favorite song with someone deliberately singing the lyrics wrong.

I wished I hadn't overheard anything at all, but I'd somehow become a master of blending in with the furniture. I'd sunk into one of our ancient spinning armchairs that my dad refused to give away and had my feet tucked up into my sweatshirt when Mom came home.

Mom shuffled into the house holding her phone to her ear, looking exhausted. Her favorite green sweater was hanging slightly off her arm, and her purse strap sank deeply into her shoulder, making me wonder what she'd stuffed it with. All of her sentences were cut short before she had a chance to get her thoughts out.

"Yes, Lydia, I'll definitely—" Mom stopped talking and tossed her keys toward the bowl on the table to grab a pen. But she missed and her key chain went clattering onto the tile floor as she struggled to write notes on the back of an envelope.

"No, you're right. I completely understand—" Mom wriggled her arm, trying to free herself from her sweater, before realizing that she was still wearing her purse.

If she'd been in a different mood, I might have said something like "Don't let the sweater win, Mom," but her next words came out in a breathy hiss, like she was trying to drain all her frustration from her body like toxic vapor.

"Yes, it will save money short-term, and I can present to your board, but—"

Then Mom just listened with her teeth clenched as she tilted her face skyward.

Apparently, Mom had been right in the beginning.

You don't say no to Lydia Brookhurst.

You don't argue.

Which is why it was so weird that Mom was the one who'd wanted to work on her account.

That's when my dad walked into the kitchen from the bedroom, without realizing I was still a chameleon blending into the gray fabric of the armchair.

"This is not the kind of business I want to run," he said when she finally hung up. "Look at you! You're exhausted. We're not so hard up that we need to appease this woman."

"I'm fine!" my mom said in a completely not-fine voice, her bangs falling into her eyes. "You don't know her," Mom said, pushing her hair out of her face. "It's not just the money." There was a strained edge to her voice, like she wanted to say more but thought better of it.

"You keep saying that, but it seems like it is. I get that it's *a lot* of money, but we're okay without it."

Dad smiled, trying to make everything seem less weird, but Mom just looked at him like he was speaking another language, and for some reason that made me really sad. I would have given anything to read her thoughts.

"Okay, well, I'm not working on her account anymore. She's inconsiderate and treats us like her staff. Screw her and her damn abstinence rings."

"I am not dropping this account," Mom said resolutely, even though she'd flinched a little at his tone.

"I'm not asking you to," he said. "But you'll be working on it alone."

He stormed off toward the garage, and I heard the chain jingle on his beach cruiser, so he was probably going to ride down the street for a coffee.

Mom stood there for a minute, staring at the purse that was still hanging from her arm, before untangling herself and heading off to her room for a shower. She'd never even picked her keys up off the floor.

Neither of them had noticed me at all.

For someone used to being the center of her parents' every waking thought and action, it was weird.

I didn't get up for a few minutes after that, just letting their argument wash over me like a storm.

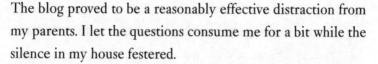

The blog proved to be a reasonably effective distraction from my parents. I let the questions consume me for a bit while the silence in my house festered.

There were some easy responses that just required re-direction to older posts, but there were always some questions that haunted me when people asked them:

Is safe sex really safe?
Yes, but only if you use protection correctly. And even then there's a chance that . . .

How do you know when you're ready for sex?
Only you can answer that.

That always makes me feel like Smokey Bear in a very "Only you can prevent forest fires" kind of way.

Can you use a balloon as a condom?
NO.

Can you still get pregnant if you use protection?

YES. Though it is less likely if the protection is used correctly. Click on this link to the safe-sex practices to prevent pregnancy and the spread of sexually transmitted diseases.

That one was for Cora. I'd told her to her face, but putting it in writing on the blog somewhere I knew she'd see it made me feel like it would get through.

I also started a new section on *The Circle in the Square* called "Yes or No," which was my attempt at answering some of the more repetitive questions with a yes or no answer and a link to more information.

Does a vagina have teeth?
No.

Do penises have bones?
No.

Do women really have three holes down there?
Yes.

Can you see sperm?
No.

Can a woman orgasm more than once?
Yes.

Is the G-spot real?
Yes.

This was oddly satisfying, but not enough to completely distract me from the horror of health class the following week. On Thursday it reached an all-time low when Coach Snowden brought out penis and vagina puppets to illustrate the importance of consent.

There was no way those puppets hadn't come from some adult erotica store, and the thought of Coach Snowden going in to purchase these "instructional materials" from the same place most bridesmaids bought penis-shaped gummies for bachelorette parties was troubling.

I found this lesson infuriating because I'd spent a great deal of time researching consent. The need for a glossary of terms relating to sex came up the minute I started writing and found that some terms were easier to define than others.

"Rape," for example, needed a better definition than any dictionary could provide, so I actually had to look to the US Department of Justice before writing that particular entry.

It was then that I learned that the definition had been unchanged since 1927, when the FBI's Uniform Crime Report Summary Reporting System asserted that rape was "the carnal knowledge of a female, forcibly, and against her will." It was finally updated in 2012.

That was horrifying.

"Carnal knowledge" is a term that originally came from the Bible, and this definition had no mention of male victims. There was also no mention of what it might be called when someone was assaulted by other sexual means, like forcing something into one of your orifices. A finger up the vagina or a razor blade up the anus would *not* have been classified as rape.

The new definition read: "The penetration, no matter how slight, of the vagina or anus with any body part or object, or oral penetration by a sex organ of another person, without the consent of the victim."

It would have been appropriate to discuss some of these issues in a class that was supposed to teach teens about consent, but instead Coach Snowden put the old definition on the board and sat quietly staring at his phone while my classmates in the first two rows played with the penis and vagina puppets.

"The vagina says, 'Buy me dinner first,'" said a football player holding the vagina puppet. The front row laughed.

Clearly this is going really well, I thought.

"The penis says, 'I swear it's just cold in here,'" said the senior girl holding the penis puppet. Everyone else laughed.

It's strange that I felt so angry in such a useless class, but I did. I was angry about the way Coach Snowden was handling a serious topic, and I was irritated with everyone who was laughing. When I looked toward the front of the room, I noticed that Jorge was leaning back in his chair watching his fellow teammates with what looked like annoyance, but I couldn't be sure. At least he wasn't laughing. He looked over at me and shrugged. He still hadn't sent me that essay he wanted me to read, and I wondered if he'd changed his mind.

"All right. All right," Coach Snowden said, trying to quiet the class. "Now that we've had our fun with that, I have a video for you to watch. Those of you who are not inclined to watch it may sit quietly." He raised his eyebrows to all of us in mock seriousness and lifted an ancient VHS tape in the air as a gigantic television was pushed through the door on a cart. Our school had not yet committed to investing in updated technology. Or books, for that matter.

My phone vibrated in my pocket, and since I was in health and not an actual class worth paying attention to, I violated my own rule about using my phone during school hours and pulled it out to read. It was Cora.

> I told David about your current love triangle and he was inspired to create this.

A few seconds later she sent me a photo of a drawing from David's sketch pad, and I had to stifle a laugh. He'd drawn a picture of Neil leaning seductively over his desk and lowering his glasses at me. There was a newspaper folded in his back pocket. The caption read: *You had me at your use of the Oxford comma, Phoebe.* Then, below that drawing, he'd created another one that was unmistakably Jorge holding a basket of fruit and offering me a single apple. The caption read: *May I tempt you, Phoebe?*

I giggled. The casual gender-flipped Adam-seducing-Eve-in-the-Garden-of-Eden thing he had created based on Jorge's fruit was pretty clever, and he'd drawn Jorge as pretty hot.

> There is no love triangle. But tell him we could use him for cartoons on the paper.

Then I added:

> Also, you're both idiots.

I was still smiling when I turned to watch the audiovisual guys set up the TV for the movie. David's cartoon had lightened my mood considerably, until the film started.

It opened with a teenaged girl wearing cutoff jean shorts and a teenaged boy wearing a leather jacket. Even with my limited understanding of the '80s, I could tell that the girl with the feathered blond hair was meant to be the victim and the boy in the leather jacket was obviously the villain in this scenario. After a few minutes of benign conversation, the girl said "no" very clearly when the leather-jacket-clad boy reached over to touch her inappropriately. A moment later, a boy in a varsity jacket stepped in and said very sternly: "She said *no*, Tony. 'No' means *no*." Then Tony walked away, and Keith (the good guy) stepped in and asked Amy (the victim) if she was all right.

They walked off happily together, and I wanted to vomit.

This was quite possibly the worst movie on consent I'd ever seen. Amy was protected from Tony only because big, beautiful Keith showed up. Tony learned nothing from this encounter and would most likely head out to continue trying to fondle whomever he wanted for the rest of his life. And Keith was the hero because he stopped the whole thing from happening. He was the reason that Amy was safe.

It was at that moment that I noticed Jorge staring at me. He was sitting back in his chair with a relaxed expression on his face, and when I inclined my head at him, he got out of his chair and walked over to where I was sitting. Coach

Snowden was reading a magazine, and the rest of the class was distracted, looking at their phones, so no one really thought this was odd.

"Who are you talking to?" Jorge asked, sitting down next to me.

"What? Nobody," I said quickly.

"You were staring at the screen and moving your lips," Jorge continued.

"Oh."

"No denial?" he asked.

"Nope. I've been caught," I said. "I was just a little appalled by this movie."

"You mean Tony's casual attempt to grope Amy, or Keith being the hero of the tale?"

"Both," I said. "The varsity-letter-wearing hero was marginally less irritating."

"Marginally," he agreed.

"What do you think is the moral of the story?" I asked.

Jorge looked thoughtful and said, " 'Hey, girl, I hope you know some blond guy who can save you at exactly the right moment, because Tony is going in for the ass grab.' "

I snorted. Then, "So, no essay?" I asked.

"Finishing it up," he said. "I need a couple more days with it."

"I thought you already had other people read it."

"Well, I haven't had you read it yet," he said. "Besides, I'm just making it shine."

I laughed and accidentally knocked my phone off the desk in front of Jorge's feet.

Smooth.

"I got it," he said, but when he touched it, Cora's text flashed on the screen, David's drawing illuminating his face in the dark classroom. Horrified, I made a grab for the phone, but Jorge had already caught a glimpse and yanked it back. His eyes shifted from the first drawing of Neil and then traveled quickly toward the one of him.

"Oh. Shit. I . . . It's Cora. She's just . . . I mean . . . Shit."

SHIT SHIT SHIT TIMES INFINITY . . .

Jorge looked at me and burst out laughing.

"I think that's the least eloquent sentence you've ever produced," he said, handing me the phone.

"I'm sorry," I said, turning bright red. "She just sent that to me. I had nothing to do with it, honestly. I'm sorry. I'm really sorry."

"I believe you," he said. "Don't worry, I'm not offended."

"Good," I said, because I didn't know what else to say. The bell rang a few seconds later and Jorge stood up to leave, throwing his backpack over his shoulder.

"See you tomorrow. I'll be the one with the fruit. Promise not to tempt you, though," he said, and was gone before I could muster a response.

"Phoebe." Coach Snowden was standing at the front of the classroom looking at me.

"Yes?" I said, a little perplexed. Until that moment I was unaware that Coach Snowden knew my name, but then I figured he might have asked someone.

"You're heading to the newsroom today?"

"No, but I can," I said. "Something you need?"

"Yeah, a friend gave this to me and asked that it be added to the next issue. Can you give it to Neil Norton, please?"

"Sure," I said, holding my breath.

As he handed me the folder, the zipper on his gym bag split open, spilling an assortment of receipts, gum wrappers, and papers all over the floor. I helped him gather them up, wondering how someone could make it to Coach Snowden's age without learning how to throw their trash away.

"Thanks," he muttered, offering me the folder once again before walking out of the room in a hurry. I got up to leave and noticed that something else had fallen out of his bag: a shiny green flash drive. It was the one he used for all his Power-Point presentations. I recognized it immediately because he always made a production of wriggling it into the computer before class started. He always put it in the wrong way and got frustrated when it didn't fit. This display was usually followed by a longing for the good ol' days and some quip about how technology was ruining us all.

I thought about calling out to him to tell him he'd left it behind, but something stopped me. Something devious and satisfying and strangely out of character for me.

Once I got into the hallway, I peeked inside the folder and saw a flyer for Lydia Brookhurst's store. There was a photo of several different abstinence ring designs, and it was similar to the other ads that she normally ran in the local papers. Except there was one tiny change beneath the usual slogan:

Choosing abstinence is just another way of choosing Jesus.
God bless.

Stay pure.
Brookhurst for Mayor

Sadly, it never made it to the newsroom.

I was feeling smug about this little victory until dinner that night, when my mom was late. Again.

Dad was sitting alone at the kitchen table, which wasn't sad unless you saw my mom's untouched sushi sitting directly across from him. He'd already mixed her soy sauce with the wasabi, and he was staring at it, like Mom had stood him up for a date.

We both knew she was at a Brookhurst meeting. I didn't tell him to go to sleep or put Mom's food in the fridge because she'd eat when she got home. I'd already eaten my spicy tuna rolls and slid my chair out.

"Homework," I said, looking at him while he played with his chopsticks.

"Better get to it," he said, still not looking up.

Neither of us wanted to talk about where Mom was and why she was there, but there was this unspoken craving for normal.

My parents have always had rules: No shoes on in the house. Defrost meat on the right side of the sink. Fruit gets washed before it goes in the fridge. Sit down together for one meal every day. No exceptions.

Dad and I had already eaten because it was late, and this was the third night in a row that had happened.

Since they weren't working on the account together anymore, it was strange to listen to their forced conversations about it when Mom came home.

When the garage door opened, my chest lifted a little, thinking they could talk, but that's when the argument started.

The only part of the conversation I could hear was Mom saying, "I am doing my job, Matt. Stop acting like that means I condone everything she says. This is a lot of money. At least enough for Phoebe's first year of college. And if the policies renew—"

"There's something else," he said, interrupting her.

My dad doesn't interrupt.

I could tell he was walking around the kitchen now. He opened the refrigerator door and slammed it closed.

"It's business, Matt. Just—"

"What are you not telling me?!"

My dad doesn't shout either.

A chair scraped against the kitchen floor like he was pushing it in, but a loud crash told me that he'd done it too hard and knocked a bottle onto the floor. I heard it hit the tile and shatter.

Probably the soy sauce.

Then I recognized the sound of the heels my mom hadn't taken off tapping as she moved to the pantry to get the broom and dustpan.

"Don't," he said quickly. "I'll do it myself."

There were a few seconds of silence where I imagined my

mom standing there watching my dad mop up the sauce and sweep the broken pieces of glass into the trash before turning to walk into the bedroom.

I can't believe I ever teased them about wanting matching reflective track jackets.

My follower count was slowly inching forward and picked up speed every time Brookhurst sent a *SHOW YOURSELF @CircleintheSquare.*

Cora texted me.

Hey thanks

For what?

You know what. David says thanks too.

David could tell me himself, I thought.

I'm not sure why that annoyed me. It was the way that girlfriends sometimes add their boyfriend's name to gifts even though they have no idea what it is. But then he sent an actual text.

Hey it's David. Thanks for sending my samples to the paper.

I sent him a thumbs-up, which I immediately recognized as an annoying, insincere response, so I followed it with a smiley face and a

> Your comics are perfect for the paper.

Luckily, Neil had agreed.

Now David was sending me sketches and asking for my opinion.

He sent an incredible one of Cora pulling on her Rollerblades. It captured her perfectly, and even though I wasn't ready to like him, that was cool.

The way he drew her was cool too. Like the focus of the sketch wasn't to make Cora look like a model. It was the way she'd tug at her sweatshirt or untangle her shoelace. The way she'd concentrate on something. And it made me realize he was paying attention.

The expression on Cora's face, that look of concentration. It reminded me of when I saw her reading the blog, looking up stuff about the pill and pregnancy. So my next post wasn't completely in response to Cora, but it made me feel better knowing she'd likely read it.

It's strange how certain types of questions seem to come in waves. Last week *The Circle in the Square* had been flooded with questions about birth control. The most common questions were whether oral contraceptives:

123

1. cause cancer,
2. make you gain weight,
3. make you infertile.

My responses were sourced from multiple doctors, journals, and trustworthy websites:

1. Oral contraceptives have actually been shown to decrease lifelong risk of ovarian and uterine cancer.
2. Double-blind studies show that if you control for other factors (lifestyle, diet, exercise, etc.), weight is unaffected.
3. There is no direct link between infertility and extended use of oral contraceptives.

Responses to this information on Twitter varied between relief and accusations of leading teens toward promiscuity and eventually hell.

This week there seemed to be an unusual amount of questions that started with "Can you get pregnant if..."

you've never had your period?
you don't ejaculate inside her?
you are on the pill and you use a condom?

Yes, yes, and, unfortunately, yes. Though the odds of getting pregnant while using a condom and the pill correctly are very slim.

I cited several sections of the blog to back up my response, including a link to the correct use of a condom, and was about to log off when another question popped up on my feed.

> Is the "morning-after" pill an abortion pill?

The answer was complicated. I had a response ready to go and could cite my source from memory, but something held me back. It was exactly the kind of answer that someone might use to criticize the blog for being political.

But then I remembered that facts alone are not political statements, and I began to type my response:

> The morning-after pill is usually described as emergency contraception. Emergency contraceptive pills work before pregnancy begins and will not be effective if a woman is already pregnant.
>
> According to the National Institutes of Health and the American College of Obstetricians and Gynecologists, a woman's pregnancy begins when the fertilized egg (zygote) implants in the lining of a woman's uterus. Implantation begins five to seven days after a sperm fertilizes the egg.
>
> So, based on this information, I would have to say no, the morning-after pill is emergency contraception. Not an abortion pill.

I submitted the response after adding a few links to the definition of "abortion" and then logged off.

But before I did, I noticed I'd gotten an email from Jorge.

> Hi Phoebe,
>
> Thanks for doing this. I know you have a bunch of other projects due for the paper (saw your staff spotlight assignment posted on the bulletin board in the newsroom) and also regular life and homework.
>
> Anyway, see attached!
>
> Jorge

My cheeks flushed a little as I opened the document to read.

The essay was about plant sex.

Okay, not really, but close.

Turns out Jorge is super into hybrid plants, and the essay was all about how many times he'd failed to create plumcots (plums and apricots) and tayberries (blackberries and raspberries) and how he'd eventually succeeded by using a cotton swab to paint pollen over each bloom and sold his creations at his own stand at the Sunday farmers' market.

Anyway, I emailed him back and said that his essay was pretty close to perfect and that we could talk about it in health class.

"He sent you an essay about plants?" asked Cora when I told her about it the next day. She was running her hand on the bottom of her Rollerblades to see if the light-up wheels she'd just gotten us worked properly.

The plan was to skate home from school, until Cora got an email.

"Yeah, it's not just plants, though. It's really fascinating and—"

But Cora's lip curled up in disgust.

"Ugh. It's from ASB," she said, looking at her phone.

"They want another photo shoot?" I asked half jokingly. I'd just gotten my Rollerblades on and was working up the energy to stand.

"Yes," she whined. "They want me to head over to the gym now, if I have time, so they can get a few different shots of all of us." She groaned and I laughed.

"Just go and get it over with. I can get home on my own, and David can come pick you up, right?"

She nodded.

"I'm really sorry," she said, running toward the gym.

I watched her slip out of sight beyond the administration building. Then I pulled out my phone to look at Jorge's essay again, and at that exact moment Nurse Reyes came striding into the hallway.

"Nurse Reyes!" I yelled, skating over.

She turned toward me.

"I'm Phoebe Townsend. I've followed up a few times with you about getting your thoughts on *The Circle in the*—"

"Yeah, I know. Sorry about that," she said. "I don't think

it's a good idea, and to be honest, I think an interview with me would get pulled before it even made it to print."

Neil had asked for splashy and unpredictable.

"It won't get pulled," I said, thinking of Mr. Edmundson, who hardly ever checked our articles.

"And I'm not sure if you're aware, but I was the one who included that blog on that list of resources for sex education. It wasn't the only resource that was pulled by the board," Nurse Reyes said.

"I'm aware," I said. "Which is why I want to talk to you."

She leaned against the doorframe of her office.

"What if we didn't mention Lydia Brookhurst specifically?"

She laughed. "I have no intention of mentioning that woman at all if I can help it," she said.

"Great, so . . . ?"

I stood there, still wearing my Rollerblades, and Nurse Reyes finally crossed her arms and said, "Fine. Come in. Are you any good on those?"

I tripped on my way through the door, which effectively answered her question.

The office was tiny, and there were no photos or any evidence of a personal life, which is kind of the thing you do when you aren't planning on staying much longer. There was, however, a huge jar of lollipops resting on her desk.

"What do you like about the blog?" I asked.

"I think it's beautiful," she said. "It's one of those things I wish I'd had available to me as a teenager. It's accessible and it's true."

"Why is it controversial, do you think?"

"I think some people are highly sensitive to facts," she said, rolling her eyes. "And it's hard to convince adults that it's important to give teenagers information about stuff we'd rather not talk about. But studies show proper sex education reduces unplanned pregnancies and sexually transmitted disease."

She told me her favorite entries in the blog.

The things she thought were missing from sex ed, like a more thorough discussion of contraceptives.

And why consent should be a lesson by itself.

But she delicately avoided saying anything against Brookhurst directly.

"What would you say to people who are uncomfortable with this information in schools?"

"That just because something makes you uncomfortable doesn't always mean it's wrong. It means you're just not used to talking about it yet. Sometimes you have to create what my abuela called un silencio incómodo. 'Uncomfortable silence.' And just watch what happens. Most people don't know how to handle it. Sometimes it's that quiet moment that gives us a chance to think."

"Off the record," I said. Nurse Reyes looked up. "Did you get in trouble for listing the blog as a resource for students?"

She looked thoughtful. "I was unofficially told not to piss off people who pay for stuff."

"Is it okay to print this, then? I mean, even if I don't mention her by name—"

"You'd better print it," said Nurse Reyes fiercely. "Believe me, even if I get in trouble, I'll be okay. Though I'll definitely miss the glamour that comes with the high school nurse title." She smiled.

I thanked her and rolled out of her office, immediately tripping over a cracked piece of cement. At least this time I landed on my backpack.

"Cora, you could have picked almost any other hobby, but no, you had to put me on wheels," I muttered to myself.

"You talking to yourself?" Jorge asked, his face swimming upside down above me. "Need a hand?"

"Uh, thanks. Where did you come from?" He lifted me onto my feet.

"Oh, actually, I was going to drive this over to your house, but then I saw you go into Nurse Reyes's office and figured I'd wait."

"Drive to my house for what?"

My stomach rumbled when I saw the Rodrigo's Taquería bag in his hand.

The smell of hard rolled tacos with cheese, guacamole, and salsa was unmistakable and intoxicating.

"Here," he said. "I wanted to give you this to say thanks for reading my essay."

"Oh my God," I said, all my attention now focused on the bag. "That smell. It's like heaven."

"Yeah. I know. I ate mine already. My parents have been friends with Rodrigo for years, so I get lunch there a lot."

"Me too," I said.

"I know," he said, smiling. Then immediately realizing that that might have come off as creepy, he added, "I noticed the bag sticking out of your backpack before the football game. How about you eat this while I drive you home?" he asked.

"Oh, you don't have to do that. I can skate home," I said.

"Are you sure?"

He looked at me. We both looked at the Rollerblades.

"Yeah, okay. Where's your car?" I asked.

He handed me the bag of Mexican food while he fastened his seat belt, and I did my best to appear like a normal human being eating it.

I bit into the first hard rolled taco and managed to keep the cheese and guacamole from dripping down my face. He turned out of the school parking lot, and I remembered his essay.

"So plumcots, huh?"

He'd definitely been waiting to geek out about this.

"There are so many unexplored hybrid combinations!"

His face lit up as he walked me through some of his favorite fruits and berries, and since I was otherwise engaged with Mexican food, I let him talk.

Until the engine died.

"Shit," said Jorge as he pulled over to the side of the road. "Awesome."

We were still about ten minutes from my house.

"That's okay," I said, wiping the grease off my hands and stuffing the trash into my backpack. "I can walk."

"Okay, I'll walk with you."

"You don't have to do that," I said. "Really, it's no big deal."

"What if I'm not accompanying you to be chivalrous or anything? I'm just going with you so I can bother you some more about the essay. I'll just text AAA, and my mom will pick me up at the Starbucks at the bottom of your street." I looked at him. "Here, I'll carry your Rollerblades." Then he lifted his arm toward the long, dusty road. "Shall we?"

"Why not?" I shrugged.

"Great, because I think this would be the perfect moment in our friendship for me to really pick your brain about your hopes and dreams," he said.

"Oh, are we friends now?" I asked.

"Well, yeah. I mean, if someone asked me about you, I wouldn't pretend I don't know you." He laughed.

"Sweet," I said, trying not to kick up too much dirt as we walked.

"So, is writing what you want to do someday?"

"I guess."

"You guess? What kind of BS answer is that?"

"I mean, yes, I love the paper. And I like writing articles, but I also like science."

And secretly want to become the world's leading sexologist, I thought.

"And you can't do science and writing?" he asked.

"That would make me sound like a five-year-old who wants to grow up to be a ballerina who is also a veterinarian."

"No, it wouldn't," said Jorge. "If you like both things, you find a way to do both."

"All right, then. What do *you* want to do? Any thoughts about your college major?"

"Nope. I have no clue," he said.

"That's brilliant," I said. "And *mine* was a bullshit answer?"
He just shrugged.

"I like growing fruits and vegetables. Actually, I think if I could do anything, I'd buy tons of land and start my own farm. Grow hybrid plants and start a blood orange grove. I love blood oranges."

There was something very soothing about listening to Jorge pledge his undying love for hybrid plants.

"I like that," I said, and I meant it. "I think that's the only part that's missing from your essay. You need to talk more about *why* they matter so much to you. Otherwise it's perfect."

"Thanks. I'm glad it meets with your approval." He bowed his head ever so slightly, but I could tell he was happy. "My grandparents would be turning in their graves if they knew." He sighed. "Actually, my abuelita would probably just haunt the shit out of me. Mexican grandmas don't mess. And she always wanted me to have a comfortable job. You know, in an office or something." He looked up and laughed. "And even if in my mom's progressive sí-se-puede, you-can-do-anything world there's nothing wrong with wanting to buy a farm, I just can't shatter her please-God-let-my-son-become-a-lawyer dream."

"Well," I said, grinning, "maybe you could do both."

"Like a veterinarian ballerina?" he asked.

"Exactly."

We made it to the Starbucks at the bottom of my street, and from there I could see my dad's car in the driveway.

"Hey, if you're not busy Saturday night, I thought we could

133

meet up at the poetry slam at Dregs & Grounds. It's extra credit for English, you know. Isn't your friend Cora reading that night?"

"Oh yeah, she is. But I can't go this time," I said. "I'll be at that journalist gala."

"Oh, fancy," teased Jorge, raising a pinkie. "Going as a lone representative for the paper?"

"Who said I was going alone?" I asked.

"Who are you going with?" Jorge said, his lip curling. I could tell he already knew the answer.

"Neil Norton."

"That guy acts like he's thirty." Jorge frowned.

"He does not."

" 'I write for the *Linda Vista High School Chronicle* because I value truth. And I hope you do too,' " he rattled off in a perfect imitation of Neil, sticking his chin out when he spoke.

"He did not say that," I said indignantly.

"No," Jorge laughed. "But he did write it on Facebook under his 'About Me' section. And his picture does make him look like a dopey real estate agent. Actually, I guess he's looked that way since we were little," Jorge mused.

"You've known him that long?" I asked, curious.

"We were best friends for a while. On the same baseball team."

"What happened?" I asked.

He looked evasive. "We grew up."

"Well, thanks for the offer," I told him. "But I *do* have plans Saturday. Have fun at the poetry slam."

For a second it looked like Jorge wanted to say something

else but thought better of it. The smile was momentarily wiped from his face as I turned to leave.

"I'll see you tomorrow," I said, turning to walk up the street. "Thanks for the tacos."

"You're welcome. Maybe leave the blades at home for now?"

"You know, I'm actually not that bad when there are wide-open spaces to move around in."

"Cool. So as long as the ground is completely flat and nothing is within twenty feet of you, you're golden," he said.

"Exactly," I said, waving goodbye.

That night I read through my notes and thought about how the staff spotlight might look like a dig at the Brookhurst campaign.

But Nurse Reyes had said to print it.

And Neil didn't care about that. He loved the blog. Right?

Facts alone are not political statements, I reminded myself.

When I logged in to the blog again before bed, my head still full of everything I'd heard that day, I didn't have any new questions, but someone had left a comment below my answer to the question about the morning-after pill.

> U R a baby killer and U deserve to die.

9

"Let me just read you this one part on sexual attraction," Cora said.

I ignored her.

She was lying on my bed staring at her phone and reading bits of *my own research* back to me. To be perfectly honest, she wasn't actually as much help as I thought she'd be. The gala was in four hours, and she was pretty useless. She didn't exactly want to talk about anything gala-related. She just wanted to prepare me for what she thought would be the highlight of the evening.

"So if he goes in for a kiss with tongue, this is what you do—"

"I don't need you to tell me what to do if he wants to French me, Cora. I need you to help me get dressed and do my makeup."

She'd brought over a bag of the clothes that her aunt kept giving her as Christmas gifts in an attempt to get her to dress more conservatively and less like a whimsical fairy princess. Cora's mother refused to let her donate the clothes because she was afraid her sister might find out that Cora never wore them.

As I dug through the bag, I set aside anything that looked like it might fall into the please-take-me-seriously category.

"Maybe I should just show you the section in the blog about kissing. It's really useful. It explains the science behind it and how it's relevant to sex. I'm really surprised that you haven't gone in and read everything yet."

"No time, you know," I lied. It was weird having Cora quote me to me without knowing it.

"Okay, so it's an event for journalists, right?"

"Right," I said.

She reached to the bottom of the bag and pulled out a silver clutch and handed it to me.

"I don't need a purse yet, Cora. I don't have an outfit."

"Open it," she said.

I looked inside to see a perfectly rolled-up black jersey knit dress with a low neckline.

"Your aunt gave you *this*?" I asked incredulously. The majority of the clothes in the bag were pantsuits and jackets that weren't unattractive, but none of them had that stunning-librarian quality I was going for. Except this.

"My aunt's girlfriend," Cora said. "She works for a clothing line that doesn't really believe in cleavage. But once in a while there is a style that sneaks through with actual potential. She must have snuck this one in when my aunt wasn't looking."

I stepped into my closet and threw it on. When I looked in the mirror, I was pleased by the transformation. My hair, which I'd just gotten used to, had grown to its perfect length. The dress hugged my body in all the right places. I'd spent my life in jeans and T-shirts. This was the first time that I was wearing something that made me look really feminine, and I was surprised at how much I enjoyed it.

"Here," said Cora, watching my reaction with a grin on her face. She handed me a tailored jacket from the zipped clothing bag and a pair of her black pumps.

"Now you will be the most beautiful nerd at the Geek Ball," she said, clapping her hands.

"I like it," I said, turning around and grinning at my own reflection.

Cora pulled out some makeup and told me how to accomplish a smoky eye. I took in what she was saying with a kind of glazed expression until she stopped midsentence and said, "You know what, here, I'll do it."

She whistled when I stepped into the heels, and got her phone out to take a picture. I leaned dramatically against the doorframe of my bedroom and elegantly tossed the back of my hand against my forehead like a fainting Hollywood starlet.

We experimented with some of Cora's accessories and spent a lot of time not talking about the thing I really wanted to talk to her about.

It seemed like she was avoiding any sex talk as well.

Every time it looked like I wanted to bring up the something that we weren't talking about, Cora would change the subject. The strange thing was that she just thought I was curious as a friend, and I was, but it was so much more. At this moment a participant in the subject of my research—that is, an actual sex-haver—was sitting in front of me. However, it wasn't entirely confirmed. All I really knew was that she had condoms.

What would she say if she ever found out I was Pom?

After Cora left, I answered a few questions from the Q&A section just before the gala. Not even my trolls seemed to be interested in the blog at the moment, which suited me just fine.

When I finally stepped out of my room, my parents were standing in the hallway, unsure if they should gush about how I looked or pretend I always dressed like this. My dad settled for kissing me on the cheek and saying, "You look good, kiddo. Not too late, okay?"

I hadn't actually told them I was meeting Neil there, but it's not like I was lying. I didn't tell because they didn't ask.

Despite my mom's insistence that I cover every visible inch of skin, she didn't believe I was a damsel in distress, which is what I was thinking as I scooped the car keys out of my dad's hands and walked out the front door, removing the jacket completely when I realized I was sweating.

Then I was off. The gala was at the Pemberton Theater in the city, where all the attendees were to be treated to a performance of *Les Misérables*. I was supposed to meet Neil outside by the white columns so we could walk in together. I valet-parked my parents' Toyota and went up to find him.

I'm not exactly sure how to describe Neil when I saw him. He's always been attractive, but when I saw him dressed in a navy-blue suit, standing by the door of the event waiting for me, the effect was overwhelming. I'd never actually experienced butterflies in my stomach before, and I vaguely remembered looking up the scientific term for that feeling but couldn't recall what it was. Instead I smiled nervously and felt my phone buzz in my purse. I ignored it.

"You look amazing," he said. "Are you ready?"

"Ready," I said, and he led me inside.

It was a sea of black and white, and I was glad that I hadn't opted for Cora's bottle-green dress instead, because that would've been a blast of color in this crowd. The table at the front of the room was lined with tiny plaques labeled with all the newspapers and magazines represented at the gala. I stopped in front of the plaque for the *Stanford Daily*.

"First choice?" Neil asked.

"Yeah," I said almost wistfully.

"Let's go meet them, then," he said, jerking his head toward a table with a Stanford banner. "Here, take these. I had them made for us so we'd look a little more professional."

I looked down at the stack of business cards he'd handed me and saw my name.

Phoebe Townsend
Linda Vista High School Chronicle
Staff Writer

"Thanks," I said. "Do you know people at the *Stanford Daily*?"

"No, but we will after we introduce ourselves," he said,

grinning. "Let's go." He took my hand and we walked over to the table.

"Hi," said Neil. "Neil Norton. I'm the editor for the *Linda Vista High School Chronicle*. And this is one of our staff writers, Phoebe Townsend."

Neil started talking almost immediately with an old man sitting at the end of the table. He had hair like cotton fluff and bright blue glasses that sat rigidly on his nose. A woman on his left extended her hand to introduce herself.

"Hi, I'm Amanda. I'm from Linda Vista originally too," she said, handing me her card. "Are you interested in Stanford?"

I somehow became another person. The reserved, quiet Phoebe Townsend, who did her best to keep her enthusiasm in check, disappeared, to be replaced with a Stanford fangirl whose first comment was about how much she loved that the school's unofficial mascot was a tree.

Amanda, who was politely listening to me ramble on, seemed genuinely interested. After I'd finished talking and Neil and I had stepped away from the table, I was horrified by how much I had shared.

"Oh my God," I said. "I can't believe I just talked that much. I never do that."

Did I really just introduce myself and tell them how cute I think the tree is? "Please let me in because your mascot is adorable"?!

"It's fine," said Neil, looking around and smiling. "They like enthusiastic people."

Neil did most of the talking at the next table, and for a moment I had an out-of-body experience where I felt like I was being absorbed by a crowd of like-minded people, but in a good way. I was becoming an older, more experienced version of myself. Then, just as Neil was thanking the *Los Angeles Times* people for the chat, I saw Lydia Brookhurst step into the hall and shake hands with a few older men in suits. Neil saw me turn in their direction.

"Shit," he said, gently guiding me around a crowd of women in matching blazers.

"What?" I asked.

"So high school papers don't typically get tickets to these kinds of events," he said quickly.

"Okay," I said. "Then how did—"

"Neil, my dear!" said a familiar voice behind us.

Neil looked momentarily like a child caught doing something wrong, but he rebounded.

"Hi," said Neil, leaning in to kiss Lydia Brookhurst, which seemed like an overly affectionate greeting for a stranger until—

"Ms. Brookhurst, this is my friend Phoebe. She's a staff writer on the paper."

"Ah yes! Phoebe's mother is doing some risk analysis for my business. How is . . ."—Brookhurst hesitated—"*she* this evening?"

"She's fi—" I started to say, but she was already waving at someone over my head. It's not like I cared whether she gave me her undivided attention, but after all the work my mom was doing for her, could Brookhurst really not remember her name? She took her coat off to reveal a gold dress that clung to her body like plastic wrap.

"I thought you said you weren't going to be able to make it tonight. Isn't that why you gave me your tickets?" Neil asked, still smiling.

"Well, a meeting got canceled, and I just paid someone a little extra at the door, and here I am. But don't waste your time on me, sweetheart. Go! Mingle. Lovely to see you, Phoebe."

I let Neil steer me to the other side of the hall and then looked at him questioningly.

"All right, let's hear it," he said.

"Did she read your interview with Pom?" I asked.

It was strange asking Neil this question, having been the secret interviewee in this situation, but he ran his fingers through his hair and looked a little uncomfortable and, if possible, more handsome.

"Yes, that's why she gave me the tickets. She showed up in the newsroom and asked me if I knew anything about Pom's identity," he said.

"Do you?" I asked.

"No." He sighed. "And then she said I was doing a fine job as editor."

"And she gave you tickets for that?" I asked. "She didn't exactly come off looking great in that interview."

"Yeah, I know," said Neil. "I'm just ignoring the fact that the tickets came from her because I really wanted to come tonight. And I'm really glad you're here with me."

"Why?" I asked. The moment the word left my mouth, I realized the question might force Neil to state one way or another how he felt about me, and I hadn't intended to put him in that kind of position.

"Because I like you," he said. Then he leaned in and whispered, "And not that it matters, but you look incredible in that dress." I found myself searching for words, but it didn't matter because Neil was smiling at my reaction. "C'mon," he said. "People to meet."

Neil and I took a tour of the room, making introductions, and after almost an hour of small talk we had collected almost fifty business cards. I looked down at the one from Amanda and smiled. AMANDA WHITAKER. EDITOR. STANFORD DAILY.

"You're really good at this," I told Neil.

"My dad is in sales," he said. "He always talks about how important it is to meet people and learn something about them. You never know when you might need that information later. You never know who's going to be able to give you a leg up when you need it."

He glanced over his shoulder and did a quick double take. Lydia Brookhurst had one arm around Carl O'Leary, the head of our local news station, and the other arm around Todd Bauerston, an anchor on CNQB. It was strange watching Lydia Brookhurst circle the room and sweep in and out of conversation like a bird of prey. She laughed on cue and seemed to offer a compliment at the exact right moment. I wondered if I was the only one who thought it was odd that she was on an invite list for this kind of event. As far as I could tell, it was journalists only, and it was weird enough with her position as a business owner. But as a local political candidate? The thought of her reading the piece I wanted to submit for the staff spotlight made me uncomfortable.

Then there was the tiny fear that she would somehow find

out that I was Pom. Something about the way she scanned the room, searching for people who might be useful.

She was so good at blending into the crowd, I didn't even notice that she was once again within earshot until I heard her say, "There's a program that can reveal his identity. You've never seen software like this, Todd. It's FBI-level software. I'd never use it to identify a minor, of course. And I don't believe for one second he's actually a teenager. But it's only a matter of time until *someone* does identify him." She laughed.

Neil, sensing that something was up, leaned in and whispered, "You okay?"

"Yeah, fine," I said, still feeling exposed. And it wasn't like Brookhurst was saying anything earth-shattering. The software she was referring to wasn't alien technology. I guess it was just the situation. Being at an event with a known enemy who didn't realize I was there.

"Do you want to go somewhere a little more private?" he asked, looking around at the crowd of people who wouldn't miss us if we disappeared. My heart leapt into my stomach as I nodded. Trying to look braver than I felt. One worry was suddenly replaced by others:

1. Despite my brief experience at camp and the piece I'd written on the blog, I'd never really kissed anyone I liked and didn't know what to expect.
2. I wasn't sure I was capable of pressing my lips to someone else's without analyzing it.
3. I didn't know what to do with my tongue.

I tucked my hair behind my ear in what I hoped was a natural, casual sort of response to what I thought would be my first make-out session ever.

The door to the theater swung open as a waiter with shrimp cocktail on a silver platter came racing into the room. Neil tilted his head toward the door, and we disappeared down the dimly lit hallway in the theater lobby before climbing the ancient stairs to the top box.

"Are we even allowed to be in here?" I asked him, looking out at the empty stage and orchestra seating.

"Does it matter?" he said, gently pulling me behind the burgundy curtain.

"I guess not," I tried to say, but the words hadn't even left my mouth before Neil's lips were inches from mine. My breath left me in short, quick bursts as I tried to relax. I'd never done anything like this before, and I could hear blood pulsing in my ears.

"They won't be coming into the theater for another hour or so," Neil whispered.

"Oh," I said.

There were a number of appropriate sexy responses I could have made here. Like, for instance, "Oh, so what should we do for a whole hour?" or "However will we pass the time?" Even though my research is purely scientific, I'm not completely oblivious to normal romantic banter. But in this case I was concentrating on not doing something embarrassing.

Luckily, Neil didn't seem to notice. He placed his hands on the small of my back and pressed me deeper into the dusty burgundy curtains. Then he began to kiss me.

Badly.

Oh God, yes, it was bad.

It might not be fair to make this kind of judgment based on my experience, but based on my research, this was bad kissing.

So. Much. Spit, I thought, horrified. He was literally just opening and closing his mouth and shoving his tongue in and out in rapid succession. *I think I'm going to drown.*

Then I imagined what Cora would say if she were there watching the proceedings: *Phoebe Townsend. Sixteen and a half years old. Found dead in top box of Pemberton Theater. Drowned in some hot guy's spit while making out. In lieu of flowers, please distribute condoms to random individuals you meet, in hopes that they, at least, won't die a virgin. And that should they engage in amorous activity, they will do so safely.*

Yes, Cora would handle it respectfully, I thought.

Lydia Brookhurst would be so pleased when the blogger mysteriously vanished. She might even see it as divine intervention.

As if the moment couldn't get any more awkward, the dust from the curtains was starting to irritate my nose. He was drowning me in spit, and I was about to sneeze in his mouth as I struggled to control his wayward tongue.

Miraculously, the urge to sneeze went away.

Then, as if sent from heaven, his cell phone began to buzz in his pocket. He tried to ignore it. It was a valiant effort to ensure that I did not feel like he was choosing to take a phone call rather than continue making out with me. I just pushed back and said, slightly out of breath, "You should take that."

He answered his phone.

"This is Neil," he said, then frowned. "Oh, hi, Ms. Brookhurst. Yes, I'm still at the party. I just slipped outside for a few minutes to—" He listened. "Sure. I'd love to meet her. I'll be right there."

He hung up and looked at me.

"She wants to introduce me to Ingrid Lyons, the editor at the *Bugle*," he said.

"Go," I said quietly. "I'll wait here."

"You sure?" he asked, but he was already shoving his phone into his pocket and buttoning his jacket.

"Of course," I said.

He leaned in and kissed me again, whispering, "To be continued." Then he raced down the stairs and out of sight as I wiped the spit off my face and touched my lips. They felt raw.

The disappointment set in. I didn't understand what had just happened. I was attracted to Neil physically and intellectually, and yet the kissing had been bad. It wasn't anything like what I thought it should feel like. I guess I just hadn't known there would be so much friction involved. Were my lips supposed to be this chapped? Perhaps we just needed practice.

What makes you think you know what kissing should feel like?

Research isn't everything, Phoebe.

I let my thoughts swirl around in my head for a while. Longer than I realized, because by the time I looked down at my watch, thirty minutes had already gone by. The doors to the main floor of the theater were open, and the seats in the mezzanine were starting to fill up.

I looked for Neil in the lobby and finally spotted him walking underneath the arm of a drunk, red-faced man who kept patting him on the back. Snippets of their conversation, including phrases like "keep it up, sport" and "we'll make a newsman of you yet," floated over the crowd. On Neil's other side was Lydia Brookhurst, who was engaged in conversation with a stern-looking woman with gray hair. They were pulled into the crowd ahead of me, and I couldn't squeeze my way toward them.

Neil actually turned around to face me for a moment, gestured apologetically, and mouthed the words *I'm sorry. I'm sorry. I'm sorry. I'm sorry.*

I watched him take one ticket out of his pocket for himself and hand the other one to Ms. Brookhurst. *My* ticket.

"Ticket?" asked the usher at the door.

"I guess I don't have one," I said, a little dazed, watching the spot where Neil had stood seconds before, imagining him getting pushed toward his seat. It was at this moment that the usher gave me a look that made me feel about ten years old.

"No ticket, no entry. Sorry, miss."

Then he shut the door in my face and I began my pathetic walk back to the valet line as I tried to piece together the events of the evening.

On the plus side, I got my car from the valet almost immediately, since everyone was watching the show. I'd also managed to introduce myself to a few people at the *Stanford Daily*, so the evening wasn't a total loss, though it was a pretty sad way to end the night.

I checked my phone before taking off and saw that there were fourteen messages from Cora.

The first one read:

> Phoebe, u there? I need help.

Cora was waiting in her driveway when I got to her house.

"I thought you'd be at the gala until late," she said.

"Can you tell me again what happened?" I asked as she buckled herself into my passenger seat.

"It came off. The condom came off. . . ."

"Okay and so—"

"Everything spilled out, okay, Phoebe! Is that what you want to hear, that I'm a complete idiot?"

"No," I said. Cora was breathing hard, and I could tell she was scared.

"Well, the good thing is you are also on the pill, so the possibility of pregnancy is low."

"But it *is* possible?" She looked at me, eyes wide.

"Yes, but not if we go get you a morning-after pill right now."

"Okay," she said, trying not to cry.

"One more thing," I said. "Since the condom came off, you're going to want to get tested. Just in case."

"Tested for what?" Cora hissed.

"Everything," I said. "Sexually transmitted diseases you might have gotten from—"

"David isn't sleeping with anyone else!" she snapped, tears suddenly rolling down her face.

"Okay," I said, making a mental note to come back to this later. "What did David do?"

"What do you mean?" she asked after I parked the car outside the pharmacy. I tried to keep up with her as she raced through the automatic doors.

"I mean, where is he and why didn't he already do this with you?"

"I don't know," Cora said before hissing, "Shit! That's Mrs. Telly from my mom's bunko group."

We hid behind a wall of feminine hygiene products and waited until a woman with long, wavy hair left the store. Then we turned to walk toward the family planning aisle. It was mercifully empty, which was a relief because Cora was a wreck.

"I need one of these," Cora said, showing me her phone. It was a link to my blog, citing the various forms of emergency contraception.

"Yep, this one," I said.

We were walking to the counter to ring it up when I heard another set of footsteps shuffling behind me. All the color drained from Cora's face, but she relaxed slightly when she realized who it was.

David was standing there looking just as bad as Cora. His clothes were wrinkled, and his absurd beanie hung off his head a little more haphazardly than usual, like a sock only half pulled off a foot.

"I'm sorry," he said. "I'm sorry I freaked out."

She stared at him for a moment before nodding. It was nice

to see that she wasn't running dramatically into his arms. I was proud of her for that.

"I'll just . . . head home, then," I said, trying to gauge whether Cora wanted me there. When she didn't say anything, I hurried out of the pharmacy. Just as I was about to open my car door, I felt her arms around me in the tightest hug she'd ever given.

"Thank you," she said. "I'm sorry I was—"

"It's okay," I told her. "Go take that. And remember what I said about getting tested. I wasn't saying it to be mean. I promise."

"I know," Cora whispered, wiping tears off her cheeks.

"Go," I said, and watched her walk back toward David.

As I saw him reach for her hand, still looking apologetic, I found myself disliking him less.

"I'll see you tomorrow at Estelle's for breakfast," she said. "Don't forget."

I nodded, waving back at her and realizing that I *had* forgotten that I was supposed to meet with her and a group of other people from Poetry Slam Night.

When I finally got home, my dad had a piece of popcorn dried to his cheek and my mom was snoring with her head thrown back on the couch. It was nice to see them together, even though nothing was really back to normal. Mom's phone was sitting inches from her lap, and even asleep, Dad had his arms crossed.

I woke them up to let them know I'd gotten home safely. After watching them toddle off to bed, I threw on my pajamas and crawled under my comforter, my sore, disappointed lips a reminder of the difference between writing about kissing and actually doing it.

Then my phone buzzed again. I was expecting a text from Neil, so I was surprised to see that it was Jorge. His text was a photo of a drawing. He had tried to draw a cartoon of me writing. It was pretty bad. He'd given me a cape and ridiculously muscular arms. I snorted.

> Nice. An excellent likeness of me.

> Wasn't expecting to get a response back from you tonight. Good time at the gala?

> No, actually. It was pretty awful.

> Care to elaborate?

> Too long via text. I'll tell you Monday.

The "..." popped up on my screen, but it disappeared a second later.

It had been a weird evening.

I resisted the urge to open my computer and write a diary entry about real-life kissing experience because (1) it had been disappointing and (2) I really just wanted to sleep.

My phone buzzed again at some point in the middle of the night, but I didn't see Neil's apology until the next morning.

> Sorry about last night. I tried to come get you but I got sidetracked by some newspaper people and Brookhurst wanted her ticket for Les Mis.

I didn't respond.

10

When I arrived at Estelle's, a small farmhouse breakfast place frequented by old people, I gave the hostess Cora's name, and she took me to a table where one other person was already seated. Jorge.

He stood when I got there and raised a hand in greeting.

"Guess we're the first ones here," I said.

Obviously, I thought.

The hostess, who had stepped back to her podium to take a phone call, turned to us to say, "That was your friend Cora. Apparently, the rest of your group had to cancel."

"Oh," said Jorge, and I imagined him being crushed by the awkwardness of the situation. I imagined him desperately looking for a way out of this. And I imagined strangling Cora later because this whole thing reeked of her.

Her behavior would fall under the category labeled *I did this for your own good, Phoebe. I am saving you from yourself.*

"So if you're staying, I can move you over here to a smaller table," the hostess told us.

"Sure," Jorge said quickly, before I could say anything in response. "I mean, if it's okay with you," he added.

155

"Sure," I responded casually, putting my bag under my arm and following the hostess to a more intimate table by the window overlooking the duck pond.

I ordered a coffee, and Jorge ordered a water, an orange juice, and a hot tea.

"You always have three drinks with breakfast?" I asked.

"Yeah," he said. "I always have something hot, but I love orange juice, and neither of those really quench your thirst, so hence the water. There's just no other way."

He said the last part seriously, and I stifled a laugh.

"I know it's not Monday yet, but do you want to tell me about the gala?"

There was something light about his body language, like he was enjoying himself. I watched him add three packets of sugar to his tea.

"Are you . . . glad I had a bad time?" I asked, surprised.

"Of course not," he said. "But I could've told you Neil is an ass if you'd asked. Why was it awful?" He leaned forward, smiling.

I frowned at him and he laughed.

A variety of responses came to mind, but I settled for the truth. I told him about Brookhurst swooping in and stealing my ticket. About the way she'd circled the event like a vulture. I told him how Neil basically ditched me, but omitted the part where he destroyed my lips, since I was almost certain Jorge could tell how chapped they were anyway, and I blushed thinking about it.

"I think I'd upgrade that to an *absurdly* terrible time," he said, and sipped his tea.

"Well, I did get to meet some newspaper people and chat with a couple journalists from the *Stanford Daily* for a while," I said. Jorge seemed to consider this for a moment.

"That was still really crappy of Neil."

He was right, but I didn't want to admit it yet, so I shrugged and looked at the menu to face my usual breakfast dilemma. I always want something sweet with something savory, but it's never the pancake plate with eggs, and I hate doing special orders because I'm sure it irritates the chef. I must have explained all this out loud to Jorge without realizing it, because when I looked up, he was grinning.

"What?" I asked.

"You're a weirdo," he said.

"I am not."

"You were just talking to yourself about your order. You mock my three drinks, and you're having a battle with yourself over how to request the cinnamon roll French toast plate and half of the breakfast burrito." He was laughing now. Then he added, "How about we split something sweet and savory?"

"Split?" I asked.

"We'll call it halfsies. I'll do half of your food, and you do half of mine."

His mouth was still curled into a grin, but his plan basically sounded like the way breakfast should happen always without question, even if it was definitely a "couple" thing to do.

So I agreed.

It ended up being the best breakfast I'd ever had at Estelle's, possibly the best I'd ever had in my life. We ordered the Greek omelet and the crème brûlée French toast.

"Best. Idea. Ever," said Jorge, who had finished his tea and orange juice and was working on his water. "How's your Spanish going?"

"Bien," I said.

"Any progress rolling your *r*'s?" He still loved that I couldn't do this.

"No, es muy embarazada."

"You know that means 'pregnant,' right?" he asked.

"Shit," I said, blushing. Jorge laughed for a while about that.

We'd moved on from the discussion of the gala and were now talking about homecoming court and laughing at Cora's reaction. Our school was one of the few that had juniors and seniors eligible for nomination, though only a senior could be crowned.

"All the other girls were so stoked to be up there," said Jorge. "And Cora looked like she'd just walked into an elevator someone farted in."

"Pretty accurate," I laughed. Truth was that I thought Cora was probably going to enjoy being on the court just a little bit, even if she never admitted it.

Jorge's ears suddenly perked up as the voices from the table behind us grew louder.

"Interesting," he said, clearly listening in.

"What's intere—" I began to ask, but he shushed me as one of the women at the table said loudly, "Well, I'll tell you, Matilda, I think Lydia Brookhurst is going about this the right way. That blog, or whatever it is, sounds absolutely filthy. According to my daughter-in-law, it is basically a sex book with all kinds of sex tips and suggestions in it. For children. *Imagine.*"

Jorge snorted.

"Imagine. A sex book for *children*," Jorge whispered in a highly offended tone.

I grinned, and then Matilda spoke up.

"Kids today have no modesty. We would've been skinned alive for reading trash like that. You read any of it, Mavis?"

"Course not. You know I wouldn't be caught dead read—"

Jorge leaned across the table and whispered, "Hey, would it be totally embarrassing for you if I messed with them a little?"

"Probably," I said.

"Can I do it anyway?"

I gave him the go-ahead with a smirk, and he continued with enthusiasm, "I mean, I had no idea the blog had sex secrets in it!" I buried my face in my hands. "Like that section where it tells you about that part behind a woman's knee that makes her orgasm!"

"Or that section where it talks about all the places we can meet up for orgies?" I added drily.

For a second Jorge looked shocked, then his face split into a grin as he stifled a laugh. The table behind us had gone silent.

"And you know the secret code, right? The phrase we're supposed to say when we arrive?" he asked.

"Of course," I said. "But it changes every week. This week it's 'banana hammock,' but last week it was 'clitoris.'"

Jorge choked on his water, and someone at the old-lady table dropped her silverware.

We split the bill when the server brought it, and somehow we both managed to keep a straight face as we walked past the table and onto the porch of the restaurant before we burst out laughing.

"That was awesome," he said. I smiled and he added, "I'll never understand why she's so pissed about that blog, though."

"Brookhurst?" I asked.

"Yeah. It's not like it's dirty. It's just about sex."

I shrugged.

"You read it?" I asked curiously, unable to help myself.

"Of course," he said, defiant. "Why?" he asked.

"No reason," I said quickly, feeling stupid for asking.

We walked across the gravel parking lot toward our cars, and I remembered that I hadn't said anything to him about his own nomination to homecoming court. When I brought it up, he lifted his head in a very regal way.

"Oh, you know," he said. "My subjects. They're looking for leadership, and I have an obligation to my people."

I smiled for maybe a second too long and realized that there was a lull in the conversation, the first one since we'd both sat down to breakfast, actually.

"That was fun," I said.

"Breakfast or talking about a dirty sex blog in front of old ladies?"

"You know, I enjoyed both," I said as Jorge laughed. "I'm actually glad Cora ditched us."

Shit. That was one step too far. He didn't say anything like that. Now you sound desperate.

"So I have a confession about that," Jorge said. "Cora was

160

going to move the breakfast to another day, and I asked her not to tell you."

"Why?" I asked.

"I wanted to ask you out, and this seemed like a good way to do it without doing it, you know what I mean? Kind of a cowardly predate, if you will."

I looked at him with what I thought was a quizzical expression on my face.

"I was hoping you'd let me take you on a real date, though. And maybe let me take you to homecoming."

When he looked at me this time, it was different than before. He had his hands in his pockets, and there was something sweet about the way he tilted his head toward me. It was almost shy for someone who never seemed to struggle with confidence.

"But if you don't want to, I will respect that. No amount of royal privilege would—"

I raised a hand to silence him.

"I'd love to be your date," I said. His grin widened.

"But you know they don't crown juniors, right? I mean, if you were looking to use me for royal connections, I'm afraid I'll just be a court member."

I registered the fact that I was closer to him than I'd ever been before, but it felt good, natural—and I wasn't anxious about it. Then I did something completely out of character. I kissed him on the cheek, letting my lips brush his skin.

Before I turned to walk to the car, I noticed the goose bumps on his neck, and I felt strange. Powerful almost.

So this is what confidence feels like, I thought.

I liked it.

That night I opened the blog and answered a few questions that had come up more than once.

Will semen make my breasts get bigger?
No.

I wasn't sure if she meant applying semen topically to her breasts or ingesting it, but since the answer was no to both, I saw no need to get clarification.

Can I accidentally break my boyfriend's penis?
Yes, it is possible to "break" a penis, though the phrase is misleading because the penis does not have bones. Blunt force to an erect penis can cause a penile fracture. See the link below to . . .

This question had surfaced on the blog a few times in various forms. In addition to anxious girlfriends, there also appeared to be a group of anxious boyfriends afraid to engage in intercourse because of the so-called destructive capabilities of the vagina.

My boyfriend has warts on his penis but says it's still okay to have sex. Is it?
NO. He needs to see a doctor and get treatment. In the meantime, please consult the safe-sex practices located . . .

I am not a doctor, but I am confident in telling women not to have sex just because their boyfriend says, "Don't worry, it's fine."

Should sex hurt?

It shouldn't hurt. There may be some discomfort during first sexual experiences, but pain associated with sexual intercourse should be discussed with your doctor.

What happens if the condom comes off?

It could have been from Cora.

I responded:

Get tested immediately and seek out emergency contraception.

Then I provided a link to the resources on the blog.

I was about to close the blog when I received another question.

Does writing about sex this much make you horny?

I deleted it.

11

Breakfast with Jorge was probably one of the last happy, non-gross moments before I succumbed to the epic vomit-fest that would be the next few days of my life, but I was still feeling okay early Monday morning when I got to school. It was curious timing because I'd just done three things completely out of character that had resulted in some unintended consequences:

1. I'd published the spotlight article about
   Nurse Reyes by submitting it on Sunday
   night to our adviser, Mr. Edmundson, whom I'd
   counted on *not* to read it before it printed Monday
   morning.
2. As soon as I got to school I'd returned Coach
   Snowden's flash drive to his desk without his
   knowledge, but not without correcting a few errors
   in his presentation.
3. I'd helped Monica Hansen write an article by
   giving her my notes.

Then at about noon on Monday, the flu hit me hard and I went home.

Even though Jorge was grossed out by the possibility of me projectile-vomiting all over his shoes, he visited a couple of days later. With a doctor's mask.

"Are you actually still sick, or are you hiding from Neil while he cools down about the article?" he asked as I opened the door for him. He looked at me, taking in my pale complexion and diseased visage, before firmly securing the doctor's mask on his face and passing me a stack of homework that Cora had delightedly handed over to him when he asked for it.

The truth was that, before I left school on Monday, I'd already talked about the article with Neil. Sort of.

I remember I was walking toward my English class, mentally answering a question about lubricant from my blog, when Neil interrupted me.

"How could you do that?" he asked, stopping in front of me.

"Submit an article?" I said, because I didn't have time to play dumb.

"Yes, submit *that* article. We have to retract—"

"Was it false information?"

"No."

"Was it written poorly?"

"No, but—"

"Then I fail to see why—"

"Not everyone can be a fucking saint, Phoebe. Sometimes we don't say things that piss off the people who pay for stuff."

That's what Nurse Reyes had said too.

He'd suddenly turned red, and I realized that it was because he was embarrassed. Neil doesn't swear.

"Actually, that doesn't sound like something good journalists would do," I told him.

"You crossed a line," he said, straightening up.

"So your interview with Pom was fine, but mine with Nurse Reyes is not?" I asked.

"It's about timing," Neil said.

"You mean you wrote your article before Brookhurst had something to offer, and I wrote mine when you realized what you had to lose?"

Neil looked different. He ran his fingers through his hair in a distracted kind of way, and even though I'd once found that attractive, now it was annoying. He was also noticeably pale and sweaty.

"Is this because of what happened at the gala?" he asked. "You're trying to get back at me because of—"

"No," I said, cutting him off. "Though that *was* rude. I actually believe in this article, so I submitted it to someone who could sign off."

Neil smoothed the front of his shirt, and I suddenly saw the resemblance to the thirty-year-old real estate agent Jorge had described.

"Well, I'm disappointed in you," he said. "I thought you were someone I could count on."

He looked like he was waiting for an apology, and instead of responding angrily the way I wanted to, I stared at him without blinking. Eventually he looked away.

"Fine," he said. "I guess I was wrong."

This time I still said nothing, but I added a smile and waited for him to leave.

Create uncomfortable silence. And watch what happens.

Nurse Reyes was right. People don't know how to handle it.

And Neil is, in fact, a terrible kisser. I realize I have no practical experience to compare it to, but an abundance of saliva and chapped lips are not signs of kissing prowess, so my conclusion stands unchallenged.

I can't believe I ever called him Cornelius. Embarrassing.

Cora said Neil left school after throwing up later in the newsroom, and I veered off course on my way to AP English to throw up in a mercifully empty bathroom.

On Twitter I noticed that Brookhurst had made a small nod to my interview with Nurse Reyes.

> **@TheRealLydiaBrookhurst:** If you wanted a professional to weigh in on Sex Education, you'd think they'd get a REAL DOCTOR to do it.

Classy.

"So he's pretty pissed," said Jorge through his mask. "I mean, if anyone has a right to be angry, it's you. He gave you the plague."

I blushed and Jorge pretended not to notice, though there might have been a hint of annoyance in his voice as he changed the subject to anything besides what I must have been doing with Neil to contract his sickness.

"I guess Brookhurst came to campus yesterday to talk to the principal about the staff spotlight on Nurse Reyes."

"She can't stop us from writing something just because she doesn't like it," I said.

"No, but she can pull her funding from the school if she wants, and the article goes against what she stands for, so naturally, she's livid."

"Is the principal going to do anything about it?"

"Technically, you didn't do anything wrong, but maybe. The political cartoon didn't help either," Jorge added. Even through the mask I could tell he was smiling, and I couldn't help but smile back.

David had taken my advice and created a political cartoon for the paper that I had slipped to Mr. Edmundson with my article.

Seriously, the man is a useless lump.

The cartoon depicted Lydia Brookhurst roasting marshmallows in a Girl Scout uniform over a pile of burning books. Not a bad start, and Cora was absolutely beaming with pride about it. She'd had it printed on T-shirts and coffee mugs through her parents' shop already and was handing them out before health class while I was sick. Apparently, they'd already sold out online, because for a small, conservative town we're remarkably feisty about our edgy T-shirts.

Which brings me to Coach Snowden.

As a blogger, I've had to get comfortable with computers and software, and that expertise has bled a little into other realms of my life.

I hadn't been in the class when the PowerPoint presentation

took over (having already succumbed to Neil's flu), but Jorge recounted what had happened:

1. The PowerPoint started and Coach Snowden immediately realized something was wrong when *real* facts and figures started appearing on the screen.

2. A giant, very realistic diagram of the female reproductive system flashed on the projector. When Coach Snowden read the description of "erogenous zones" and the direct links to the sex blog that described the purpose of the vagina in terms of female pleasure during sex, he knocked over his travel mug trying to turn it off, spilling cold coffee all over the students in the front row.

3. It turned out he couldn't disable the PowerPoint. *How very interesting and very embarrassing for him. Perhaps that was the intention of the creator?*

4. The PowerPoint presentation continued by discussing masturbation for both males and females. *Male and female masturbation? Perish the thought!*

5. It was at this point that Coach Snowden lost it and proceeded to shout, "LOOK AWAY! DO NOT LOOK AT THAT VAGINA. I DON'T KNOW WHAT'S GOING ON, BUT THIS IS NOT MY PRESENTATION! EVERYONE OUT OF THE ROOM!"

6. Pandemonium.

7. Everyone was kicked out of the classroom and

forced to wait in the hall until Coach Snowden could figure out how to turn the PowerPoint off.

8. The vice principal was called, and the Audiovisual Club tried to explain to an irate Coach Snowden that they could not turn off the PowerPoint because all the other programs were frozen. This happens sometimes after an update. They could only turn off the monitors and let it run its course on his computer.

9. The rest of the period was spent in silence while Coach Snowden sat in the front, his cheeks bright red. At some point the sound from the PowerPoint came back on just in time for a narrator to provide the definition of "clitoris" in a British accent, and Coach Snowden scrambled once again to mute it.

10. The bell rang and Coach Snowden stormed out of the room before anyone else.

"So no one knows how it happened?" I asked Jorge.

"Nope. No one knows. Coach Snowden swears that he had his presentation with him the whole time. He also swears that he did nothing to his flash drive." He shook his head and stood up to leave.

"Thanks for dropping this off," I said, looking at the papers I could easily have downloaded from all of my course portals online.

"No problem. Cora said she'd rather not breathe your foul, putrid air for a while anyway."

"She's sweet like that," I said.

"Oh," he said, pulling something from his pocket. "I almost forgot. Nurse Reyes gave this to me. She came to health class to find you, but since you were out, I offered to drop it off."

"What is it?" I asked.

He pulled out a red lollipop. I laughed.

"She said to tell you she really liked your piece."

"Thanks for delivering the message," I said, twirling the lollipop in my hand. He stood there shifting his feet a little.

"Something else?" I asked.

He pulled down his mask and leaned toward me so quickly I had no time to react. Then he dipped his head gently and kissed me on the cheek before drawing back and straightening up with a very serious expression on his face. His lips were soft, and though they'd barely touched my skin, the exhilaration that flooded my body from this one tiny gesture was so much stronger than from my misbegotten kissing disaster with Neil.

Jorge pulled his mask back up and said, "And that's the last time that happens until you're less gross. Seriously, I don't need to get infected."

Then he was gone.

Which brings us to the third out-of-character event.

Enter Monica Hansen.

Monica, who remained like an evil, shadowy presence in my life, had apparently stopped by my house while I was sleeping. I'd politely told Neil I couldn't finish an article on college acceptance letters I was working on due to violent vomiting. Neil then sent me a text message asking me to give my notes to Monica, who would be completing the assignment for me.

I wasn't thrilled with the idea of giving Monica anything or letting her into my home, but as another wave of nausea hit, I left the stack of paperwork with my mom and asked her to give it to Monica on Tuesday when she arrived.

When I woke up, the notes were gone. She'd left a pink Post-it behind that said *Thanx*, with an *x*, and I realized how much the *x* bothered me. Like adding the *ks* was too much trouble and she was saving time. But as far as exchanges with Monica went, it was fairly normal . . . until the follow-up email.

The subject line read "Interesting Reading Material!" She had attached a photo taken through the crack of my bedroom door. In the background I could see my body as a bulging lump wrapped in blankets, and in the foreground my laptop was wide open to the home page of my blog.

My breath caught in my chest when it occurred to me that she'd snapped this photo behind my mom's back. Thankfully, I'd logged out of the blog editor screen at least.

There was no response necessary for this. I could have tried, "LOL. Yeah." Or something with more bravado, like, "Nothing I didn't already know from experience," which no one would have believed. But I decided to settle for ignoring and deleting the email.

All the photo proved was that I read the blog. But if she'd caught me with the edit screen open . . .

I breathed.

It would have jeopardized my anonymity for sure.

I was proud to be writing something that seemed to be helpful. But if people found out it was me, well, that would get more attention than the blog itself because I was a teenager and a girl.

Judgment for knowing too much would be expected.

Rattled by Monica's email, I went to the blog to see if there were any questions I could answer before bed.

Only one came up.

> Hi. I'm not sure if it's normal to ask you but my parents don't know I'm gay and I don't have anyone to ask, so here goes: How do gay people have sex?

I stared at it for a while. None of my research materials or the stuff I'd collected from the gynecologist's office would help me answer this.

Later that night I walked out of my room with every intention of sinking a soupspoon into a jar of Nutella, when I heard my parents talking.

"I thought you hated Brookhurst," my dad said. "What does it matter what Phoebe writes?"

"I know her. That article was a direct attack, and that's how Brookhurst sees it. It isn't worth it."

"To write an article that might make her look bad?"

"You don't know what she's capable of."

I stepped backward into my room and forgot about the Nutella.

12

Reading this kid's question about gay sex had made me realize this was the first time I'd gotten a question that embarrassed me. Not because I was embarrassed to answer it, but because I *could not* answer it. I hadn't done any research on the subject at all, and none of my materials could help me put together a cogent response.

It was the first time since starting the blog that I felt outside my comfort zone because I was providing an answer to a question that had absolutely nothing to do with my own curiosity. I mean, I was curious, but the answer wasn't going to be in response to any questions I had personally, because in the back of my mind I'd always sort of known that I was attracted to men.

I'd never considered the question before, which disappointed me.

How had I never considered it?

Every resource I'd normally check failed me. Obviously, nearly all of the gynecological materials were completely useless. Every sex ed textbook I'd managed to snag excluded LGBTQIA folks, which made me realize if it was this hard for me, a cisgender (as in, my gender corresponds to my sex assigned at birth) heterosexual woman, someone used to writing about sex and pulling information about sexual material, it would be nearly impossible for someone who didn't know where to begin asking questions, who didn't have anyone close to them to ask, and who didn't have resources readily accessible.

I started pulling titles of books from the online archives of the library. Lists of authors who could answer questions with details I didn't have. And for a minute I thought that would be enough. A list of books would be a great place for this kid to start.

But it wasn't enough. As much as I wanted it to be, I knew it wasn't enough.

I thought I could answer the question about gay sex more completely with a solid response here. I looked at the list of books and magazines I'd put together, but that kid had not asked me for a list of stuff to *read* on the subject. They'd asked me how gay people have sex, which led me to examine the very definition of sex.

Using the information I'd gathered, I prepared my response.

> Thank you for the question.
>
> The Merriam-Webster dictionary defines a "sex act" as "an act performed with another for sexual gratification."
>
> This is a good start, but there are important details missing from this definition. So here is my best answer:

Any act between two or more *consenting* people involving arousal could constitute sex.

Key points: consent matters and intent matters (a regular pelvic exam with a gynecologist does not equal sex, for example).

Also (and this is important to note):

Sex is not defined by penetration, orgasm, or the possibility of creating offspring. It can include those things, but they are not strictly necessary to denote sexual activity. And there is no sex hierarchy where some sex acts are considered more legitimate or more "real" than others.

Sexual activity generally refers to the body parts that we use to have sex. But it can include whatever experience—not necessarily physical—brings you pleasure.

Sex between two people can occur anally, when one partner puts their penis into their partner's anus. It can involve penetration of one or both partners or no penetration at all. Sex can also occur through mutual masturbation.

Sex can occur between people of any gender identity and sexual orientation. Men can have sex with men, women, or any other gender. Women can have sex with women, men, or any other gender.

See the complete definitions of anal sex, oral sex, and mutual masturbation by clicking **here**.

Please note that sex does not look *one* way. It could also include acts not listed here.

> While this may be a tangent to your original question, it's also worth noting that sex and gender are different. Click **here** for definitions of gender identity, gender binary, genderqueer, gender-fluid, and transgender. . . .

It still wasn't enough. I had answered a few questions in a very broad sense and provided links to some definitions on the blog, but I knew there was so much more to discuss. The problem was, I didn't know what I didn't know.

> I hope this provides a start to help answer some of your questions, but I'd also like to refer you to the following resources that might also offer the more specific details you need. This is, of course, not a comprehensive list, but it might help with some of the other questions you may have.

I included my list of books, magazines, and queer groups that might be able to help, and looked back at my response before adding a line about safe sex:

> Please also note that safe-sex practices apply here. See **link**. Condoms and dental dams should always be used to prevent the spread of STDs.
>
> Regular testing for those who are sexually active is also highly recommended.

Before closing the entry, I added:

> I realize that this response is still lacking, so if you have other, more specific questions, please feel free to write again and I would be happy to research.

I included a few links to some important articles I'd come across, including a very important one published in *Teen Vogue* that explained that as long as it is between two consenting people, anal sex is completely natural.

My favorite quote from the article states: "There is no wrong way to experience sexuality, and no way is better than any other."

I felt okay for a second, thinking that I had at the very least given the kid who'd asked a few answers, but then the response posts started coming in almost immediately.

Some people responded positively and others promised to never read my blog again.

I deleted the homophobic comments, and waited for Brookhurst to respond. She must have been distracted, because she responded to multiple blog entries.

> **@TheRealLydiaBrookhurst:** Please tell me why we are wasting our time trying to teach young men about a woman's period in health class. They. Do. Not. Care.

@TheRealLydiaBrookhurst: @CircleintheSquare
your post on mast*rbation is offensive. If you
stand by this filth, why are you hiding behind this
account?

Then she spotted my most recent response.

@TheRealLydiaBrookhurst: @CircleintheSquare Are
we really still having conversations about gay sex?
When are we going to focus on NORMAL?

I still get a lot of questions about what's "normal."

> Is it normal to have a curved penis? A larger left
> boob?
> Is it normal that I've had a lot of sex but never had
> an orgasm?
> Is it normal to be afraid of sex?
> Is it normal to not want to have sex?
> Is it normal to not be attracted to anyone?
> Is it normal to be attracted to lots of people?

"Normal" is hard to explain. For these questions the answer has always been yes.

But Brookhurst had even more to say about the latest entry, and tweets alone would not suffice.

On my way to school on Tuesday I did just that.

It was a conservative radio show that no one really listens to except around Christmastime, when they play carols 24/7, but Brookhurst was railing on *The Circle in the Square* with unnatural aggression.

"Well," said the host, "this Pom person, whoever they are, obviously believes that our school sex education is lacking somehow. That's why they felt the need to write this—"

Brookhurst interrupted.

"You know what," she said, "I don't understand that. It isn't a great big secret where babies come from, and it is the state's job to provide some form of sex education, but it isn't the school's responsibility to teach what is, in my opinion, *questionable* material. We, the citizens of this town, are in charge of the content. Whatever happened to letting parents decide what the kids need to know and when they should know it?"

"So then you propose—" the host started before Brookhurst cut him off again.

"An abstinence-only plan, yes. Sexual risk avoidance. We need to teach responsibility. We need to teach teens *not* to have sex, not *how* to have sex. That means keeping his you-know-what out of her you-know-where."

"Until they're married?"

"Exactly! That's how we keep the unplanned pregnancies

180

from happening. Exercise some self-control. There's your birth control right there! It isn't that difficult. I will never understand why these liberal educators insist on shoving their twisted views on our children."

"You also made several comments about homosexual activity," he said, not really asking a question.

Brookhurst cleared her throat for this one.

"It is impossible to understand a mind that can justify explaining such an act to impressionable young people in excruciating detail. As a woman of faith, I am appalled. God loves us all, but I've said it before and I'll say it again: hate the sin, love the sinner."

And on that note, with the promise of God's damnation, I turned off the engine and walked to class, my phone already buzzing with a text from Jorge.

Are you better yet?

13

I believe the jump in followers was due to the radio address.

In other news, my mom and I had been avoiding each other since the Nurse Reyes interview came out. Talking about it would have made us both uncomfortable, so shoving our feelings way down where no one could see was the obvious choice.

Super healthy.

I couldn't help but notice that she was upset about it, though. She had weekly video conferences with Brookhurst about her business, and I overheard the end of one that included Lydia's comment: "And if certain 'journalists' would stop sensationalizing this election, I wouldn't have to deal with so much misinformation."

She hissed the *s* in "misinformation" like a snake, and I saw her put air quotes around the word "journalist."

I waited for my mom to defend me or say something. Anything, really.

But she just nodded, holding the phone.

I tried not to let that bother me.

I'd stayed up too late answering blog questions, and when I woke up, I realized I'd also forgotten to charge my phone and transfer my laundry into the dryer. Almost-dead phone and funky-smelling clothes. An excellent start to the day.

It was Thursday. Normally, I would ride to school with Mom and Dad, but Cora had come over early to take me, thinking I would still want some distance from the cloud of awkward surrounding me and my mom.

Sometimes Cora really gets me.

Just as we arrived at school and I could feel my stomach begin to unclench, I got a text message from Mom in all caps, because she always accidentally turns that on somehow.

> PHOEBE MY COMPUTER CRASHED AND I BORROWED YOURS. I'M SO SORRY I DIDN'T ASK SOONER BUT YOU WERE ALREADY GONE. I'LL BRING IT BACK AFTER MY MEETING WITH BROOKHURST THIS AFTERNOON.

Panic. Undiluted panic coursed through me.

> Do you need my password to log on to the computer?

The text looked so calm and friendly on the screen, but really I was dying inside. My phone's battery was at one percent.

NO. IT WAS ALREADY UNLOCKED. THANKS.

Then my screen went black. I breathed through my teeth as one thought pulsed to the surface of my mind.

I recapped the source of my panic in my head.

1. My mom had borrowed my computer, which was essentially like someone borrowing my eyeballs.
2. My computer was unlocked—probably because I had been playing music—with the edit screen of my blog open.
3. FML.
4. I should be able to log out remotely through my phone, but it was dead, because *of course it would be dead*. I never let it get below a 75 percent charge, and the one time I forget it in my backpack . . .
5. I needed to get into the library.

"What's wrong?" Cora asked when she realized I'd stop moving, talking—possibly breathing.

"I need you to cause a diversion of some kind. I need to use the school computers without anyone seeing, and I need you not to ask questions."

I knew I sounded like something out of a really bad spy movie. I could see the wheels in Cora's head turning, and I was counting on the strength of our friendship and the memory of the almost-baby night to convince her without too much further conversation.

"Let's go," she said, grabbing my arm as the bell rang. We moved toward the library, weaving through the swarms of kids running to class.

I saw Jorge wave uncertainly at us as we turned a corner, and I only had time to wave awkwardly without any explanation.

The library was empty, but I could hear the librarian shuffling textbooks.

"I need him out of the way," I whispered to Cora.

"Okay, but he can live, right?"

I stared at her.

"Okay, we're not joking today," she said.

She tied her hair in a ponytail, pulled off her sunglasses, and ran to the librarian. A man.

He was still innocently stacking textbooks on his cart when Cora approached.

"I am so, so sorry," she said, her voice shaking ever so slightly. "I just got my period and I need a tampon right away."

I covered my mouth with my hand and watched as the poor man's face dropped. He looked like he'd never heard any of those words in his life.

Then the real performance began when Cora pretended to cry.

"I'm really so sorry. It's my first one," she sobbed, "and I was squatting on the floor near the graphic novels, and it just happened. I didn't mean for anything to get on the carpet but . . ."

Ugh. Cora, that's disgusting. But good work.

The librarian, who had now turned a vivid plum color, led Cora to where the cleaning supplies were as she continued to splutter "I just hope it doesn't stain" and "I'm so, so sorry." He looked like he just wanted her to stop talking.

Blessing Cora, I set to work logging in to my desktop remotely. I wouldn't trigger any of the computer lab's security settings as long as I didn't access *The Circle in the Square* directly.

Graphic novels were located in the opposite direction from the computer lab. I calculated that I should have at least a few minutes to log in remotely and exit the blog before my mom could accidentally broadcast my latest response about the vagina's natural lubricant to her very conservative clients.

I logged in to the first available computer, bypassing all the instructions on "safe internet use."

Then I went in to access my desktop remotely, and just as the picture of my family on our last trip to Oahu flashed on my screen, a pop-up disabled the website with a warning:

> You are viewing sexually explicit material on a
> school computer. This is grounds for suspension.
>   Please remain seated until a librarian can
> assist you.

Yes, that's exactly what I'll do. I'll sit here quietly and wait to be suspended, I thought, the sweat pooling in my eyebrows.

Then, from a distance, I heard Cora spilling the cleaning supplies all over the floor.

"Oh, I'm so sorry!" she said in a whisper-yell. "This has been the worst day ever."

The librarian looked like he wanted to die. He hadn't even blinked in my direction, so I mouthed the phrase *key card* to Cora as obviously as I could without attracting his attention. She nodded curtly and then did the most spectacular thing I've ever seen done outside *Mission: Impossible*.

She slipped theatrically in the puddle of soap she'd just spilled, and instead of falling dramatically, she knocked the librarian just enough for him to stumble in the soap but not enough to topple him over. "Oh my goodness," she said. "Let me help you."

Then, as she steadied him on his feet, she lifted his key card out of his breast pocket and tossed it gently behind a bookcase three feet in front of her.

I ran for it, dove behind the bookcase, and waited for them to move back toward the graphic novels, where Cora would have to somehow create a gross, mysterious stain on the carpet. I swiped the librarian's card in the computer and cleared the error message, but there was another problem.

A pop-up told me that my mom was trying to use my computer at the same time I was.

SHIT, SHIT, SHIT.

"Log out. Log out. Log out," I breathed.

It seemed to take an eternity for the computer to exit the blog.

I entered the series of passwords and finally closed the program, but just as I was about to stand up and run for the door, I saw a yellow box checked on my remote desktop. Some kind of tracking software.

My heart did a double backflip, but there was no time to

worry about that as I ran for the door, slipped on the soap Cora had spilled, and slid into the exit turnstile. I threw the key card behind me on the floor near the book scanner and prayed the librarian would just assume he'd dropped it.

Cora appeared around the corner of the library about five minutes later, unzipping her hoodie.

"You were—"

"I know," she said, putting her sunglasses back on and smiling in a very self-satisfied way.

"I'm just in awe."

"You're my person," she said, squeezing my hand.

Then we walked in silence toward my health class, where I would have to explain why I was so late.

"What did you do when you got to the graphic novels and he saw there was no stain?"

"I *am* on my period," Cora said simply.

I just looked at her.

What.

"Go big or go home," she said.

"I just—but—"

She was wearing shorts, so it was, in fact, possible.

Then I stopped thinking about it.

Coach Snowden didn't even notice I was late. He and the football players were discussing strategy while the other students played on their phones.

Jorge looked at me curiously when I walked in, and I winked.

Did I really just wink? I'd been running through the hallway. What if he thought I'd been trying to get to the bathroom because of chronic diarrhea or something equally gross? Winking was not the appropriate response to that.

But then he smiled.

Okay, we're fine, then.

I took a deep breath and picked up my phone to text him an explanation, then remembered that it was still dead.

14

My laptop was returned to my room without any discussion of my almost heart attack, which meant my mom had no idea what I'd gone through to close the blog.

I had been so busy worrying about her opening the blog on my computer that I hadn't even begun to worry about her accidentally opening the folder with my diary in it.

It was password protected, but only if I was not too dense to close it properly.

Otherwise my mom would have been treated to such gems as *Personal note and note for research: vagina elasticity.*

What in the actual hell would she have made of that?

Then my dad interrupted my pointless worrying.

"I'm pretty sure the Brookhurst campaign is over," said my dad at breakfast while my mom was getting ready. I wasn't fully awake yet, so I just looked at him in disbelief. "You know Helen Rubinowitz? The woman she's running against?"

I nodded.

"Well, Brookhurst said a few not-very-nice things about her at that gala event, and someone recorded it."

"What did she say?" I asked.

He turned his laptop screen toward me with the written transcript.

> Well, you know some women don't think they
> need to put in the effort to make themselves look
> presentable. Just look at the woman I'm running
> against, for heaven's sake. Poor thing. She fell out of
> the ugly tree and hit every ugly branch on the way
> down, for sure. No wonder her husband left her.

"Wow," I said.

"It gets worse. Also keep in mind that Rubinowitz is a widow. Her husband did not leave her by choice. This is not going to play out well."

I looked down and continued to read Brookhurst's statement.

> Look, it's common knowledge that beautiful women
> are more successful. If you're a dog, you aren't
> going to get far. That's the truth.

I would really have loved to agree with my dad, but since the Brookhurst campaign began, the town dynamic had shifted. Even though she couldn't get rid of Food Truck Village—yet—there was nothing to stop restaurant owners downtown from hanging those signs in their windows: 100% AMERICAN. PROTECT OUR ROOTS. SUPPORT THE REAL LINDA VISTA.

Nearly all of them were accompanied by a B4M button. One sign even added: DELETE THE BLOG. CONTACT US.

Then, when I flipped on the local radio station on the way to school, people were actually calling in to *defend* her.

"She didn't mean what she said. Obviously, she wouldn't have said it if she'd known someone was recording it. What a vicious thing to do to someone!"

"Look, she tells it like it is. She didn't say anything everyone wasn't already thinking. You've seen Helen Rubinowitz, right?"

"At least Brookhurst is personable! Have you ever heard Rubinowitz talk? I'd rather read the ingredients on a box of Raisin Bran."

Later, when I got home and opened Twitter, I noticed Brookhurst had posted a list of nauseating campaign promises. I told myself I'd look at it later.

"Have I told you lately how amazing it feels to not be carrying a tiny parasite?" Cora asked.

"Yes," I said. "Quite a few times, actually."

Cora had a lovely way of describing pregnancy, and if it weren't technically true, I might have defended fetuses everywhere, but teeny-tiny humans do rely on their mothers' bodies to grow and develop. They take up space and nutrients and sometimes make their moms physically ill in the process.

So "parasite" makes sense. Even if it's a little mean.

Her pregnancy scare had had an interesting effect on her. For as long as I'd known her, she'd been adamant about getting exactly what she wanted when she wanted it, without too much consideration for consequences. However, it seems when the consequences are a possible living human being growing in your uterus, they become much more threatening.

I'd told her to read up on the effects of the morning-after pill before she took it. I wanted her to know that bleeding would happen, and it might throw off her cycle for a while, but she'd apparently read all about it on *The Circle in the Square*, which was comforting.

David was wearing headphones and sketching while Cora leaned up against his shoulder. If he could hear anything she was saying, he didn't act like it.

Jorge had gone to grab a couple of breakfast burritos for us, and Cora looked at me significantly when he sat down, allowing his legs to brush up against mine.

"It's going to be cold in the newsroom from now on," said Jorge, taking a bite of his burrito while handing mine to me. "Frigid cold."

I gave him a noncommittal head bob.

"I'm serious," he said. "Neil is the kind of guy who loves you when you agree with him and make him look good. But once you don't—"

The bell rang.

Cora nudged David and they both walked off to art class together, but Jorge and I stayed where we were. Our legs were still touching as we sat on the concrete steps outside, and I'm pretty sure that neither of us actually wanted to move. We'd been in close proximity a lot, but we hadn't kissed. To be honest, it was starting to get to me.

"See you later," he said, throwing his backpack over his shoulder. His eyes lingered on my face, and I imagined what it would be like to touch him without feeling nervous and wondered under what circumstances I would be capable of doing that.

When I got to the newsroom, I discovered that Jorge had been right about the chill.

Neil was sitting on the front desk, surrounded by a group of girls, all talking excitedly about homecoming. His eyes flicked casually to the back of the room when I walked in and then back to his group. I noticed that the seat I usually occupied was now taken by Monica Hansen, who was looking up at Neil with a sickly, self-satisfied expression. She was sitting with her usual smug indifference to everyone in the room, but there was something triumphant in her gaze.

"All right, everyone, this issue is all about homecoming," said Neil in a forced peppy voice that didn't sound like him. Nobody else seemed to notice, because the room was immediately filled with scattered applause and a few cheers from the front row.

"I've already handed out all the assignments for the upcoming issue, so go ahead and check out the online portal for what I need from you. Most of you already know because we discussed it." He winked at Monica, who smiled.

The room buzzed with conversation for a while, and I

opened a school laptop to look at what assignment he'd picked for me.

Phoebe Townsend—Proofreading—Horoscope

He was clearly still angry. Proofing the horoscope was a newbie assignment at best.

I scanned the rest of the assignments for the issue and saw that Neil was interviewing Brookhurst, but what was even more interesting was that Monica was writing an opinion piece with the working title "The Sex Blog—You Are What You Read," which, given her connection to the Abstinence Club at school, sounded ominous.

Neil had once complimented Pom's work, telling everyone in the newsroom he thought it was well researched. Now he was letting Monica write a piece that no doubt discredited it.

The horoscopes for the issue were each two sentences long, so it took about five minutes to finish and submit my assignment.

I tried to find a free minute to talk to Neil, but he was surrounded by people who'd come up to talk to him about their work or about homecoming.

Finally the bell rang and I walked quickly to catch up with him, even though he was clearly ignoring me.

"Neil?"

"Phoebe," he said with no expression on his face.

Weak chin, I thought. *Wonder why I never noticed it before.*

"So I completed my assignment for this issue."

195

"Good for you," he said condescendingly. "I'm sure our horoscope readers will appreciate your efforts. They'll be thrilled to know that Sagittarius is in great shape for finals and Leo will finally talk to their crush."

He sounds like an idiot. Did he always sound this stupid?

"Right," I said. "Well, actually, I was wondering if I could do an interview with Rubinowitz, since you're already doing one with Brookhurst. You know, for balance."

"No room," said Neil, fastening the snaps on his leather bag.

Of course he thinks he's too good for a backpack.

"I think that maybe—"

"Look, Phoebe, to be honest, your work has slipped lately. Maybe I put too much on your plate. Maybe your attention has been elsewhere. I don't know. But I have a job to do."

He walked off, and a minute later I was recounting the whole thing to Jorge and Cora. And also David, who might have been listening but was mostly just drawing in his sketchbook.

"I told you," said Jorge, leaning against the lockers.

"What an asshole. I heard his interview with Brookhurst is going in a few local papers too. They're her contacts, after all," Cora said, looking over David's shoulder at his drawing before he pulled it away. "So what are you going to do if Neil won't let you do the Rubinowitz interview?" she asked.

"Nothing, I guess," I said. "It's not really my responsibility to make sure she gets an interview. I was just—"

"Yes. It is," said David, still not looking up. I blinked. "It's your responsibility because even though it is for a stupid school paper in a town that is pretty close to putting creationism on the syllabus for biology, you have the ability to balance this out and provide both sides. If you don't do it, you can't be sure anyone else will. And that means you're basically letting Neil control the story. Actually, letting Brookhurst control the story." He finally looked up at me. "Why don't you interview Rubinowitz anyway? My uncle is the editor at *Walnut Press*. It's just a local paper, but it has a decent circulation. I bet I can get him to publish it."

We all stared at him.

"I can listen *and* draw," said David blandly. "I'm not ignoring you."

Jorge looked at David approvingly. I wasn't sure he'd ever heard David speak before then.

"Call her office," David said.

That part was surprisingly easy. The assistant at Helen Rubinowitz's law office was only too eager to set up the interview that afternoon, making it seem like the candidate could use all the publicity help she could get.

When I arrived at Rubinowitz's law office, it was clear to see what her biggest hurdle in this election would be. Lydia Brookhurst was vile, but she was outspoken, flashy, and completely charming when she wanted to be. Rubinowitz, on the other hand, was reserved and straightforward, the consummate professional. Almost everything she wore was black, and she preferred to let her experience speak for itself, while Brookhurst loved to sing her own praises.

"Phoebe," she said in a quiet voice. "I understand you want

to interview me." There was a warmth about her that made her seem human in a way Lydia Brookhurst could never pull off.

"Yes," I said, looking around at the assortment of framed degrees on her wall as I sat down in a creaky chair on rolling wheels.

I pulled out my notebook before noticing that she also had framed crayon drawings and photographs on the bookshelf behind her desk. There were several photos of small, doughy, nondescript babies who must be her grandchildren, a boy in a yarmulke, and a little girl wearing Minnie Mouse ears at Disneyland.

"Can you tell me why you're running for mayor?" I asked, still trying to get comfortable in a chair that was trying to roll away from me.

"I found out Lydia Brookhurst was running."

Something seemed to stir in her eyes when she said Brookhurst's name, something dark and unpleasant that gave her the appearance of a person who had just smelled something foul.

"That's a strong statement to make. To run for office simply because someone else is. Would you like to elaborate on that?" I asked.

She cleared her throat. "The first part of what I'm about to tell you is off the record," she said, looking at my notebook. "But I want you to get the full picture."

I put down my pen.

"I know Lydia Brookhurst better than a lot of people, and there are things about her character that make her particularly dangerous."

"Her character?" I asked.

"She regularly cheated in school. It was common knowledge to people who were close to her that her family erased the allegations and went so far as to forge test scores for college admission.

"And there was a nasty habit in her family of making vague and not-so-vague racist comments about non-Christian holidays. Her father was especially creative about using slurs people had never heard before."

I thought about how Lydia's father had a gold plaque with his likeness engraved on it in the middle of Main Street.

"There are other stories too. Aside from the beauty pageant stories that most people already know, I remember that on Pet Day she casually dropped a classmate's hamster into the python tank when the girl refused to change the date of her birthday party." She sighed deeply. "If you have enough money, you get away with all kinds of things."

I stared at her.

"I am telling you these things because there were no punishments issued for any of them," said Rubinowitz. "I want you to understand why I am running."

"But why would we leave this off the record?" I asked. "Isn't this worth mentioning?"

She shook her head.

I blinked at her, my pen desperate to capture all the details I'd just heard.

"But—"

She shook her head again and slid a piece of paper across the desk to me.

"Her obsession with Pom is strange and completely unnecessary, and I'm aware of what she's said about me and how I look, and that isn't important either. This," she said, tapping the paper, "is the list of programs she intends to cut funding for once she gets elected. *This* is what we need to focus on."

I ignored the surge in my stomach at the mention of the blog and looked down at the list. It was the one she'd just tweeted that I hadn't looked at yet.

It read:

LGBTQIA Support
Homeless Employment
Immigration Assistance

And then . . .

"'Creative arts scholarships'?" I asked. "Why would she attack scholarships?"

"Some of them are need-based, which she obviously does not understand, but the real reason she's opposed to that one is because she can't omit the fund for the arts."

"Why would she do that?"

"I can only guess," said Rubinowitz, her mouth in a hard line.

"Okay," I said. "So guess."

"She was once asked to present the award for an art merit scholarship at a banquet at her family's orchard. Fancy event. Big tented canopy with waiters and everything. Lots of press." She leaned forward significantly and said, "She wasn't involved in the organization at all. She was just presenting. But the winner was a lesbian with short purple hair who had recently published a humorous story about coming out to her very religious grandmother.

"The title of the piece, 'My Gay Vagina,' which Lydia had to read out loud to a group of very rich, mostly conservative people, made her squeak in embarrassment. Lydia followed it up by shouting, 'Oh, not *my* vagina,' before practically running offstage without handing the student the award."

"I see," I said, trying not to laugh.

"So she's never publicly commented on why she would cut that particular program, but for anyone who was there that night and for anyone who knows her—that was the reason. She was embarrassed, and she's never really been a friend to the LGBTQIA community."

"Were you there? At the banquet?"

"Yes," said Rubinowitz. She held back, so I pressed on.

"Were you invited?"

"Yes," she said.

"By whom?" I asked.

"The recipient of the award," she said.

"And how do you know her?"

"She's my granddaughter."

"So you were the religious grandmother?"

"So it would seem," she said, and smiled.

An hour later my notebook was full, and I was ready to write the article.

During the interview I'd gotten several texts from Cora asking me (1) *When are we shopping for homecoming dresses?* (2) *Why are you taking so long to respond?* (3) *Seriously, why do you even have a phone if you don't respond to texts?* (4) *WTF Phoebe.* Then, ten minutes later, (5) *FUCK. Respond. Some of us have shit to do.* (6) *Oh yeah. The interview. Sorry.*

Then I got a text from Jorge asking me how it went.

> I think I can write something good with this.
> Heading to library now to write first draft.

The public library near my house was nearly empty, which was exactly what I was hoping for. My favorite squashy chair was unoccupied, and I sat down quickly, then let all of my notes flow into my laptop for what felt like hours, until a long brown arm reached over my shoulder and grabbed the computer, lifting my Word doc to his gaze.

"Hey—" I said, ready to shout, before I realized who it was. "I'm not done yet."

Jorge ignored me and sat down to read the four pages I'd written. His eyes narrowed, and I couldn't help but stare at him as he scrolled through my words with razor-sharp attention.

When he was done, he smiled and said, "By now I should probably expect your stuff to be great when I read it, but I'm always impressed by how great it is. Seriously, Phoebe, you can write anything."

"Not according to Neil. I'm slipping, remember?"

"Neil is an idiot. Come with me."

He zipped my laptop into its case and scooped all my notes into my bag before reaching out and offering me his hand. I took it and we walked to the back of the library, where a small spiral staircase wrapped through the reference section and up to a small room of old magazines that no one ever visited.

My heart pounded in my chest because I knew where he was taking me, and all I could think was *Thank God this is happening.*

When we got to the empty room, he set my backpack on the floor and gently put his hands on my waist before asking, "Can I kiss you?"

I paused for a second, pretending to consider the question, and he put his hand under my chin as if to say, *Please?*

Yes please! I thought, then nodded.

It was electric. His lips were buttery soft, and they moved with delicate precision, teasing me toward him and then slowly pushing back. For a few moments I forgot to breathe and had to stop and lean my forehead into his chest while I caught my breath.

He laughed.

"You're supposed to keep breathing when you kiss someone," he said. I didn't bother telling him that I had very little experience with kissing someone like this. But it didn't matter because he was a little breathless too, watching me with bright eyes, like he'd gotten away with something.

Kissing had come up frequently during my research as a means of two people using smell and taste to assess each other as potential mates. It's the equivalent of sampling someone's sweat and saliva like wine, which definitely makes it sound way grosser than it is.

Jorge pulled me closer into the shadows of the room and

dipped his lips into my neck, which I found I quite enjoyed. *He does smell good,* I thought. And we stood there in the semidarkness of the dusty magazine volumes for an unknown amount of time.

Then a muffled scream echoed in the silent room.

The wispy, thin librarian had climbed soundlessly up the spiral staircase, let out an embarrassed squawk when she saw Jorge's hand inching up under my shirt, and turned to flee from the room.

"The library is closing!" she whisper-shouted at us, practically leaping down the steps.

We laughed until it hurt, and when we walked out of the library holding hands, she deliberately avoided eye contact.

"We completely embarrassed her," said Jorge.

"Well, it could've been worse. She's lucky we weren't naked," I said. Then paused and said quickly, "I mean—"

"You mean we *could've* been naked up there?" Jorge asked with mock outrage.

"Not today," I said, leaning in to kiss him. I enjoyed the moment when his mouth split into a grin while it was still pressed against mine.

Maybe it was the kissing, or the fact that I always have a hard time sleeping when I'm in the middle of a story draft, but I stared at my bedroom ceiling for a long time before giving up and getting out of bed to rummage through my original research stuff from the estate sale.

It's what I've always done when I can't sleep.

I'd been through all of it many times throughout the years, but every once in a while I like to pull out a box and make sure I haven't missed something big, some giant secret that will explain some ancient sexual mystery I haven't read about yet.

A well-worn envelope of baby photos flopped out of a disintegrating cardboard shoebox from a shoe store that had gone out of business before I was born. I had never spent much time looking at the baby pictures, because they seemed irrelevant to my research, but still, it had been a while since I perused the fat, cherubic faces, so I flipped through them one by one, noting that based on the birth date scribbled on the back of each photograph, all of these babies were at least ten years older than I was.

A little girl with bright red cheeks wearing a Strawberry Shortcake onesie. A little boy with spaghetti all over his face, and the message *Thanks, Doc!* written on the back. A set of twins wearing matching tennis uniforms. A little boy with giant Coke-bottle glasses. A baby girl who'd obviously refused to smile for the picture.

It was therapeutic looking through the familiar baby faces again, but just as I got toward the end of the stack, I spotted a small green envelope that I'd never noticed before.

The only reason I noticed it now was that it was stuck to the inside of the box.

I opened the envelope carefully.

Dear Dr. Mullen,
I couldn't tell anyone when it happened. I don't know if I made the right choice.
My parents can never know.

No one can ever know.

If it weren't for you, I probably wouldn't be here.

Thank you for saving me.

A.L.T.

I wondered who A.L.T. was. All I knew for certain was that she had been in trouble and needed a doctor's help.

It made me happy to think she'd gotten it.

I folded up the letter and slipped it back in with the baby photos before opening my laptop one more time to make a note of this in my diary.

When I was finished, I saw that there was another message from Neil.

Dear Pom,

Would you be interested in doing another interview for our paper?

—Neil Norton

I attached a link to his interview with Brookhurst, where he'd veered away from tough questioning in order to paint a flattering picture of her, and replied:

No, thank you. I'm really not interested in biased journalism.

15

Three things happened after Neil requested a follow-up interview through my blog.

The first thing that happened was that I finished my Rubinowitz interview and emailed it to David, who responded with *Will send rt away. Cheers.*

He'd been growing on me. I'd managed to convey to Cora that their public make-out sessions were a tad "slurpy," and she and David had toned it down a bit. He'd also started talking more, which was nice because the quiet, brooding-artist thing was starting to make me want to pull his stupid beanie over his face. It was actually nice to hear him participating in a conversation instead of casually occupying space in my peripheral vision.

The second thing that happened was that Jorge invited me over to his house to see his "secret" garden.

Sounds dirty but isn't. It was just a garden.

He has a greenhouse that he's been working on with his dad on the weekends. They've been planting together for the past two years, but I doubt he's told anyone how much he loves it. I don't even think his dad really knows how much he loves it.

"I started with the easy vegetables," he said, walking me through the greenhouse.

"There are easy vegetables?"

"Zucchini, radishes, tomatoes . . . Radishes actually only take about three weeks to mature, so in the beginning I grew a ton of them. Problem is, no one likes them. They're mostly decoration. I hardly sell any when I bring them to the farmers' market. And zucchini are like mutant vegetables. We gave a lot of ours away to neighbors and homeless shelters because we had so many. Some we just ditched on doorsteps. My mom went a little overboard and baked tons of banana-zucchini bread. Then my dad lost it when she started including zucchini in every meal, and refused to look at them for a while. And the tomatoes . . ."

It was adorable watching him get excited about vegetables, and to be honest, the greenhouse itself was structurally pretty cool. There was a wooden-plank walk under our feet and three long tables of plants, with hanging fans in each corner of the outdoor room. A swing chair sat between two potted lemon trees in the space farthest from the house, and there was another row of small troughs filled with bushes of some type of berry. Everything was labeled in Jorge's minuscule handwriting, and the empty baskets in the corner hung ready to harvest the crops.

He gestured sadly at a large green ceramic pot that held a mature peach tree he'd lovingly nursed back to health. He explained that he'd saved it from a neighbor's trash can and was sure it would have fruit this year and—

I kissed him midsentence, before he could make any more excuses for the peach tree's size or demeanor. Unfortunately, it was at the exact moment that his dad walked in. He turned beet red and headed back into the house like he'd just witnessed a crime.

"We should stop doing that to people," Jorge said. "Poor Dad. He can't handle kissing. He walked in on my older sister making out with her boyfriend on the couch once when she was home from college, and he didn't speak for, like, two days."

I wondered how my parents would react to me kissing.

When something terrible happens, I always remember where I was and what I was doing. I just wish in this case I had been doing something more serious.

I was answering a question about farting during sex, which is, of course, very common, and that means the question comes up a lot too because it's embarrassing and people spend a lot of time worrying about it. At least, that's what I think based on how many questions I've received about it.

If it's a woman asking the question, it might not be a fart. It could be air that's gotten trapped in the vagina and is let out slowly, sometimes called a vart or a queef. Also common and embarrassing.

And, according to my research, avoidable if you try not to elevate your lower half too much, which lets air in.

Regular farting is also common during sex due to pressure on the abdomen or shifting positions. It just happens, and it still made me laugh a little while I answered the question, because farts are just funny.

Unless they're yours. Then they're mortifying.

But the smile was wiped off my face almost immediately when I looked down at my phone and saw a text from Jorge.

> They trashed the Food Trucks.

I didn't know who "they" were, but I didn't need to. I threw on my jacket, got in my mom's car, and drove to Food Truck Village, where a crowd of people was already huddled. I spotted Jorge standing with his dad near what was left of Rodrigo's Taquería.

A powerful smell of acrylic filled the air as the remains of the trucks stood limply next to piles of shattered glass and trash. Someone had splattered red paint across the hoods of all the trucks and thrown the cans through their front windows. It looked like the owners had already salvaged what they could, and all that was left to do was to clean up the mess.

Jorge didn't speak, but his face was tight. His dad was talking to Rodrigo, the owner of Rodrigo's Taquería, and a few people walked up to the owners of the other trucks to offer their condolences and ask what they could do to help. It was like a death.

I covered my mouth as the wind blew the harsh smell of acrylic paint in our direction, and when I looked up, I saw Jorge crying. Fat tears rolled down his cheeks.

I reached out and touched his fingers lightly, and he reached back and let me hold his hand.

We were never going to find out who was responsible. It

was always going to be one of those things that people felt sad and angry about without any real details to back up the incident. And that's what we would call it from now on. The incident.

No one saw who had done it. The only evidence at the scene was a paint-splattered Brookhurst button and some pamphlets that touted the "100% American" message that Brookhurst had never *publicly* supported but never publicly condemned either.

"Let's go somewhere," I told Jorge.

"Where?" he asked. His eyes were still fixed on the shattered glass, and his feet looked like they were rooted to the spot.

"C'mon," I said.

He looked over at his dad, still talking to Rodrigo, and I whispered, "They'll be okay for a bit."

Jorge followed the pressure of my hand without asking questions. We got into my car, and I drove to the only place I could think of that would be both distracting and quiet.

He looked at me when I pulled into the nursery parking lot.

"Let's go talk to some tomatoes," I said, trying to make him smile.

"Is that what you think I do?" he asked, but his lips almost lifted to a grin when he got out of the car.

We walked through the rows of plants until Jorge's shoulders relaxed and he became visibly more himself.

"You know what's weird?" he asked finally. I looked at him. "She never really told anyone what to do about the food trucks. Just like she's never really told anyone what to do about Pom. But everyone knows this is because of her. This celebrating-our-roots, one-hundred-percent-American xenophobic bullshit.

"And it's pretty amazing how quickly angry people get together when a rich person on a stage tells them what to be afraid of and who they can blame for their problems."

"We'll get Food Truck Village back up and running. People will see through this racist garbage. She can't do this."

"She already did, Phoebe," Jorge said tersely. "But this is what happens when people like Brookhurst get a tiny bit of influence." He reached out to hug me, and we stood there between the succulents and the agapanthus. "I hope Pom stays anonymous. I would not want to be them right now."

We stood there for a few more minutes.

"Are you cold?" he asked, rubbing my arms where goose bumps had appeared.

"No," I said. "I'm fine."

When I got home, I saw that my dad had already started dinner. I walked toward the sound of the frying pan with every intention of bringing up the food trucks, but then my mom came in from the garage, and in a matter of fifteen seconds I watched her step to the table, take off her jacket, and pull what was unmistakably a Brookhurst button off the lapel and stuff it into her pocket.

I stepped backward out of the kitchen and told my parents I wasn't feeling well, which wasn't exactly a lie.

What reason could she have for wearing that button? I thought.
Work is one thing, but that's over the line.

My question was answered almost immediately by local news coverage and a statement from my parents' religious nonprofit clients, the Heavenly Bodies people, who said, "While we believe the food truck incident is regrettable, we do not hold Ms. Brookhurst responsible and *still* support her campaign."

So she wore the button to a Heavenly Bodies meeting.

That night my parents didn't argue about my mom working for Brookhurst. As far as I could tell, they ate in silence.

I waited until they went to bed before I got leftovers out of the fridge.

That's when I realized I hadn't looked at the paper since Neil assigned me the horoscope.

I always went online to see the uploaded links as soon as they were posted to the *Linda Vista High School Chronicle,* and even though the horoscope was hardly journalism, I went to look anyway.

Neil's most recent piece popped up first.

THE CIRCLE IN THE SQUARE:
ABANDONING THE MORAL HIGH GROUND

By Neil Norton

Apparently, *The Circle in the Square* was no longer a "trove of information."

Now it was just a detour on the highway to hell, a point that was made clear by the final lines of the piece:

The blogger Pom, author of the infamous sex blog
The Circle in the Square, has declined my offer for a
second interview, which begs the question:

What do you have to hide, Pom?

Wow. You're a hack, Neil.

16

Comments on *The Circle in the Square* and Twitter had started spiraling into weird messages in all caps that had nothing to do with sex education.

> PROTECT OUR CHILDREN!

> LET PARENTS DECIDE WHAT THEIR KIDS SHOULD BE READING!

> BLOCK THE BLOG!

> SEXUAL RISK AVOIDANCE IS THE ONLY OPTION!

> STAY PURE! VOTE BROOKHURST!

Our town's used bookstore, the one I'd gone to for collections of *Calvin and Hobbes* as a kid, had a Brookhurst sign in the window.

That one hurt.

And Brookhurst was, of course, enjoying the show.

> **@TheRealLydiaBrookhurst:** Wouldn't it be a shame if we all found out who Pom is? Guessing he doesn't want anyone knowing he writes this trash.

I logged off Twitter and went back to the blog.

About 70 percent of the questions I receive are about sex, but the other 30 percent still address body issues.

The most common for girls seems to be about the aesthetics of their vaginas. Whether their labia are an appropriate color or size. Do men actually care about this? I don't know. Once again, it all just comes down to whether they are "normal."

I usually repost a doctor's response with several medical drawings showing women of all shapes and sizes, and still there are concerns that their bodies are somehow deeply flawed.

Then come the questions about labiaplasty (altering the folds of skin surrounding the vulva) and breast implants, which I answer with as much medical information as I can.

Cora's response to this would be somewhere along the lines of "Leave your lady bits alone."

For guys, there is an abundance of questions about penis size and shape, though I did receive one inquiry about whether having foreskin was unusual.

The general answer to nearly all of these queries? "Yes, you're normal."

David's uncle was thrilled to publish my interview with Rubinowitz. He'd actually been at the journalist gala as well. I just hadn't met him. But after looking at his *Walnut Press* photo online, I would've known he was David's uncle. If he'd been wearing a beanie, the family resemblance would have been uncanny.

When the piece came out, it was circulated widely online and in print by several groups in town. Book clubs and library foundations. The food truck owners. Cora's parents. Jorge.

Neil was predictably quiet about the whole thing, but I saw a copy of the newspaper wedged into his bag, so I knew he'd read it.

I knew Mom had read it too, though I hadn't spoken to her since I saw her take the Brookhurst button off her jacket. My dad, on the other hand, held it out to me and winked.

"Nice work, kiddo."

I smiled, wondering if he'd talked to Mom about it, but pushed the question aside to look at the interview again.

Brookhurst might be dazzling in person, but Rubinowitz was a powerhouse of information, detailing her plans to overhaul public spending and increase job growth in Linda Vista. She also denounced Brookhurst's plans to cut funds to important programs in order to support "other business ventures" as "pathetic attempts to help rich friends."

Rubinowitz made no comment regarding Brookhurst's disparaging remarks on her appearance, even though I'd desperately wanted her to say something.

Maybe something like: *I think women have value beyond how they look.*

Or: *I think it's more important to discuss a political opponent's platform, rather than their dress size.*

Or: *Lydia Brookhurst is a dumbass. Don't vote for her.*

"It's not important what she thinks about how I look. I don't need to comment," Rubinowitz had said when I called to ask about it again.

The first face-off between Brookhurst and Rubinowitz would be the upcoming debate. As it edged closer, the town turned uglier than I'd ever seen it before. Huge BROOKHURST FOR MORALITY lawn signs went up in front of a ton of houses, and Lydia leaned hard into condemning the blog while saying virtually nothing about the food truck incident.

There was a different feeling near Food Truck Village too. The businesses directly across the street had become a hub for Brookhurst supporters. There was an anger mixed with what I think was a tiny bit of fear. Those stores and restaurants had latched on to Lydia's campaign, so now when she was attacked, *they* felt attacked too. It didn't matter if they didn't think she was perfect; it just mattered that she felt like one of them, a homegrown businesswoman.

When Cora and I took a walk, Tony from Tony's Burgers and Cecilia from Linda Vista Flowers were standing in front of their stores, handing out Brookhurst buttons. A bunch of people took a button, walked into the flower shop, and found a seat in a folding chair. It looked like it was set up for some kind of meeting.

When Cecilia caught us staring, she scooped up her buttons and retreated into the store, her mouth pulled tight against her bony face.

That night I opened *The Circle in the Square* to take a look at the Q&As. This was one of those instances where the question wasn't necessarily about sex directly but was what I'd started calling sex-adjacent.

> My mom thinks getting the HPV vaccine (the one that is supposed to guard against cervical cancer) just encourages girls to have sex at a younger age, but a few of my friends are getting it before they go to college and I'm wondering if I should too. Should I get the vaccine?

My response said:

> Yes, you should.
> I can't say that 100 percent of doctors agree (because there might be a creationist who

happened to go to medical school out there), but I can say *the majority* of doctors and medical experts would advise their patients to get this vaccine.

This was not a new question. Human papillomavirus infection can cause cervical, vaginal, and vulvar cancers in women. Since the introduction of the HPV vaccine, many parents have come out against it because they feel it gives their kids permission to engage in sexual activity. The CDC website states that 85 percent of people will get an HPV infection in their lifetime and that resulting cancers can include cancer of the penis in men and cancer of the anus and throat in both women and men. Vaccination is advised for all adolescents.

It's weird to me that so many parents would prefer to think that their kids would not have sex, rather than just give them something to keep them safe if they do.

And of course, I knew Brookhurst would have something to say about it when I posted.

@TheRealLydiaBrookhurst: @CircleintheSquare HAVE YOU NO SHAME? OF COURSE THE HPV VACCINE ENCOURAGES SEX!

@TheRealLydiaBrookhurst: @CircleintheSquare YOUR MEDICAL ADVICE IS ASTOUNDING GIVEN THE FACT THAT YOU HAVE NO MEDICAL DEGREE.

> **@CircleintheSquare:** *whispers* If medical degrees
> mattered to you maybe you'd listen to doctors who
> recommend the vaccine . . .

Side note: Cora and I did eventually go shopping for a homecoming dress. Hers is silver and mine is black, despite her insistence that I wear color.

17

On the night of the press conference and debate, Cora and David came with me. Jorge said he'd try to come for the end of the debate if he could, but he and his dad were helping with some food truck renovations.

The room was packed with more people than I'd ever seen at a town event before. BROOKHURST FOR MORALITY flashed above us on long pale blue banners with gold letters, while plain RUBINOWITZ FOR MAYOR signs stood limply against the walls.

There was a forced calm in the air, obviously a direct result of the food truck incident. Snippets of conversation floated around us, but it was hard to pick out more than some regret that the incident had happened and some assurances that it was a fluke thing.

"It's not like Brookhurst trashed the trucks."

"She doesn't support vandalism!"

"It's just lucky nobody got hurt."

My parents waved at me from the front of the room and sat down to watch the debate next to River and Astrid. They were friendly and they greeted each other warmly, but anytime they are all in the same room, it's like some weird crossover episode of my life.

Cora and David led me to a row in the back of the room, crowded with kids from Linda Vista High who were all trying to get extra-credit points for their US history and government classes.

I saw Neil sitting with the press, in front of the laptop that controlled the projector, acting as if he were the only person in this room covering the event. Monica Hansen was sitting to his left and had just finished whispering something in his ear when he turned in my direction. For a second our eyes locked, and he seemed surprised to see me there. I half raised my hand in greeting before he pointedly turned away to pretend he hadn't seen me at all. Cora, noticing this exchange, made a series of rude, graphic comments that caused the old woman in front of us to look at us with outrage. Cora, unperturbed, flashed her a smile as David guided us to three open seats.

Behind the stage, the projector had illuminated a painting of Linda Vista from when the town was founded. In the bottom right-hand corner was a timer, which was supposed to keep track of each candidate's responses. Neil clicked something on the screen, and the timer began to count down to the start of the debate.

The moderator, Mrs. Patch, a retired history teacher, was exactly five feet tall. She walked to the podium, then made a point to pull out her step stool to give herself a little more height. A few people laughed when she did this but promptly stopped when she turned around to glare at them. She cleared her throat and the questioning began.

The usual comparisons were already being made. Helen Rubinowitz was soft-spoken and plain, everything Lydia Brookhurst was not. While Lydia was thoughtful with her responses, the way she avoided presenting any specific evidence was strange. It was notably stranger when her supporters cheered after every single response, despite its inaccuracy.

The debate felt different from any other town hall event I'd ever attended. There was a level of anger in the crowd that made me uncomfortable.

Once the local-government-related questions had been answered, the moderator cleared her throat again and said, "Ms. Brookhurst, you have commented at length about your feelings concerning a local sex blog for teenagers."

Someone in the crowd shouted, "Filth!" Someone else shouted, "Block the Blog!"

Mrs. Patch, who did not flinch at any of this, waved her hand calmly for quiet and continued speaking.

"Blocking *The Circle in the Square* would be impossible for practical and legal reasons, as it has not infringed on copyright or broken any other laws. Can you tell us why you have been so vocal about your opposition to it? What is it that you are trying to accomplish?"

"This is going to be good," Cora whispered.

Brookhurst's composure did not falter; in fact, the placid grin on her face grew wider as she smoothed her dress.

And ignored most of the question.

"Thank you for the question," she said. "I think it is important to note how crucial it is for teenagers to get information regarding this *sensitive subject*," she said, lowering her voice, "from their parents and not from the internet. It is absolutely appalling how Pom presumes to educate our children on sexual activity that is promiscuous, dangerous, and, in some cases, *unnatural.*"

Several people applauded Brookhurst's response while Mrs. Patch tried to push her to answer the actual question she'd been asked.

"Ms. Brookhurst," said Mrs. Patch, talking over the crowd, "that isn't what I—"

The crowd was still buzzing and Brookhurst used it to fuel the rest of her statement.

"The fact that he has written this highly questionable material anonymously just proves that he is too much of a coward to own up to this smut. And we deserve better than this. Our children deserve better than this. And I am going to give it to you!" She shouted the last statement, and her supporters all lost control, rising to give her a standing ovation. Brookhurst raised her hands to quiet them.

It was easy to see what she might have looked like in her high school years. She was still the consummate pageant winner in all her glory, basking in the stage light with an almost indecent pleasure.

Applause gave her life, and the steady hum of approval encouraged her to patrol the stage like she owned it. After a few minutes of this, the quieter voices of dissent were stamped out.

"I mean, just listen to some of the filth from this blog." She reached into her purse and pulled out a bejeweled phone. "Feel free to follow along!" she said merrily as hundreds of people fumbled for their phones.

"Ms. Brookhurst, we are not here to listen to you quote

blog posts," Mrs. Patch said sternly, and Lydia's supporters booed. Brookhurst put her phone away with a mock apology.

"I'm so sorry. You're absolutely right, Mrs. Patch. And you are doing such a fine job as moderator tonight. Isn't she doing a wonderful job? Can we give Mrs. Patch a hand?"

Cheers erupted again as Mrs. Patch's eyes narrowed at Brookhurst.

"And, yes, we must absolutely get back to the debate, but I have another matter of business to attend to."

Mrs. Patch looked outraged as Brookhurst waved a young girl from the Junior Olympic acrobatics team to the stage. I recognized the Brookhurst logo from the disastrous homecoming court performance.

The girl smiled, pulled out a gold envelope, and handed it to Brookhurst before doing a magnificent backflip off the stage to wild applause.

"What the fu—" Cora started to say, but David shushed her.

All eyes were laser-focused on Brookhurst and the envelope in her hand.

"It looks like Pom accessed the blog from a public-school computer, making it so much easier for us to find his identity with our tracking software." She flipped the envelope over in her hand like a cat playing with a mouse. "In the end he wasn't all that clever, was he?"

There's no way, I thought.

Rubinowitz tried several times to intervene, but it looked like her mic had been disabled, because all I could see was her opening and closing her mouth and staring in shock at the now-roaring crowd.

My heart caught in my chest as Brookhurst continued. "I have his identity here, in case any of you are curious." The envelope glinted in the light as she held it up for everyone to see. Then she clutched it protectively to her chest. "But you're not interested in who Pom is, right?"

The crowd roared with laughter, and somewhere behind me a man started the chant.

"WHO IS POM? WHO IS POM? WHO IS POM? WHO IS POM?"

Brookhurst began tearing the envelope slowly, savoring every second.

"This is Pom," she shouted. "Let's congratulate him, shall we?"

There was an unmistakable glee in her voice that ignited a low rumble of approval in the mob she'd created. I couldn't breathe.

"I have to leave. I have to use the bathroom," I told Cora.

"Now?" Cora asked. I could tell she was half-repulsed, half-intrigued, by what was going on, but she still scooted back for me to pass her. I pushed past as many people as I could, eager to get to the back doors before something happened. But by the time I got to the end of the row, Lydia Brookhurst was speaking again.

Just as I bumped into a woman decorated in BROOKHURST FOR MORALITY pins, I heard Lydia Brookhurst declare in a triumphant voice . . .

"Phoebe Townsend."

Everyone knew it was me.

It was worse than a naked dream, because even in those dreams I know I'm dreaming, so I can casually walk around observing other people's reactions to my nakedness.

This was real.

There was a dull buzzing in my ears as the crowd processed the words they'd just heard.

"Did she say Phoebe Townsend?"

"That's not possible."

"How could she have written *The Circle in the Square?*"

"It's always the quiet ones with the dirty minds, you know. . . ."

I could not move. I wanted to. I'd never wanted to run away from a place so badly in my life, but I could not bring myself to put one foot in front of the other, and the longer I waited to get out of there, the more people turned toward me. Pointing. Whispering. Looking to their friends so they could point and whisper too.

"Let's go," said a voice. I smelled something like industrial cleaner and noticed that Jorge was standing beside me with remnants of Clorox all over his shirt. For a second I registered the fact that he must have walked in around the time Brookhurst said my name. He took my hand.

I followed the gentle pressure and let him guide me out of the hall. Cora and David had leapt to their feet to part the crowd in front of us, and I somehow regained the use of my legs, still not fully aware of what was going on. The dull buzzing in the crowd got louder as more people realized I was there, but somehow Jorge managed to navigate our way out of the room before anyone stopped us.

Shock is a strange thing. It does strange things to the body. But I usually respond to it the same way I respond to pain or fear. I search for the facts to comfort me. But this time I couldn't pull them up. My mind was blank and I felt lost. I kept thinking about my parents in that room next to Astrid and River, and when I jerked my head back to the crowd, Jorge whispered, as if reading my mind, "They'll be fine. Let's get you out of here."

Jorge walked me to his car, opened the passenger door, and tucked me inside. He probably would have put my seat belt on too if I'd let him. Once he closed the door, he had some kind of hushed conversation with Cora, and it was a little bit like I was a child being rescued from something beyond my control.

On any other day that might have been annoying, but I was in the mood to appreciate being taken care of, and the last thing I wanted to do was think.

Jorge got into the driver's seat, looked over at me with concern, and then turned on the engine.

We didn't speak the whole ride home, even though I could

see his lips moving out of the corner of my eye. He was trying to come up with something to say, but he kept stopping himself. Eventually we pulled into my driveway, and the motion-sensor light on our garage cast an orange glow on the front half of the car.

He turned off the engine and looked at me.

I avoided his eyes.

"Phoebe?"

I said nothing. I knew if I spoke, I was going to cry. And letting someone see you cry is worse than letting them see you naked. Much worse.

"So, you're Pom?"

I couldn't help it. I pulled my knees into my chest, wrapped my arms around them, and started to cry one of those slow, miserable cries that feel like you're letting all the air out of your body in a mixture of anger and complete despair.

Details filled me up like scalding water. The fact that everyone, including my parents, knew that I was Pom. The fact that Lydia Brookhurst had publicly announced my name. The fact that everyone would be asking why I did this and what I hoped to accomplish and debating whether I should have done it in the first place. The fact that everyone was going to think I was some kind of pervert.

Hot tears poured down my face, and I vaguely registered Jorge trying to soothe me, until finally he lifted me out of my seat and onto his lap, where he wrapped his arms around me. I pressed my face against his chest and continued to cry big, ugly, embarrassing tears. I vowed that the minute I was done, I would run from the car and never look back.

233

Jorge just sat there holding me. Every so often he stroked my hair and kissed my cheek, but he didn't say a word. He reclined his seat and let me cry until I couldn't anymore.

I was pretty sure I was crushing him, but every time I tried to get up to move, he just adjusted his arm and whispered, "I'm fine. Don't worry."

Everything leading up to this moment felt wrong. I felt like something had been stolen from me in a very public, very obvious way, and I couldn't even find the words to explain what I was feeling. Humiliation? No, not entirely. Anger? Sure. But that wasn't all.

"Lost" might be a better word.

My anonymity had given me the freedom to research something with curiosity, and my exposure had made me aware of the eyes that were now watching me. Well, were *always* watching me. It's just that now they knew whom they were looking at.

"Are you sure you're okay? Maybe I should stick around until your parents get home," Jorge said, still holding my hand.

He looked at me anxiously but still hadn't asked me any questions that would force me to provide more than a three-word answer.

"I'm fine," I said. "Thanks."

I kissed him, and after I watched him drive off, I turned on all the lights in the house. Mom and Dad came home about ten minutes later and knocked on my bedroom door.

"I just want to be alone right now," I told them. And I heard them have a whispered argument before they retreated to the family room.

I learned a lot in the hours that followed the press conference. And every lesson was painful, including the moment a weird new account posted my address for the world to see. Even now, looking back twinges a little bit because I don't really think I believed that people were capable of meanness for the sake of meanness.

But the truth is, they are.

Humans are absolutely capable of great, overarching cruelty.

Oscar Wilde once wrote, "Man is least himself when he talks in his own person. Give him a mask, and he will tell you the truth."

I am aware of the irony of this. The fact was that I was able to comfortably "tell the truth" on my blog because no one knew who I was. Because I was wearing my own mask.

The difference is that I wasn't hiding to say awful things.

And this isn't very profound, but that's why the internet is everyone's mask. You'll never see how cruel someone can be until you hear what they say when they know no one will ever be able to prove that they said it.

I guess I was stupid because I didn't think to close *The Circle in the Square* to comments right away or delete my Twitter account. I should have thought of it, but I was distracted. If I had been smart, I would have closed them immediately, before anyone could give me their opinion, or vent, or do whatever people feel comfortable doing on the internet.

It got bad quickly.

Someone posted an old photo of me on Twitter. It was from when I won our middle school spelling bee. It had been printed in the local paper, and my parents had it framed in our living room. Underneath the photo someone had added a caption:

> Maybe if she didn't look like this she would get to fuck someone instead of spending all her time writing about fucking. Damn.

Two hundred people had already liked the comment. Someone else wrote:

> I still don't get why she felt the need to create this blog. Is it really appropriate for someone her age?

Twenty-five likes already.

Then a few commenters defended me. One was Cora, with creative foul language and elaborate descriptions of where the critics could stuff their opinions and other miscellaneous small objects.

But it was the last comment that struck me the hardest.

> Look, Phoebe, if you don't want anyone to call you nasty then don't write about sex, hon.

That one got 346 likes.

Three hundred forty-six people liked the idea of telling a girl to shut up if she didn't want anyone to call her names.

Up to that point I had still been pretending that all of this was happening to someone else, but the commenter had used *my* name, and that was what brought me back to reality.

Everyone knew it was me.

19

"Phoebe?" Mom asked quietly through the door again. "Can we come in?"

Something in my chest tightened.

"Okay," I said.

My dad followed her in, looking as lost as I felt. "How long has this been going on?" she asked, sitting down on the edge of my bed.

I looked up at her, feeling anger rush to my face, but it was doused immediately with what felt like ice water when I noticed that she'd been crying too.

I didn't speak. I couldn't speak. No words would come out of my mouth, so I just stood up and walked over to the largest drawer in my bed, where my secret stash was hidden.

I proceeded to hoist every book, diagram, model, and poster out of hiding until my room was flooded with sex. The giant vagina model seemed to be glaring at my father, who politely looked away. The cover of the illustrated *Kama Sutra* sat innocently on top of a stack of medical journals that momentarily distracted my mom. Her eyes opened wide as she looked around the room, failing to grasp what it was she was actually looking at. I sank down on the edge of my bed, wrapped my arms around my knees, and didn't look at either of them.

"Phoebe," she said, a little louder this time. "How long—"

"Since I was fourteen," I said.

"But . . . why?" she asked.

It was a reasonable question, to which I still had no answer, so for half an hour I explained to my parents *how* this had happened, since I couldn't really explain the *why*. While they sat in the middle of my research materials, I told them how I'd gotten my resources. About starting *The Circle in the Square*. How it had gone viral. How I'd made a Twitter account and then opened the blog up for questions when Neil wanted an interview.

"And Lydia Brookhurst," Mom said finally, "has been railing against this blog. Your blog. From the beginning." It wasn't a question, but I felt like I needed to confirm it for her anyway.

"Yes," I said.

My mom sat for a minute collecting her thoughts before getting up and kissing the top of my head like she did when I was small.

"C'mon, Matt," she said.

"Where are we going?" he said, still trying to avoid eye contact with the giant plastic vagina.

"To work," my mom said quietly before turning back to me. "Phoebe, you've done nothing wrong. We'll be back soon. There's something we need to take care of." She leaned forward a little and looked like she was listening for something. She walked to the window and looked out. "I think Cora is here," Mom said.

I heard a door open and close down the hall and then familiar quick footsteps coming toward my room.

"Hey," said Cora, knocking gently on my bedroom door.

"Hey," I said back.

My parents left without another word, and Cora flopped down on the floor among the piles of sex education materials. She sat cross-legged, looking around at the scattered debris as if she were taking inventory of my life. Her eyes darted around the room until finally she looked up at me.

"Why did you let me keep thinking I knew more about sex than you do?" she asked.

"Technically, since you've had sex, you—" I started to say, but Cora interrupted me.

"No, I mean actual knowledge about this stuff," she said, and she looked a little angry. "Why didn't you tell me you were Pom? You couldn't trust me?"

"That isn't it," I said.

"But you still didn't tell me?"

"I didn't tell anyone," I told her.

"I thought I was different."

"Look," I said, "it wasn't because I didn't trust you. It wasn't because I was embarrassed to tell you about it. It has nothing to do with you. It was something I started researching because . . . it's fascinating. And doing it without telling anyone made it feel like a legitimate research pursuit completely free of judgment. Like nobody was looking over my shoulder or telling me I was doing it wrong. Or doing *something* wrong."

She considered this as she leaned against my wall and continued to look around the room.

"That's an enormous plastic vagina," Cora said.

"Yes, it is," I agreed.

Silence.

"What's that?" she asked, pointing to a small metal instrument hanging out of one of my boxes.

"Oh. It's an antique speculum. You know, the thing gynecologists use to open up your va—"

"Got it," said Cora quickly.

Silence.

Cora studied the evidence of my hidden life.

"Oh, that's where you got your pen name," she said, looking at the painting of Eve with the pomegranate. "Pom. I get it. Oh, and"—she turned her head and seemed confused—"what's that?" she said, pointing to the framed piece of abstract art.

"Pretty sure it's a vagina."

We both stared at the colors of the painting and tilted our heads a little.

"Why does it look so angry?" Cora asked, studying the painting.

And we both started laughing again despite the bubbling awful feeling that had settled in my stomach.

"So where's David?" I asked. "Don't you two have that art class together right now?"

"You really think I'd go to art class after all that? And anyway, David didn't go to the class either. He's at home icing his lip."

"Why?"

"He got in a fight with some guy who called you a pervert, and it turns out neither of them can fight, so they threw pretty weak punches at each other for a few seconds, until David shoved the other guy, got tangled in his legs, and smashed his lip into some folding chairs."

"Wow," I said. "Really?"

"Really," she said. "I mean, I'll have to talk to him about not tucking his thumb into his fist when he punches. He definitely needs to work on his technique. But his heart was in the right place."

"Yeah," I said. "It was."

I folded my hands in my lap, and even though I felt horrible, I was glad Cora was there.

She nodded and took a deep breath with a semi-horrified look on her face.

"I'm thinking about every time I quoted the blog and trying to wrap my head around the fact that David learned how to give me an orgasm . . . from you."

"You're welcome," I said, and we both started laughing and could not stop. Behind her head was a diagram of a penis, and just as she was about to stop laughing, she looked at it, pretended to honk the testicles, and started laughing again. It was completely absurd, and had it been any other day, I probably would not have laughed, but there was something so liberating about sitting there with Cora, ignoring the rest of the world, just laughing about something stupid and immature. We laughed until we cried, and then suddenly I was just crying, not laughing, and Cora came over and put her arms around me.

I hadn't expected to cry again. So far I'd been able to hide the sadness and disappointment, but laughing with Cora opened me up a little. After a few minutes I stopped, straightened up, and looked at her with a renewed sense of calm.

"Okay, so you're like a sex expert, then," Cora said.

"No," I said, wiping my eyes. "I'm a person who has done a lot of reading. And I can answer some questions. I think you get to be an expert when you get a PhD or something."

"Is that something you want to do someday?"

"Yes," I said. "It is."

It felt good to say that out loud.

"Phoebe, that's awesome. You're halfway there."

Cora and I spent several hours going through the materials I'd tossed all over the floor and putting them back where they belonged. When we were finished, there was no evidence that I researched anything that anyone might consider inappropriate.

"I think I liked it better filled with all your dirty sex crap," she said. "In fact, I think this deserves a special place of honor."

She pulled out the abstract vagina art and leaned it up against the wall on my desk.

"There," she said. "Angry vagina implores you to continue your research."

I grimaced. It was a hideous painting, but I'd never been able to bring myself to throw it out. It felt like an important piece of anatomical information that I would never understand, and for that reason I should hold on to it to remind myself that there were things that I would never really understand.

My mom had called and said they were going to be late and asked if Cora wanted to stay the night. I was still unclear about what they were doing, and my mom was cagey about their whereabouts. It felt like our family dynamic had been altered somehow during the past few hours, and there was no anger on their part, but there was something else. Sadness maybe.

At two o'clock in the morning we inflated the air mattress for Cora and turned out the lights. The glow-in-the-dark stars that had been on my ceiling since I was five still glowed back at me, but not quite as brightly as I remembered.

"Have you talked to Jorge since he drove you home?" Cora asked in the dark. I could hear her still trying to get comfortable on the air mattress.

"No," I said. I hadn't looked at my phone since he dropped me off either. Though I was pretty sure that if I looked now, there would be messages from him checking to see if I was okay.

"Don't worry," Cora said. "He really likes you. I can tell."

"I know," I said. "Actually, I think he loves me."

"What?" said Cora. "Did he tell you that?"

"No," I told her. "But I guess I just feel it."

It's not something you're supposed to say out loud. You're supposed to say it to yourself, or wait until someone says it to you and then pretend you didn't know, because assuming that someone loves you is a dangerous act of hubris that opens you up to all kinds of tragedy.

But it would have been dishonest somehow to grudgingly nod at Cora and agree that, yes, I did think he *liked* me. Someone who *likes* you doesn't let you sob into their shoulder.

I thought that was love, but then again, I'd never been in

love before. I'd only studied sex, which even I knew was not the same thing.

I'd gotten used to hearing Jorge speak his mind about everything. I'd grown accustomed to listening to his opinion on nearly every subject the minute a new topic presented itself, and the sound of his voice could soothe me in a way nothing else could.

Cora watched these thoughts cloud my face for a few seconds before she reminded me she was there.

" 'Kay, we should probably go to sleep now," she said.

"Probably should," I said.

"Good night," said Cora. "I love you."

"I love you too," I said before turning on my phone to read Jorge's texts, which were actually just a series of really bad stick-figure drawings of me drinking coffee and holding up signs promoting safe sex. Nothing like the kind of stuff David drew, but accurate nonetheless.

The last one was of him kissing me on the cheek, holding up a sign of his own.

It read: MY GIRLFRIEND WRITES THE BLOG. SHE'S PRETTY BADASS.

I smiled because he'd never said that before.

But I didn't feel badass. I felt naked.

20

> **@TheRealLydiaBrookhurst:** I apologize for anyone who may feel hurt with the recent revelations during the debate.

I'm not sure what I expected to happen. To be fair, it's not like I could have foreseen any of this. I didn't have a contingency plan for what might happen or what I would do if my identity became public. I just always assumed I would be safe from exposure.

But.

Even if I had foreseen the great reveal at the hands of Lydia Brookhurst, I never would have expected the response.

My parents had gotten home late the night before, and I hadn't even heard them come in. It was strange leaving for class, knowing they were home but not hearing the familiar sounds of the two of them moving around in the kitchen. Cora drove me to school.

We stepped into first period, and even though all eyes

turned to me, there was no time for anyone to say anything. Though my English teacher, Ms. Price, did put her hand on my shoulder briefly before passing out the exams.

I filled in bubbles and listened to the recorded instructions, and at the end of the two hours we were excused.

The hallways outside were unusually loud, but I didn't notice until we turned the corner. A crowd had formed in front of my locker.

"Excuse me," said Cora. Then she stopped dead and stared at the locker, eyes wide. Everyone else was muttering behind her, but I couldn't see what they were looking at.

"Phoebe . . . ," Cora murmured quietly. It wasn't like her to whisper. And when I finally got a good look, I saw why she had spoken softly.

The lockers were old, rickety metal boxes that had been around since the school was built. Mine was in the middle row, four lockers from the left. Across the front someone had carved the words PHOEBE LIKES DICK.

Above that someone else had used a Sharpie to write the word SLUT, and just below that someone else had penned CUNT.

"Phoebe," said Cora.

"I see it," I told her.

"Let's go." She tugged my arm.

"Not yet. There's someone I'd like to talk to."

"Phoebe, c'mon. Now is not the time to—"

I ignored her. I don't actually remember the walk from my locker to the newsroom. Every step I took was in a daze, with Cora trying to keep up behind me. She kept speaking, but I didn't hear her.

Anger coursed through me like poison.

I turned the corner, but before I opened the door to the newsroom, the sound of angry voices erupted into the hallway, followed by the sound of someone being shoved into a wall. Jorge was unleashing a flood of impressive profanity at Neil, who was struggling to free himself.

"I didn't know it was Phoebe!" Neil shouted. "And I wasn't the one who doxed her."

They didn't see me when I walked through the door. I could tell Jorge was livid even though I couldn't see his face. His shoulders were pushed down away from his ears, the way a bird of prey might brace itself to gouge out something's eyes.

"You helped her do this," Jorge spat. "You're pathetic."

"Fuck you," said Neil. "I didn't help her do anyth—" Then he saw me. "Phoebe," he said, and his expression changed.

"Phoebe." It was Jorge this time. He looked worried. Like he might have crossed some invisible line. He reached out for me, but I didn't take his hand. I was too angry, and there were too many things I wanted to say to Neil, and a couple of things I had to know for certain. Cora was still standing somewhere behind me, but she hadn't said a word since we walked in.

"When you did the interview with Pom"—my voice had an unnatural edge, because I could feel myself just a few moments away from losing control, and I wanted to hold on until I could get away from school—"did you already know it was me?"

"No," he said, dropping one hand to his side. "I had nothing to do with what happened. I swear, Phoebe, I—"

"What did she promise you?"

248

He said nothing. It was the first time I could remember Neil struggling to answer a question.

"For the interview you did. She obviously promised you something," I said. "A job? Recommendation? Some connection you need?"

His eyes darkened, and there was a weakness in his features that was enhanced by the awkwardness of the moment. I couldn't tell exactly what it was.

"An introduction to someone important?" I asked.

"Carl O'Leary," he said.

The head of our local news station. He'd been at the gala.

"Was it worth it?" I asked. He said nothing. "You weren't the one who exposed me, Neil. I'm not blaming you for that. But you know what kind of person she is."

"Phoebe, it's complica—"

"It's interesting," I said, "that you would help someone knowing they're fundamentally wrong, just because of what they could do for you. I wonder if anyone she introduced you to knows that your loyalty is for sale."

He opened and closed his mouth a few times before I left the room, Cora following close behind me.

I barely registered that someone else was trying to get my attention as I made a beeline for Cora's car.

Monica was making her way toward me from across the parking lot, but I got into Cora's car pretty quickly and was home before I realized we'd even started moving or that I'd left Jorge behind with Neil and hadn't looked back. I hadn't had a real conversation with him since everything went down.

I looked at the last text he'd sent me and noticed the "..." on my screen. It disappeared and came back again, like he was struggling to find words.

When Jorge showed up at my house later that evening in his football track pants and a white shirt, he dove into what was clearly a speech he'd been practicing the whole way there.

"Delete it," he said, stepping through the door and closing it quickly behind him. He looked around the room before focusing his attention on me. I took half a step back from him.

"Jorge, I don't kn—"

"Close it. Do whatever you need to get rid of it." He walked over to the couch and sat down, his elbows leaning on his knees as he ran his hands through his hair and fixed his eyes on me with a pleading look.

I stood there staring at him, and I couldn't form a response before he started talking again.

"She knows who you are. Where you are. How to humiliate you."

This wasn't news to me—none of it was—but he still looked up at me again like he was explaining something very simple to someone very dense.

"Look. There's nothing she can say that hasn't already been said. It's all talk. That's it. Just talk. I can handle that," I told him, sitting down on the cushion next to him. I reached my hand out to touch him, but the minute I did, he jumped out of his seat like he'd been burned. I pulled my hand back, stung.

"Jesus Christ, Phoebe. They destroyed the food trucks. Brookhurst supporters did that. And it was just because she gave some people somebody to blame. 'Just talk' can ruin lives. Don't be stupid."

I looked at him and realized his backpack was still over his shoulders.

"Now she's doing it to you. She's riling up her idiots. She's getting ready to paint you as some kind of attention-seeking sexual deviant. You think it stops at the campaign? There have been rumors about her being shady for years," he said through gritted teeth.

"Then, good!" I said. "It's good this is happening! Who cares what they say about me at this point?"

"You are still not getting it!" Jorge said, holding on to his backpack straps. "It's more than that. It's dangerous."

"What do you mean, 'dangerous'?" I was sitting on the couch right in front of him, but he couldn't seem to hold still.

Finally he threw his backpack down and pulled a crumpled-up sheet of white paper from the front pocket. It was folded in half.

"Someone just shoved this in my duffel bag during practice," he said, looking sick. I unfolded the paper and read:

> You really shouldn't leave that girl on her own.
> Filthy mind like hers. You don't write about that stuff
> unless you're asking for it.

It left a sinking feeling in the pit of my stomach, but to me it wasn't worse than the other awful things I'd read or the words carved into my locker. When I tried to tell him that, he lost it.

"That is an assault threat, Phoebe!"

My parents emerged from wherever they'd been hiding in the house.

"What's going on?" my dad said, looking at Jorge.

Jorge bowed his head a little. "I'm sorry I shouted, but this isn't worth it anymore. None of this is worth it."

"I thought you were proud of it," I said. "Of me. What happened to thinking this blog was pretty badass?"

Jorge shook his head while my parents shifted awkwardly into the kitchen, but not completely out of earshot.

"Yeah, it was, when it wasn't dangerous!" He grabbed the note and held it up in his fist. "This is not badass anymore. Just delete it."

"I can't do that," I said without thinking. It was the quickest, most honest response. Of course I couldn't delete it. It was a part of me. My research. My time. Everything. It was the only thing that was quintessentially me.

"Then I can't watch you do this to yourself. I can't watch other people throw hate at you over this blog. I can't . . . keep you safe." For the first time since he'd walked in, he looked sad. "Phoebe, please, the blog is not worth this."

"Maybe not to you," I said, fully aware that my parents were still listening and that something had just risen up between us, pushing Jorge farther away. I could tell he felt it too.

He walked over to me and leaned in, kissing me on the cheek.

"Bye, Phoebe," he said quietly before pulling his backpack

on. Then he glanced quickly in the direction of my parents, who pretended to be busy as he left.

"What was that about?" my mom asked.

"I think it's over," I told them, still staring at the door he'd just walked through.

Followers Blocked: 1,003

"Phoebe," said my mom as I walked through the door. "It's for you."

When I looked at her, she just said, "Don't worry. You can take this one."

Our landline had been ringing a lot over the past twenty-four hours, which was unnerving because hardly anyone called it. Mom had been screening all the calls because we'd gotten some creepy ones and more than a few messages on the answering machine, which my dad had forwarded to the police.

I still couldn't get over the fact that they'd been so calm about all this. That they didn't freak out or demand an explanation. But I guess that fits. They try not to talk about uncomfortable stuff.

Mom was still standing there holding out the phone, and I couldn't help but wonder who had managed to make it past her defenses.

"Hi, Phoebe—it's Amanda Whitaker. We met at the gala. I'm the editor for the *Stanford Daily*. Just wanted to say I'm sorry about what happened, and I was wondering if you'd be interested in giving an interview."

I looked at my mom. How could she think I'd want to give an interview? Amanda seemed to sense hesitation.

"I think it would be a good idea to get all the facts out there before the election."

I still didn't say anything, so she added, "I'm in town for a couple days, and your mom mentioned that you might be free around noon for lunch. I made a reservation at Sushi Monster, so if you choose to come with your mom, it would be a good opportunity to reach some people, I think. You don't have to make a decision now—just come if you can."

"Okay," I said.

"Okay," she said. Then she hung up, and I looked at my mom.

"Before you say anything," she said, "it's completely up to you if you want to go. But your dad and I think it's a great idea."

"You do?"

"Of course," she said, sitting down at the kitchen table and holding a cup of tea out to me. She'd been preparing for this discussion.

I sat.

"I just wanted you to know that I read the blog. Every entry. And I don't think I ever told you I was proud of you for writing it," she said, looking down at her teacup.

"I didn't . . . I didn't think you would be," I said, staring at her and remembering how she'd once worn a Brookhurst button to a Heavenly Bodies meeting. She avoided my eyes.

"I'm sorry," she said. "I was trying not to make waves with

our clients. I didn't want to lose their business. It was cowardly. And I'm sorry."

She put her hand on mine.

"Still doesn't seem like something you'd be proud of," I said.

She flinched a little, like I'd hurt her, which I didn't understand.

"We didn't hide things from you growing up, but we didn't exactly invite questions either," she said. "And that was *my* fault."

I looked at her, and she folded her hands on the table in front of her.

"It wasn't just about the business with Lydia. There's more to it," Mom said.

There was silence while I waited for her to continue. I looked at her while she clasped and unclasped her hands, clearly uncomfortable but determined to explain herself. Everything that came out of her mouth next seemed to emerge with great effort, like it had been buried for a long time.

"I got pregnant when I was in high school."

My jaw dropped, but I didn't interrupt.

"I had been with my boyfriend for almost six months. He really wanted to, you know, go all the way, but I wasn't sure," she continued. "Eventually I agreed, and a few weeks later when I missed my period, I thought my life was over."

I stared at my mom.

"No one had ever talked to me about safe sex. I thought condoms were for prostitutes, and my boyfriend assured me that pulling out would keep me from getting pregnant." She took a deep breath, her cheeks red.

"It didn't. And when I told him, he said that it wasn't possible and that I must have been sleeping around with someone else."

"But then, what happened to—" I started, but Mom interrupted me.

"I miscarried a few weeks later. Without telling anyone. Your grandparents never knew what had happened. And I was so ashamed because I was so relieved."

I reached out to grab her hand.

"Then where does Brookhurst come in?" I asked.

"She knew," Mom said, taking a deep breath. "My boyfriend was a very young assistant coach. A very young, *married* assistant coach, and Lydia knew everything that had happened. I still don't really know how. She just made it her business to know things she shouldn't. And she hung it over me for years. Even after he moved and took a job somewhere else."

Tears rolled down my mom's face as she spoke, and I squeezed her fingertips.

"Does Dad know?" I asked.

"He does now," she said. "He was right that working with Lydia wasn't really about the money, but I was still ashamed. It was this unspoken threat, because I knew she could reveal me at any moment. I didn't want your dad to think less of me, and that was stupid."

She forced another smile, and it was like I was seeing my mom for the first time. We'd both been keeping secrets.

"I'm so sorry that I never told you, Phoebe. And I'm sorry

for keeping you in the dark about so many things. I guess I just thought that if we gave you the bare-minimum information and didn't really discuss it . . ." She trailed off.

"It's okay, Mom," I said.

I didn't ask her why she felt that not talking about sex would protect me or what she would have done if the pregnancy had progressed. I just squeezed her hand.

"No, it isn't. But we really are proud of you, sweetheart. You've created something brilliant and necessary, and it will make all the difference to someone who doesn't have anyone to talk to about this. And I'm sorry you didn't. . . ."

"I'm sorry you didn't either," I said.

I smiled, still holding her hand, and noticed the clock over her shoulder.

"Is Dad coming home late?"

"He had a few things to finish up."

"On a Sunday?" I asked. My dad rarely worked late without Mom and hardly ever on weekends.

"Oh, it's not work. He's volunteering with the Rubinowitz campaign. Knocking on doors. Making phone calls. That kind of thing."

"Really?" I said.

"And we've used all our business contacts from the Thursday class we teach to get Lydia's abstinence rings pulled from every jewelry chain in the state."

"What?!" I said, stunned.

"That's what we did on debate night," she said. "Our clients were staunch Brookhurst supporters, but then the comments

258

about Rubinowitz came out, and the food truck incident, and then that. When we told them what she did to you, they listened. They understood.

"And they also support a full investigation into her use of campaign funds, which your father and I just started."

I stared at her, still stunned.

"Yeah, it's a shame," Mom said, raising her cup of tea to her lips. "Lydia Brookhurst is really going to lose a great deal of money."

She put her teacup down and wrapped her arms around me, and for the first time I felt like I'd had an actual conversation with my mom, not about something stupid.

About something very real.

It was impossible not to feel a little uncomfortable answering questions about sex in front of my mom while we all ate sushi.

Mom actually did her best to look away whenever something awkward came up (which was often) and Amanda pressed me for details.

"How did you feel when *The Circle in the Square* went viral?" she asked.

"Shocked. Because I never expected it to become so huge."

"How have things changed since people found out you're Pom?"

I thought of Jorge. And my locker. And all the awful comments I'd gotten through Twitter.

"I think *I've* changed the most. Because before, I was writing something I felt strongly about without worrying about what people would think. Now that people know, I have to remind myself that this is still worth doing. Even if the responses suck sometimes."

My mom smiled at me, and Amanda nodded reassuringly.

She asked about my process. My research. Where I got the inspiration from.

She laughed when I told her about all the stuff from the gynecologist's office.

Once our sushi was finished and she'd run out of questions, she reached into her bag and pulled out her phone.

"Just so you know, these are from people who support you and your research. They are behind you one hundred percent. And these are just a few examples. There are thousands of them."

I looked at her screen, where she'd screenshotted a few comments from Twitter. Followers sending me messages of encouragement.

> Phoebe don't stop writing this.

> Phoebe/Pom, whoever you are. You're awesome.

> Phoebe, you saved me.

After writing in secret for so long, I was amazed at how powerful it was to see someone using my name.

"Some people are like Brookhurst. But there are lots of people who aren't," said Amanda. "You can always write to her directly through the blog. Say what you need to say."

We shook hands and Mom drove me home. We didn't talk in the car, but it was a comfortable silence.

When I got home, I took Amanda's advice, posted a letter on *The Circle in the Square,* shared it on Twitter, and turned off the comments.

Dear Ms. Brookhurst,

I don't know you. Not personally, anyway.

Nor can I say that I've paid much attention to you throughout the years before this election, even though I've heard your name come up in conversation about our town since I was small.

This is what I know:

1. You are a businesswoman.

2. You are wealthy.

3. You have a great deal of support from people who admire you for being 1 and 2.

Almost a week ago, during the debate, I was publicly credited as the anonymous writer of the sex blog *The Circle in the Square.*

You had made no secret of your desire for me to reveal my identity so other people could hold me accountable for my work.

But that wasn't the reason, was it?

It was so you could point and give your supporters the opportunity to openly shame

me for writing something you believe to be
unacceptable.

On Tuesday someone wrote "slut" on my locker.

Someone else urinated through the slats of my
locker, and by the time the janitor managed to pry
it open (someone had broken the lock), my books
were ruined.

Though, luckily, the notes that other individuals
felt compelled to write were in perfect condition, so
I'll share a few with you.

> Hey Nymphomaniac—Hope you finally get
> laid
>
> You are a dirty slut
>
> Dear Pom—BROOKHURST FOR
> MORALITY!
>
> You are a slut—We know who you are. And
> we know where you live.

It's strange the kind of hate you invite when
you're a girl who talks about sex.

My parents tried to hide most of the hate mail,
but I saw it before they could stash it out of sight.
It's on its way to the police station with the rest of
the threatening stuff we received this week.

It's interesting to me that while you claimed
you regretted saying my name at the debate,
you actually went on Twitter to clarify that had my

parents been more involved in my life, they might have put a stop to this from the beginning.

You actually tried to blame my parents for your own malicious behavior.

But let's take me out of it for a minute, because while I've got your attention (limited though it may be), I think we should also have a chat about some other things.

1. You like to comment on other people's appearance because you are all style and no substance. Helen Rubinowitz is a good person who doesn't get distracted by insults; she has no need to respond to your comments. So I'll just say you are a terrible human, you suck at life, and someone should have taught you manners. Jesus would be ashamed of you.

2. While you didn't vandalize Food Truck Village yourself, you didn't condemn the people who did, even though the evidence indicated that the perpetrators were most likely Brookhurst supporters.

The food trucks will come back without your help, and their businesses will take root in this town. We've already started crowdfunding for the repairs and are halfway to our goal. Feel free to stop by the Food Fest a month from now, all proceeds to benefit the food truck owners and establish a *permanent* outdoor pavilion for diners.

3. You have indicated that as mayor you will move to divert funds from arts scholarships, specifically those that benefit the LGBTQIA community.

They will continue to make art without your help, and their impact will be epic.

You are a disgrace. And hopefully you will lose this election because you have no redeeming qualities.

Stay away from me.

Stay away from my family.

Stick to selling your abstinence rings.

Stay pure.

Phoebe Townsend

Cora was quiet after we rehashed everything later that week, and I glanced at my phone out of habit, even though Jorge hadn't texted since that night.

I'd started texts to him and then never sent them.

Hi. I saw a grapefruit yesterday and thought of you.

Hi. Is arugula hard to grow?

Hi. I miss you let's talk about squash.

I'd seen him in health class, of course, but he sat with other football players now and didn't look in my direction at all.

"You agree with him," I said. It wasn't a question. If she disagreed, I'd know immediately, but she was chewing on her cheek, considering the last blob of boba stuck in her straw.

"I don't agree with him," she said finally. "But I get it."

"That's a nonanswer," I told her. She fixed me with a very Cora-ish *Bite me* stare.

"Telling you that you have to end the blog or he's out—that's messed up," she said. "But the stuff people have been sending is scary. And I get that he wants you to be safe."

We finished the rest of our boba and walked past Food Truck Village. There were still huge scratches on the pavement where clean-up crews had scraped glass and debris from the ground. Walking past them now felt odd, like walking past a cemetery. Any other day this place would have been packed with people waiting to buy lunch, so the silence was eerie. Even the restaurants nearby were conspicuously quiet. People were just avoiding the place altogether. My stomach made an involuntary burbling noise, as if it was remembering the smell of carnitas.

"Did they finally give you a new locker?" Cora asked, interrupting my thoughts as we settled into her car.

It was uncharacteristically clean because David couldn't handle the empty kombucha bottles rolling around on the floor like tumbleweeds.

"No. Not yet," I said. "Mrs. Lowery gave me cupboard space at the back of third period for now."

"Do you use it?" Cora asked, glancing at my bulging back-pack.

I shrugged. Going into the back of a classroom instead of to a locker like everyone else was annoying, and it drew attention. Just like my poor locker, actually.

"Well, I need to run back to mine," Cora said. "I forgot my bio notes."

"You don't have bio on Monday," I reminded her.

"I know," she said quickly. "But David sketched a picture of me on the back of my mitosis notes and swears it's better than the project he's trying to finish for his drawing class. Now he wants to turn it in, so I have to grab it. Wanna come with?"

Not really, I thought.

But I shrugged and she turned the key on her Chevy Volt.

We drove back to an empty campus. It was Friday and it had been a half day. Naturally, everyone had bolted already, which was a huge relief as we turned the corner to our row of lockers, where mine was immediately visible.

I'd never really loved it because it was in the middle row, so I was always waiting for the top and bottom rows to clear out before I could get in, but at least it was functional. Now it was like this gross, scarred thing in the middle of a perfect row. The janitor had to remove the door completely, and then the empty space just sat there like a gaping hole, drawing attention to the fact that something had been forcibly removed.

Cora didn't even glance at it as she turned the dial on her combination and pulled out the notes to look at the sketch. She took her time examining it before putting it into a folder and slamming the locker shut.

"It's actually not his best," she told me, "but I won't tell him that. Let's go."

I was a few steps ahead of her as I turned my head back to look at my sad locker, and in the moment that I looked away, I walked headlong into Jorge, who had just emerged from around the corner with his football stuff.

We bounced off each other, and for a second I almost smiled, but then everything came flooding back. Both of us stood there like complete strangers who used to make out.

There was a small bruise just above his eyebrow. He caught me looking at it and tried to push his hair down to cover it.

"Oops, forgot my stats book," Cora said, backing away as quickly as possible.

She was so eager to give us a minute to talk that she'd made up a fake subject.

She didn't even take stats.

Jorge shifted uncomfortably and then finally met my eyes. I wished he hadn't.

For almost two weeks I had timed all of my movement through school knowing exactly where he might be so I could avoid him.

Obviously, the first thing out of my mouth was totally smooth:

"You're not supposed to be here right now," I blurted out.

"Where am I supposed to be?" he asked.

In my arms?

I searched for an answer that would make sense.

"Away from here," I told him, regretting my tone. I didn't mean to sound harsh. He'd just caught me off guard.

"No problem," he said, casting his eyes to the ground. "See you around."

The truth is I miss you. I miss the way you smell. I mean, not right now because you've just been running around and . . . gross. But generally, you smell really good.

I miss the way you get self-conscious about your hair. I miss the way you geek out over vegetables. I miss the way you used to text me stupid memes before you went to sleep.

I even miss fixing the stupid tag on your shirt whenever it's sticking out.

But most of all, I miss your voice.

I watched him leave and immediately started walking in the opposite direction, toward the parking lot. Cora, who had been listening to everything, said nothing when she hurried to catch up with me. She looked guilty.

"You knew he was going to be here?" I said, taking a few huge strides as she ran to catch up.

"Football practice wasn't canceled," she confessed. "I thought we might run into him. Not literally, but you know what I mean." She sighed and stuck her arm out to stop me. "I'm sorry. I was just trying to help. I thought maybe if you were in the same place at the same time, you could talk."

It had worked before. . . .

"Good plan. Where'd he get the bruise?" I asked.

"It was some teammates after school," she told me. "I overheard it from Monica, actually. Something about them asking him what it was like to date a girl *with experience.*"

There was definitely more to the story, a lot more, that I still intended to ask her about, but my phone had started to vibrate in my pocket. I looked down at the screen and saw that it was my mom.

"Hey, Mom. I—"

I listened to my mom's panicked voice for a few seconds.

"Okay. I'm on my way," I told her. "It's going to be okay."

When I hung up, Cora was worried. "What's wrong?" she asked.

"Can you drive me home?" I asked. "Someone smashed my mom's car window."

22

My laptop was gone.

It was the only thing stolen out of my mom's car after the window was broken, even though her purse was right there. She'd borrowed it again for work and left it in the backseat while the car was parked outside our house.

But it was such a strange theft.

Had someone been waiting for the opportunity to grab something from our car? Had they been watching my mom?

Had they been looking for the laptop specifically?

I'd never even considered the possibility that someone would want to steal it.

"I'm so sorry about this, honey," Mom said, even though it wasn't her fault.

I made a mental list of the documents I'd saved. There were school files, photos, stuff from camp, and medical documents I'd had to scan. But I already knew what they'd zero in on.

My diary folder had a password lock, but it wasn't exactly a digital fortress. Someone who was devious enough to steal a laptop could easily find someone clever enough to unlock it.

Yes, that was where they'd go first. What would they find most interesting?

My own thoughts about being a virgin?

Questions I'd asked myself about my own body? My breasts. My vagina.

Questions about masturbation and arousal?

Thoughts about Neil.

Thoughts about Jorge.

I felt like someone had stolen a piece of me.

I woke up with a stomachache on election day. Helen Rubinowitz had called to thank me again for interviewing her, to see how I was doing after the great reveal at the debate, and to tell me how much she liked the interview I'd done with Amanda.

I told her about my stolen laptop, and I imagined her pursing her lips.

We both knew there was no evidence.

"Just wait," she said. "Don't lose hope. This election isn't over. She won't get away with all this."

I decided to lean into that hope.

When I got to school, there was a crowd of people gathered around the stairs leading to the quad.

A few of them started applauding as I walked up.

At first I thought it was going to be another gross moment courtesy of Lydia Brookhurst, but then I saw Cora. Her face split into a huge grin when she saw me, and she raced over to put her arm in mine.

Waving her hands dramatically toward a sea of people digging through cardboard boxes, she said, "My parents are totally on board with this, by the way. It's our simplest design and it already sold out." She reached into her bag. "You're lucky I saved you one."

The T-shirt was black. In white typewriter font it said: I READ THE BLOG. Below that was a picture of a circle in a square.

"It couldn't be something overtly sexual, so this was perfect. So far we've been brainstorming what to do with the proceeds of the sales. Something good for the cause, you know. Like scholarships for women who want to go into research-related fields. Donations to Planned Parenthood. Phoebe? Hello? Do you like it?"

I was smiling and trying not to cry.

"This is brilliant," I said. And I meant it.

"Well, I can't take all the credit. It was Jorge's idea to do a T-shirt. Something to show everyone we were on your side. We were talking all about it before . . ." She trailed off and I nodded.

The back of the shirt read: BE SAFE. REMEMBER THE CIRCLE IN THE SQUARE.

There was also the website address.

Then Cora pulled out a parcel wrapped in white tissue paper and handed it to me.

272

"This one is for you too," she said. "But you don't have to wear it if you don't want. I just thought maybe if you were feeling brave, you might, you know . . ."

She stopped talking as a few people approached her with cash for T-shirts. I pulled the ribbon off the tissue paper. It was the same T-shirt, but this one was white and said I WRITE THE BLOG.

Weirdly enough, it felt like something I *should* be wearing. It was the equivalent of the scarlet letter I would have chosen for myself, because it felt like I had nothing left to hide, if that makes any sense. The shirt was an admission of something that everyone already knew, but wearing it would mean that I was not ashamed.

I put it on over my tank top as Cora returned to handing out T-shirts.

Jorge was nowhere to be seen, and my chest tightened a little as the bell rang.

After school I sat in my room for a while staring at the wavy lines of the abstract vagina art while my parents discussed takeout options in the other room. My window was open a crack, and I could hear a low humming sound coming from outside. I was going to ignore it, thinking it was a neighbor mowing their lawn, when I heard something thump against my window. Something small . . . and blue?

Then it happened again.

And again.

When I got up to look, I smelled something, subtle at first, then—

Lemons? I thought.

But it wasn't just lemons.

I went to my window, and there on the grass of our front lawn was a message, spelled out in what appeared to be *all* the fruit from Jorge's garden:

I'm sorry. You were right.

He'd been blasting the scent with a fan pointed toward my window.

Jorge was sitting on the ground next to it, wearing his football hoodie, and he stood up when he saw me at the window. I threw the door open, but my mouth tightened into a thin line when I remembered our last discussion.

On the ground was a basket of blueberries, which he'd been chucking at my window.

"I wasn't sure the lemon smell was going to be strong enough," he said, gesturing at the blueberry basket and the rest of his harvest lying on the ground. Then he tossed me something from his pocket.

A peach.

"Finally got a peach from that tree," he said proudly.

"Are we going to make this fruit thing a habit?" I asked him, turning the peach over in my hands. Then he put his hands up and unzipped his hoodie to reveal a shirt Cora had obviously made especially for him. It read: I KNOW WHO WRITES THE BLOG. SHE'S PRETTY BADASS.

"Nice shirt," I said.

My eyes were immediately drawn to the bruise above his eyebrow. When I looked like I was going to ask about it, he waved me off.

"I was scared," he said simply. "And I shouldn't have been. Because this is important."

He tried to smile at me but faltered when I frowned at him.

"Please don't just say something because you think it sounds good," I said. "I don't want to be lied to."

He looked hurt, and the tiny, angry monster still hiding inside me was satisfied.

Good. You should feel guilty.

"I'm not lying. I meant that . . . and I'm sorry I didn't say that immediately after finding out it was you. I should have."

I closed the space between us and put my arms around him.

"Is it weird that it's me?" I asked, my face buried in his neck.

"No," he said. "Just one more badass thing about you. Writer. Researcher. Sex expert."

He shrugged and then tilted his head like he wanted to kiss me. There was still a trace of guilt in his eyes when I reached my hand up to his cheek and raised my lips to his.

He smiled, then kissed me a little more enthusiastically, breaking the rest of the distance between us.

"Let's go inside," he said, and I winced as I got a better look at the bruise.

"Are we just going to leave all this fruit here?"

"Oh shit, no. Help me pick this up. Farmers' market is to-morrow. This stuff is still good."

Jorge and I went inside to wait for election results. The outcome was being televised, but Brookhurst had arranged to make a public apology while the polls were still open.

When I saw her on the screen, she looked tired and her smile seemed forced. It was the most conservative outfit I'd ever seen her wear, and I think it was clear from her expression that she believed she was *wearing* her apology.

I'd been invited to receive it in person, but obviously, both of my parents thought this was a bad idea, and I can't say I wanted to be there anyway. Cora, on the other hand, insisted on seeing it in person.

"I want to watch her squirm," she'd said. "And I want to watch her stupid face when she loses."

I could see her sitting toward the back of the room with David when the camera panned over the crowd, and I noted with a tiny hint of satisfaction that there seemed to be the same number of people witnessing this grotesque apology as there had been at the debate.

Cora had gathered a group of people, all wearing the new shirt. They sat in the back row together, creating a sea of black, and none of them were smiling. David was even wearing a black beanie to match.

"Ladies and gentlemen," Brookhurst began, "I'd just like to say how profoundly sorry I am for the events of the debate. I am obviously only human and therefore must beg forgiveness from time to time."

Spattering of applause.

"And I just want everyone to know that even though I found—well, still find—the material highly questionable, I never meant to expose a minor. I am just not that kind of woman. It could very easily have been a member of the school's staff. After all, let's not forget, there are adults who have been very vocal about their support of the blog."

More applause. But then something happened.

Before Brookhurst could begin speaking again, a voice in the crowd said, "Can you please repeat that, Ms. Brookhurst?"

Monica Hansen was standing in the center of the seated audience, looking forward at Brookhurst. An election official near the stage raced over to her with a microphone. A man sitting to Brookhurst's right stood up and said, "Ms. Brookhurst is not taking questions from the crowd at this time. This is just a reading of her public statement. I'm sure you can ask someone near you what was said or wait for it to be printed in the local paper." He wore a limp, placid smile and quickly turned his attention away from Monica.

Without moving to sit, Monica lifted the mic and said, "I only ask her to repeat herself because I'd like to know if she is going to lie again."

Silence.

Brookhurst's eyes opened a little wider in shock, but it vanished from her face almost immediately, to be replaced by her trademark smile. Though it was arguably twitchier than usual.

"I'm not sure I follow," said Brookhurst. "But I'd be happy to discuss it with you further in private after I finish my statement."

She tried to cut Monica off, but the moment Brookhurst

took a breath, Monica spoke up again and said, "You said that you never intended to expose a minor. But several high schools throughout our county claim that their Christian and abstinence clubs were sent emails from groups associated with the Brookhurst for Mayor campaign, asking them to anonymously report classmates who might *be* involved in the blog or *know* someone involved in the blog. Are you saying that these emails, obviously targeting minors, weren't from you? And since it's common knowledge that the writer of the blog is a teen, even if you publicly questioned their age, how can you say that it wasn't your intention to expose them?"

"I have personally never sent an email like that in my life," said Brookhurst a little too quickly.

"Then are you saying someone else sent it on your behalf without your knowledge?"

The crowd, which had been muttering a moment ago, suddenly went silent.

"Cut the cameras," said the man who'd spoken earlier. Several loud shouts of protest erupted through the hall as the screen in our family room went dead.

I ran to grab my phone.

Texts from Cora:

> They turned off the cameras!

> OMFG she looks pissed. I have never seen her look so pissed.

> WTF happened to Monica?

Jorge and I stared at the blue screen of the monitor while messages from Cora kept coming in.

> Some reporter said "Ms. Brookhurst is it true that your abstinence rings have been pulled from all the major jewelry stores in the state following the events of last week?"

> Another reporter said "Do you have a response to the letter that Phoebe Townsend posted on her blog?"

> "Do you have any further comments on the food truck incident?"

> This is so delicious. She doesn't know how to respond. She's avoiding all the questions, and even her crowd is struggling to make excuses.

My parents, who'd decided to go to the public-apology portion of the broadcast, came home before the winner of the election was announced. Both of them were wearing the shirt, and both of them were in good spirits.

My dad dropped a large pizza on the kitchen table, and the

four of us sat down to eat and discuss the apology, the election, and the success of Cora's T-shirt project. My mom asked Jorge about his vegetable garden, and my dad even asked some well-intentioned questions about football, but both of them took turns raising their eyebrows at me regarding his presence in our house.

Despite everything that had been going on, it was a nice evening. Well, nice enough.

But for now everyone was pretending.

To be honest, it was nice seeing them back to normal and on the same team again.

An hour later, when nearly all the pizza and garlic knots had been consumed, we tuned in to watch the results come in live.

Helen called me again before it started.

"How are you holding up?" she asked.

"I'm okay," I told her. This was mostly true.

"Well, no matter what happens tonight, I'm really grateful for your help," she said. Then the announcer came on and we hung up to watch.

My parents sat on the couch next to me and Jorge. Dad actually looked relaxed, more relaxed than he'd looked in days. He'd been so completely immersed in last-minute campaigning that this was the first time I'd seen him sit down at home.

Jorge took my hand and squeezed as the announcement began.

The announcer was a short, bald man with thick black

glasses and white hair like cotton candy. He spent a few minutes describing the differences in the candidates' political platforms before he was handed a small white envelope with the results. Photos of Lydia Brookhurst and Helen Rubinowitz flashed on the screen side by side, once again emphasizing the stark contrast between the two women.

He opened the envelope and looked directly at the camera before speaking:

"The winner is Lydia Brookhurst."

Penis captivus is a rare occurrence in intercourse when the muscles in the vagina clamp down on the penis, making it impossible for the penis to withdraw from the vagina.

I'm not sure why that was the sex fact that surfaced immediately during the initial shock.

"Phoebe, are you okay?" Jorge asked.

I wasn't.

I'd momentarily left my body and was flying around the house reciting facts from the blog to myself as the weirdest, most sex-positive ghost who'd ever existed.

The vagina is a self-cleaning machine with the capacity to have an erection similar to that of a penis. There are eight thousand nerve endings in the clitoris, while the penis has only four thousand. Vaginas can expand up to 200 percent during intercourse and childbirth. Female orgasm is designed to induce pregnancy, because the movement of the vaginal walls pumps sperm toward the uterus, into the cervix. . . .

Then I somehow resurfaced.

"I can't believe that after all that . . . she still won," Jorge said, astonished.

I'd never heard my dad swear so vehemently before. After the second "holy fucking shit," my mom escorted him to the backyard to calm down because the veins in his temples looked like they were going to pop.

They didn't come inside for a long time, and when they finally did, my dad could not stop shaking his head and whispering, "She was a joke. She was supposed to be a joke."

I'd never seen him look so dejected, like a friend had punched him in the stomach.

I understood why.

It meant that there were quite a few people around us who, after everything that had happened, still agreed with Brookhurst. People who thought that certain library books should be banned if a few people were offended by them. People who believed that some ancient idea of morality should govern what students learned in school. People who thought that a girl who wrote a blog about sex was a pervert.

"This won't last," said Jorge. "She has zero experience and no idea what it takes to get things done."

I hoped he was right, but an hour after the announcement, Brookhurst gave a public address in which she reinforced her platform to begin work on her main campaign promises:

1. A ban on all food trucks on Main Street. All those wishing to operate food trucks would need to reapply and seek permission from the new Mayoral Food Truck Council.

Because the only way to erase the memory of the incident is to erase the trucks completely.

2. An end to funding for local scholarship programs deemed questionable and the reallocation of funds to small-business initiatives.

Because "questionable" means "queer." And "small-business initiatives" means her friends who own businesses on Main Street.

3. A school board movement to completely revamp health education to be abstinence-only or, as Brookhurst likes to call it, sexual risk avoidance education.

Because after all this, they still think removing information about sex is going to stop people from having it.

The results were awful, but there were some good moments in the days that followed.

"Her entire store was rainbow-bombed," said Cora proudly.

"What does that me—" Jorge started, but before he could finish the question, Cora handed him her phone, and we all looked at the pictures of Brookhurst's newly decorated storefront.

Someone had made a gigantic papier-mâché dove. In its beak was a huge bra with the words I READ THE BLOG painted over the cups.

Jorge laughed, and I scanned the photo for more details.

Giant neon rainbows hung artistically from the windows, and there was not one speck of visible space on the sidewalk that wasn't covered in wildly colorful art—most of it depicting naked people dancing and having what looked like a pretty good time.

"A few LGBTQIA groups have already taken credit for it," said Cora. "But the pink stuff—that's from a bunch of women's groups."

Plastered over the giant sign above Brookhurst's store were pink posters of her quotes about Rubinowitz before the campaign.

Beautiful women are more successful.
If you're a dog, you aren't going to get far.

"That's not even the best part," said David, looking at the phone and zooming in on one of the pictures. Underneath the posters someone had artfully included at least one hundred tiny piles of something covered in rainbow glitter.

"Dog shit," said David approvingly.

It actually *was* kind of beautiful.

When I got home, my parents were sorting mail. Some of it they had thrown directly in the trash, but they'd set aside quite a few pieces for me to read.

There were still a lot of negative letters to weed through, but I held on to the good ones. It was nice to know that not everyone thought I was a sex-crazed weirdo.

A lot still did.

But, as it turned out, Stanford University was not one of them.

At least, not according to the letter I received in the mail the very next day:

Dear Phoebe,

We at Stanford were very pleased to learn about the existence of *The Circle in the Square* and have been following your story with interest.

After discussing your research with Amanda Whitaker, we would like to commend you on your exceptional work and sensitivity to an important topic.

We were less pleased to learn about the circumstances concerning *The Circle in the Square*'s completion and the incidents that led to your decision to close your blog to questions.

Personally, I hope this is only a temporary decision. I wish that as a young woman I had had a resource like *The Circle in the Square.* It would have given me the outlet I needed to ask questions when those around me were unwilling to provide answers.

There are individuals who might seek to judge a young woman who focuses on sex with scientific curiosity, but we believe that you are a remarkable researcher with a promising future ahead.

It is our understanding that Stanford is high on your list of potential colleges. While we cannot comment on admissions procedures or probability

286

of acceptance, we would not be disappointed if
you chose to apply in the fall.

Best of luck,
Wynona Bellio
Stanford University Admissions

I read the letter several times before showing it to my parents, who started making plans to visit me at the school when I got in, which completely freaked me out because (1) I hadn't gotten in yet, (2) I didn't want to jinx it, and (3) I didn't want to admit how happy this made me.

Inside the envelope was a small note on an index card from Amanda that said only:

Thanks for doing the interview.
Please keep up the good work.
—Amanda Louise Till-Whitaker

It wasn't until later that night, as I was looking at Amanda's signature again, that I realized the letters looked familiar. I pulled out the box of baby photos and the green envelope I'd opened weeks ago.

The letter had been signed "A.L.T.," and the tall, slanted *T*s looked similar.

I didn't show the letter to anyone. It felt like something I never should have seen anyway. But when I thought about it later, I imagined what Amanda might have been feeling when she wrote it and the circumstances that had prompted it.

I mean, she said she was from Linda Vista.

It was one of those moments when the past and the present collide in ways we don't fully understand. I didn't plan on writing back to tell Amanda about the letter that I thought could be from her, because it was deeply personal, but I did wonder how all these tiny threads had come together and why I held them in my hand.

Was it her?

24

"Is there anything you have to add, Phoebe?" Coach Snowden didn't say it like a jerk. In fact, he may have even bowed his head a little when he spoke. I had known it was going to be awkward when I came back to health class, but there was no avoiding it. I was required to finish this stupid, completely useless class.

"Is there anything you'd . . . um . . . like me to add?"

A few people laughed, but Coach Snowden quieted them sternly. More sternly than he'd ever quieted anyone for laughing in his class.

"Maybe you'd like to come up and talk a little."

Really? I thought. *You want me to come up and talk a little about how I've been publicly humiliated and how my parents have to sift through our mail for threats? Or you want me to come up and chat about how I love sex, in a classroom filled with my peers, who may or may not have carved insults on my locker?*

I stared at him. Jorge nudged my foot under the table.

"Go if you want," he said. "Nothing to lose." Then he mouthed, *It's okay.*

I rolled my eyes at him, but the rest of the class had already turned to stare at me. I stared back, my face starting to feel hot.

I walked up to the front of the room and approached the tall stool with the cracked leather seat normally occupied by Coach Snowden.

"What would you do if this was your class?" he asked.

It was the perfect opportunity for people to be obnoxious, but it didn't happen. And I wasn't exactly sure why it didn't.

So I considered the question, fully aware that I was on display for the rest of the class, which was unsettling until I noticed that two people, whom I knew by sight but had never spoken to, were wearing the shirt Cora had designed.

"I'd answer questions," I said.

"Do you think people would actually be able to ask about sex in a classroom?"

I didn't see who had spoken.

"I'd have people do it anonymously. That's what worked for the blog."

"Give it a try," said Jorge, scanning the classroom.

I looked at him, then I looked at Coach Snowden, who had gone to his desk and pulled out a pad of white paper. He handed a sheet of paper to everyone in the class and sat back down.

"Write down your questions. Don't sign your names."

And they did.

Jorge collected all the papers, and for the rest of the class period I answered questions and no one said anything weird or inappropriate. Not even when the subjects were uncomfortably personal.

I removed all emotion from my voice and used the same language Pom would for the blog.

"Yes, that can get you pregnant."

"No, the penis does not do that."

"Yes, the vagina absolutely can do that."

There was silence while I did this, and I even noticed a few people taking notes while I spoke, which was strange to see.

Then the bell rang and everyone filed out, but not before thanking me.

"Thanks for doing that, Phoebe."

"That was awesome."

"Thanks, Phoebe. You don't really look like someone who knows a shit ton about sex."

Okay, so the last one was not a compliment, but I let it slide.

Jorge put his arm around me at the door, and Coach Snowden walked toward us.

"Thanks for doing that, Phoebe."

"You're welcome. I'm not entirely sure why you let me, though."

He pretended to look around the hall for invisible spies. "I'll level with you. This is the class they give you because nobody really cares about it. I live and die by my sports teams, but basically if you show up to health class, you pass. Nobody takes it seriously. Even the sex part. Nobody expects to learn anything about sex from a class." He took a deep breath. "But you treat it like a serious thing, and I thought maybe someone should see that. And I thought you should know that Nurse Reyes has agreed to come back in as a guest speaker too.

Maybe next year she'll be teaching the class." He shrugged, and I didn't know what to say. In the universe of high school, it probably didn't matter much. Even if I were able to answer questions for a day, it wouldn't really change anything, and there were still people who were going to think I was a perv.

But it was a nice gesture, and Coach Snowden might not be as stupid as I originally thought.

That night I watched as my parents continued their manic crusade to destroy Brookhurst from our family room couch. Mom was lying on her back, highlighting paperwork from their attorney. Dad was covertly searching homes for sale on his phone with one hand when he thought I wasn't looking, and massaging my mom's foot with the other.

Ordinarily, I'd be grossed out by the affectionate foot touching, but I was in a mood to appreciate that they were on the same team again. Dad's laptop was open to their current client list, and he was taking a break from phone calls for the time being.

I just couldn't help but feel like their attempt to ruin her was pointless.

"She won," I said, tugging at the pant leg of my *Avatar: The Last Airbender* pajamas while I reorganized my stack of Spanish flash cards on the floor. "Yeah, you probably hit some of her sales, but her business will bounce back. She's untouchable. Plus, she probably doesn't even care about the investigation anymore."

My mom laughed, accidentally dropping the paperwork on her face.

"She cares," she said, sitting up to offer my dad her other foot. "She just hired more lawyers. Trust me. This is only the beginning." Then she laughed again, and my dad and I looked at each other, concerned.

"Fi, the investigation hasn't turned up much yet. Everything they've found has been small."

My mom scoffed. "Nobody seems to remember she goes by her middle name," she said, holding her index finger in the air.

It was my dad's turn to laugh. "Fi, you can't be serious. No one cares about that."

"Wait. What's her first name?" I asked.

"Anne," they said together.

"Why would she go by something else?" I asked. My mom shrugged and rolled her eyes before collapsing into my dad's shoulder.

"Anne is a very common name. And it was her grand-mother's. Rumor was they never got along. Even after she finally changed her last name."

"Wait. She changed her last name too?" I asked, suddenly interested.

"Yes, but everybody knows that. Brookhurst is the family name associated with all the money. Her father's last name was Timmons, but all the kids are Brookhurst," Mom said, closing her eyes and yawning. "But maybe your dad is right. And nobody cares about that."

I blinked at her, something clicking into place in my head.

"But she is hiding something," Mom said. "A lot of

somethings. And we're going to keep digging until we find them."

Dad kissed the top of her head and kept scrolling through his phone while I scampered back to my bedroom.

I closed the door and sat on the edge of my bed, letting the truth come crashing down on my head.

Lydia Brookhurst was also Anne Lydia Timmons.

A.L.T.

She once sent a letter to a local gynecologist, thanking her for her help with something she couldn't discuss with her parents. I dug into the box and found the letter.

Dear Dr. Mullen,

I couldn't tell anyone when it happened. I don't know if I made the right choice.

My parents can never know.

No one can ever know.

If it weren't for you, I probably wouldn't be here.

Thank you for saving me.

A.L.T.

I finished reading and sat there, soaking it all in.

The large, obnoxious cursive *L* in the middle was exactly like the one she'd left on that Post-it for my mom when she came to our house.

Then I noticed the date on the letter. It couldn't have been Amanda after all. She wasn't old enough.

After everything Brookhurst had railed against and all her

protests for abstinence-only sex education, had she been the one who, by the sound of it, needed an abortion?

Somewhere behind me, my dad's old computer made a loud ping, and I realized it was an alert from *The Circle in the Square*. Someone had sent a message.

Dear Phoebe,
I wish you could have been there to accept my public apology, but I do hope you will let me apologize in person for any pain I may have caused you.
    If you are available to meet tomorrow, I'd love for you to stop by our main store.

Lydia Brookhurst

The timing was eerie, but one thought surfaced in my mind.

I had her exactly where I wanted her.

25

The letter was in my pocket when I went to meet Brookhurst.

"You didn't have to come with me," I said to the two people who never would have let me go alone.

Neither Cora nor Jorge answered me. Cora was tucked into the backseat of Jorge's car, wearing a F*&K POLLUTION T-shirt.

"She's trying to get you to convince your parents to drop the investigation by blackmailing you with whatever is on your laptop," said Jorge, who was wearing a Nike fútbol shirt.

"What if Brookhurst isn't the one who stole the laptop?"

Both Cora and Jorge looked at me.

"Right," I said.

Obviously, I didn't think Brookhurst was running around like a ninja smashing my mom's car window, but there was no doubt in my mind she was behind the theft. I knew she wanted the investigation over. My hand clamped over the letter in my pocket.

Jorge pointed out the spots on the ground where Brookhurst hadn't been able to remove the glitter, and then sniffed approvingly because there was still a faint dog-poop smell in the air.

"Dear God," said Cora as we walked through the entrance

under a sign that read: HAVE A BLESSED DAY! The place was covered in tiny white cherubs, and the walls were lined with Bible passages written in gold script. There was a wall of Christian knickknacks and bumper stickers that advocated everything from safe driving to creationism. Cora jumped a little when an obnoxious chime went off announcing our arrival.

Then a voice rang out from somewhere near the tower of Jesus figurines.

"Phoebe!" Brookhurst said. "I'm so very glad you could make it."

She was wearing a lavender off-the-shoulder sweater and pearl earrings, and her smile was as fake as her hair color.

"Aquí vamos a estar," said Jorge, before glaring at Brookhurst and following Cora to the display of abstinence rings and angel pendants. They both looked at me, and Cora sent a text that read:

> If that bitch tries to baptize you, scream as loud as you can

Brookhurst led me to a table where tea and scones had been arranged on garish lavender plates, in what appeared to be an attempt to complement her outfit.

"Have a seat," she said, smiling. I sat, aware that there were a few people in the store watching us.

"So," she said. "Again, I just wanted to apologize for any pain I may have caused you. It certainly wasn't intentional, and I hope we can move on from this bit of unpleasantness."

It is never an apology when people say they are sorry for any pain they "may" have caused, as if there is some doubt that they were, in fact, an asshole.

"Thank you," I said.

"And I was sorry to hear that your laptop was taken."

It was an interesting comment because no one would know the laptop was the only thing that had been stolen. Clearly, Brookhurst was trying to get to the point of the meeting.

If I had been in a movie right then, this would have been the part where the hero notices a green glint in the villain's eyes or a forked tongue or something.

"Yes, it is a shame. Luckily, all my documents are backed up."

"But there are probably personal items there you wouldn't want becoming public," she said, pouring me tea we both knew I wouldn't drink.

We looked at each other and she smiled.

"I hope that from this day on we can be allies, Phoebe. Sex education is an important thing as long as responsible heads prevail."

"Sexual risk avoidance education is not sex education," I said calmly.

Her eyes flashed, and her smile faltered for half a second.

She sighed, then leaned back in her chair with a cup of tea. "You know, it isn't really the blog itself. It's what you're condoning by making that information readily available."

I had my hand on the note in my pocket, but then something hit me in the pit of my stomach, something I hadn't considered before.

Here was someone who didn't care about people.

Someone who had hurt me and my family.

Someone who had just threatened to embarrass me with my own journal entries.

Someone who was callous and shallow and malicious.

And still I could not blackmail her with this note. I could not give her the speech I'd wanted to give about how I'd nailed her with this letter to a doctor she'd visited when she was young.

If I did that, I would be shaming her for the abortion she probably had.

I took a deep breath, stood up from the table, and said, "Do what you want with my laptop. *Your* secret is safe with me."

In the second of hesitation before her eyes shot wide open, I could tell she was replaying my words in her head. The chime at the door went off again as a few people wandered into the store, and for some reason this unsettled her.

I said nothing else and continued to watch her grow more uncomfortable. Then I felt a perfect, fake Lydia Brookhurst smile rise to my cheeks. She cringed when she saw it.

"What would you know about my secrets?" asked Brookhurst.

"I know enough," I said, turning to leave.

"Are you threatening me?" she hissed. There were people around, so her face did not lose its usual placid friendliness, but there was ice in her voice.

"I don't make threats," I told her. "And I meant what I said. I don't care what happens with the stuff on my computer."

Lydia's lips twisted unpleasantly, like she'd just tasted something sour.

"Have a blessed day," I said, smiling at her.

Cora and Jorge met me at the door.

"¿Lista?" Jorge asked.

Yes, I was ready. I nodded and we walked out.

It had been Nurse Reyes's suggestion to create uncomfortable silence and watch what happens.

Most people *do* fall apart.

26

TWO WEEKS LATER

"We can't use that, Matt," my mom was saying in a bored sort of voice as they scanned their emails at the kitchen table.

"Why the hell not?" he asked. There was an assortment of takeout laid out next to them while they worked. My dad was picking at the last of his Korean barbecue while my mom took small, calculated bites of her sushi burrito. They made a point of buying from the food trucks whenever possible.

"Because her breast augmentation wasn't linked to campaign funds, and it would be in poor taste to reveal that."

"She made a speech about women in Hollywood who—"

"I don't care what she said. We're focusing on the finances," my mom said, cutting him off. Dad looked put out.

"Like it would be such a huge reveal," he muttered.

"Anyway," said Mom, "I'm more interested in the stuff we just got. We're really close to linking her to the incident at Food Truck Village."

They were arguing, but they were also playing footsie under the table, and I was torn between needing to look away and wanting to enjoy the moment. When I told them I was heading to Food Truck Village to meet Jorge, they said in one voice: "Text us when you get there."

When I pulled up to the food trucks, I sat in the car for a minute and watched as crowds of people walked across what was once an empty parking lot. The new playground at the edge of the seating area had been built, and some people were securing benches to the ground. I spotted Jorge beside a row of pots, gently lowering a tomato plant into the soil, next to a few berry bushes he'd donated as well.

Before getting out of the car, I noticed someone nearby helping power-wash the parking lot where the cement had been damaged. Monica Hansen was blasting bits of shattered glass off the ground with a savage expression on her face. When she looked up, she caught my eye for half a second and got back to work. People are complicated. I guess it's comforting that not everyone falls into neat categories of good and bad.

I texted my parents. *I'm here.*

"Do you regret not going to homecoming?" Jorge asked me.

"No," I said, watching him from the swing chair in the corner of the greenhouse.

Jorge's hands were covered in dirt. Two of his yellow popper tomato plants were overflowing with fruit, and he was gently plucking each of them off the vine and settling them into a basket. I had been fired from this particular job for squashing them, so here I sat, watching him harvest his own produce.

His garden had grown in the past few weeks because we'd been spending so much more time there than anywhere else. He was also in contact with a few people in Hawaii who were trying to get him cuttings from their backyard Haden mango trees. Not to mention that Jorge and his dad had come back from a few specialty nurseries with more exotic trees and shrubs in the past couple of days. Even Jorge's mom, who'd been reluctant at first, was starting to get into hybrid plants too. She'd found male and female kiwi berry vines, which Jorge had been trying to track down for months.

"Blood orange trees, Phoebe! And guava! And mango!" he shouted, his face euphoric.

Even though he swore he needed my help, it was clear that he was trying to distract me. Mango is *my* favorite, not his. And none of them on the mainland taste quite as good as the ones from my cousins' backyard trees.

Homecoming had come and gone, and neither Cora nor Jorge had participated, even though they were on the court. We didn't talk about the fact that the school had intercepted a threatening call and the principal thought it would be best if I didn't attend.

"So are you ever going to respond to Secret Agent Toni?"

"Eventually," I said. "Are you going to stop calling her that?"

"Probably not. I mean, you have a literary agent and don't tell anyone about her, so the name fits. And I'm witty as hell."

I actually let Toni's email sit in my inbox for a full twenty-four hours before responding, and she ended up calling me before I even had a chance to hit Send.

"Phoebe, did you get my email?! What are you waiting for?"

I'd only had an agent for a month, so I wasn't sure how I was supposed to respond to the news that a major publishing house wanted to turn *The Circle in the Square* into a book, a guide for sex questions and answers. They wanted sex therapists and sexologists to weigh in and share their expertise.

They liked that I'd started hosting Twitter takeovers with LGBTQIA and disabled advocates for more-inclusive sex education curricula and wanted to include that in the book.

I still couldn't believe the whole thing was happening within the framework of *my* blog with *my* research.

"This is huge and completely not the way things usually happen in the publishing world. The publisher wants this book out now!" Toni said. She spoke quickly, the way I imagined everyone from New York was supposed to talk to keep from wasting anyone's time. "But it's happening. They want to make it a book. And they want to include some of the hate mail."

I understood why. It's dramatic and it makes for a good read, but I wasn't sure I was ready to let the world see that ugliness.

Even though a lot of media attention had died down since the election, it was still bad enough that my parents had finally decided to move. Not far, just far enough so they didn't feel the need to camp outside my bedroom every night.

Guess I wasn't the only one who still had nightmares.

"Phoebe, are you still there? I need to know what you want to do. Do you want this to be a book? I thought that was the goal, to get it into as many hands as possible."

"It is," I said, but I knew it would mean more publicity for me.

"Then tell me what you want to do."

I thought about the hidden sex education stuff under my bed and all the kids who had nobody to answer their questions. And Cora. And David. And everyone who had ever sent me a question. And about the floppy penis at camp that had started it all.

"Make it a book," I told her. "We'll make it the biggest, messiest, most honest sex book on the planet."

She laughed and we hung up.

EPILOGUE
THE SUMMER

We'd had the conversation. Multiple conversations, actually. About how we wanted it to happen. Where we wanted it to happen. What we expected. What we didn't expect.

It was still awkward on the day of, knowing my parents would be gone and wouldn't be back for hours. And that we had the house completely to ourselves for the first time since my family had moved.

But knowing about sex isn't the same as having sex, which I learned on Friday, June 17.

"If you've changed your mind, we don't have to do this now. I'm not in a rush," Jorge said for what felt like the fifth time. He knew I was pretending to be confident but that I was secretly nervous about the whole thing, which was stupid, since it wasn't like we hadn't done anything sexual over the past few months. It also wasn't like I didn't know what to expect.

Healthy sexual relationships are based on constant communication, telling your partner exactly what feels good and what doesn't. It doesn't help anyone if you lie about how you're feeling. In fact, it just slows everything down. It makes it harder to have a meaningful relationship if you pretend you like something that your partner is doing.

So before we had sex, we talked about it. A lot. Probably to the point of making it completely unappealing, but I really wanted to make sure that we understood each other. For example, we both agreed I would be on the pill for about three months, and he'd still wear a condom.

We'd taken our time and ticked off most of the sexual-act boxes. Things we'd both agreed to do and not do.

But there was one that we did still want to explore.

We looked at each other, and without knowing why, we both looked away.

Really, shyness now? I thought.

"I haven't changed my mind," I told him.

"Okay, but if you have, then . . ."

He trailed off when I reached out and unzipped his pants.

It was warm outside, and the windows in my bedroom were cracked open slightly as the fan on my ceiling whirred above us.

We were naked in seconds, and I shivered a little thinking about what was coming next. I don't think "nervous" is the right word to describe what I was feeling, but I couldn't come up with a better descriptor. I couldn't wrap my head around a logical reaction to the moment, so I decided that I didn't need to have one.

Jorge looked at me, scanning my completely naked body for the first time, and then smiled.

"You are really beautiful," he said.

I'd wanted our first time to be on a bed in a place I was

comfortable with. Jorge thought this was a good idea, that it would probably ease some of the tension.

I ran my finger down his chest and let my hand linger at his waist for a minute before turning onto my back.

He eased himself on top of me but propped himself up on his elbows, letting his lips gently brush mine before finding my tongue. My heart was beating faster than I thought possible, but I wasn't nervous anymore. I was ready.

He looked at me for a brief moment before it happened, and I smiled, letting him know it was okay.

And it was better than I thought it would be.

When he was inside me, he let out this low, happy sigh just as he found the spot between my neck and ear. He kissed it and said, "I love you."

It wasn't the first time I'd heard that either, but it felt different somehow, now that love was a physical and emotional act.

I whispered it back to him, and the rest of the afternoon passed in a dreamy sort of haze that I knew I would remember for the rest of my life.

Much later, when we were comfortably wrapped in my sheets and Jorge's head was resting on my chest, I thought about the events of the last few months. The failed library ban that Brookhurst had tried to champion. The growing number of pranks that continued to plague her store. Her now-failing jewelry business because of all the negative publicity she'd received from trying to humiliate me. And the overwhelming success of Food Truck Village downtown, which had captured statewide attention, making our town a hub for multicultural cuisine even though Brookhurst had done everything in her power to block permits for the Food Truck Village restoration project.

In fact, her time as mayor had really just given our local paper the freedom to capture her embarrassment.

People still sent me nasty messages, even threats once in a while, but I'd learned to tune them out and report the particularly awful ones.

I'd also spent a lot of time thinking about the question I could never quite answer.

Why did I become Pom?

Scientific curiosity?

Wishful thinking?

Or maybe I wrote the blog because I believed it wasn't something I was supposed to write.

Those might all be true in part, but now I would also have to add:

Because I enjoy sex.

Which might be even more scandalous.

Acknowledgments

This book would not exist without the following individuals:

Jodi Reamer, my brilliant agent, who pushed this story into the universe. Thanks for believing in this, Jodi.

The entire team at Random House, starting with:

Polo Orozco, my talented editor, who patiently guided this book to exactly where it needed to be. Polo, working with you has been such a gift. Thank you times a billion for checking my Spanish, for polishing this story, and for doing it all with such kindness and creativity. *Gigantic socially distanced hugs*

Angela Carlino (cover designer), Alison Impey (art director), and Jen Valero (interior designer), whose artistic talents illuminated the cover and design of this book. I am honored to have your art so beautifully entwined with mine. Janet Foley for skillfully managing the editorial process of this novel. Sara Sargent for taking the final steps with this story and guiding it to bookshelves everywhere. Barbara Bakowski, Alison Kolani, and Erica Stahler, my magnificent copyeditors, who made sure that not everything in this book happens on a Thursday and that my characters are not mysteriously present in scenes when they should be elsewhere. You are angels.

Also, a huge thank-you to the marketing, publicity, and sales teams at Random House for getting this book into the hands of readers.

Dr. Kristin Dardano, for her candid responses to *The Circle in the Square* blog posts and her recommendations that ultimately helped me craft answers that were both accurate and inclusive. Alejandra Olivo, for reading enthusiastically and providing her honest reflections on Jorge and Nurse Reyes.

Dr. Christina Lee, for reading one of my earliest drafts and for helping me fine-tune Phoebe's responses regarding birth control and emergency contraception. Also, major gratitude for taking care of me (and my babies) through all three of my pregnancies. ☺

My fantastic beta readers: Nick Naveda, Brooke Tabshouri, Kortney Hughes, Mike Gravagno, Mark O'Brien, and Jenny Howard. It seems like a lifetime ago that we had that brunch and tore this story apart, and I'm so grateful for your comments, your support, and your friendship. THANK YOU!

My sisters, Athena and Cassandra, who read, laughed, and helped me brainstorm titles.

My in-laws, Doug and Margaret, who continue to support my artistic endeavors with babysitting help, practical wisdom, and love.

Mom and Dad, for all the tiny moments throughout my childhood that eventually led to this life of writing. I love you.

My husband, Doug, and our kids, Alex, Charlie, and Jamie. Thank you for mostly ignoring it when I talk to myself and for filling my life with so much joy and laughter.

And finally, to Heather Flaherty, who loved this story when it was just a very ugly draft. Heather, if you hadn't laughed and told me to keep going, I never would have finished it.

About the Author

JULIA WALTON is the author of the award-winning *Words on Bathroom Walls* and *Just Our Luck*. She received an MFA in creative writing from Chapman University and a BA in history from the University of California, Irvine. Julia lives with her husband and children in Huntington Beach, California.

JuliaWalton.com